CA...
WITH SIXKILLER'S LACKEY

"What's your whole name, boy?"

He said, "I ain't sayin' 'nother word 'bout myself. You kin ast till you turn blue in the face."

I blew out a mouthful of smoke. I said, "Well, the hell with it, Lew. Hang the little bastard. I ought to be able to get the circuit judge to sign the papers today so we can hang him sometime tomorrow morning."

He'd come off the bunk, his face going kind of pale. He said, "You can't hang me, I ain't done nuthin'."

I pulled my revolver and pointed it at him. I said, "You sit right back down or I'm fixing to save the county the price of some rope. . . ."

Lew unlocked the cell and we went into his office. He was laughing so hard he had trouble pouring some whiskey. Lew said, "How far you willing to go?"

I said, "That boy come in here talking about murder and robbing. You figure out from that how far I'm willing to go. . . ."

Books by Giles Tippette

Fiction

THE BANK ROBBER

THE TROJAN COW

THE SURVIVALIST

THE SUNSHINE KILLERS

AUSTIN DAVIS

WILSON'S WOMAN

WILSON YOUNG ON THE RUN

THE TEXAS BANK ROBBING COMPANY

WILSON'S GOLD

WILSON'S REVENGE

WILSON'S CHOICE

WILSON'S LUCK

HARD LUCK MONEY

CHINA BLUE

BAD NEWS

CROSS FIRE

JAILBREAK

HARD ROCK

SIXKILLER

Nonfiction

THE BRAVE MEN

SATURDAY'S CHILDREN

DONKEY BASEBALL AND OTHER SPORTING DELIGHTS

I'LL TRY ANYTHING ONCE

SIXKILLER

GILES TIPPETTE

JOVE BOOKS, NEW YORK

**To Gary "The Synagogue
Cowboy" Goldstein
From the neighborhood**

SIXKILLER

A Jove Book / published by arrangement with
the author

PRINTING HISTORY
Jove edition / May 1992

ISBN: 0-515-10846-4

Jove Books are published by The Berkley Publishing Group,
200 Madison Avenue, New York, New York 10016.
The name "JOVE" and the "J" logo
are trademarks belonging to Jove Publications, Inc.

PRINTED IN THE UNITED STATES OF AMERICA

10 9 8 7 6 5 4 3 2 1

═══Chapter One

IT WAS LATE afternoon when I got on my horse and rode the half mile from the house I'd built for Nora, my wife, up to the big ranch house my father and my two younger brothers still occupied. I had good news, the kind of news that does a body good, and I had taken the short run pretty fast. The two-year-old bay colt I'd been riding lately was kind of surprised when I hit him with the spurs, but he'd been lazing around the little horse trap behind my house and was grateful for the chance to stretch his legs and impress me with his speed. So we made it over the rolling plains of our ranch, the Half-Moon, in mighty good time.

I pulled up just at the front door of the big house, dropped the reins to the ground so that the colt would stand, and then made my way up on the big wooden porch, the rowels of my spurs making a *ching-ching* sound as I walked. I opened the big front door and let myself into the hall that led back to the main parts of the house.

I was Justa Williams and I was boss of all thirty thousand deeded acres of the place. I had been so since it had come my duty on the weakening of our father, Howard, through two unfortunate incidents. The first had been the early demise of our mother, which had taken it out of Howard. That had been when he'd sort of started preparing me to take over the load. I'd been a hard sixteen or a soft seventeen at the time. The next level had jumped up when he'd got nicked in the lungs by a stray bullet. After that I'd

1

had the job of boss. The place was run with my two younger brothers, Ben and Norris.

It had been a hard job but having Howard around had made the job easier. Now I had some good news for him and I meant him to take it so. So when I went clumping back toward his bedroom that was just off the office I went to yelling, "Howard! Howard!"

He'd been lying back on his daybed, and he got up at my approach and come out leaning on his cane. He said, "What the thunder!"

I said, "Old man, sit down."

I went over and poured us out a good three fingers of whiskey. I didn't even bother to water his as I was supposed to do because my news was so big. He looked on with a good deal of pleasure as I poured out the drink. He wasn't even supposed to drink whiskey, but he'd put up such a fuss that the doctor had finally given in and allowed him one well-watered whiskey a day. But Howard claimed he never could count very well and that sometimes he got mixed up and that one drink turned into four. But, hell, I couldn't blame him. Sitting around all day like he was forced to was enough to make anybody crave a drink even it if was just for something to do.

But now he seen he was going to get the straight stuff and he got a mighty big gleam in his eye. He took the glass when I handed it to him and said, "What's the occasion? Tryin' to kill me off?"

"Hell no," I said. "But a man can't make a proper toast with watered whiskey."

"That's a fact," he said. "Now what the thunder are we toasting?"

I clinked my glass with his. I said, "If all goes well you are going to be a grandfather."

"Lord A'mighty!" he said.

We said, "Luck" as was our custom and then knocked them back.

Then he set his glass down and said, "Well, I'll just be damned." He got a satisfied look on his face that I didn't reckon was all due to the whiskey. He said, "Been long enough in coming."

I said, "Hell, the way you keep me busy with this ranch's business I'm surprised I've had the time."

"Pshaw!" he said.

We stood there, kind of enjoying the moment, and then I nodded at the whiskey bottle and said, "You keep on sneaking drinks, you ain't likely to be around for the occasion."

He reared up and said, "Here now! When did I raise you to talk like that?"

I gave him a small smile and said, "Somewhere along the line." Then I set my glass down and said, "Howard, I've got to get to work. I just reckoned you'd want the news."

He said, "Guess it will be a boy?"

I give him a sarcastic look. I said, "Sure, Howard, and I've gone into the gypsy business."

Then I turned out of the house and went to looking for our foreman, Harley. It was early spring in the year of 1898, and we were coming into a swift calf crop after an unusually mild winter. We were about to have calves dropping all over the place, and with the quality of our crossbred beef, we couldn't afford to lose a one.

On the way across the ranch yard my youngest brother, Ben, came riding up. He was on a little prancing chestnut that wouldn't stay still while he was trying to talk to me. I knew he was schooling the little filly, but I said, a little impatiently, "Ben, either ride on off and talk to me later or make that damn horse stand. I can't catch but every other word."

Ben said, mildly, "Hell, don't get agitated. I just wanted to give you a piece of news you might be interested in."

Ben was something rare. He was four years younger than me, but he knew more about horseflesh than any man I'd ever met. He was also as fast with a gun as I reckoned it was possible to be. However, Ben lacked one element in his character that only age and experience would cure—judgment. He was too hot tempered, too quick to act and then count the cost later. I'd tried to school him, but it hadn't done any good. Ben was Ben; you either took him as he was or you didn't take him at all. But he was my brother, and I might romp him around a little, but hadn't anybody else better try it. I kept hoping he'd find a woman like my Nora and settle himself down, but he still seemed content to cast his seed among saloon wenches, and I wasn't in any position to be giving him advice on that score. Not with my own past to be thrown up in my face.

I said, "All right, what is this piece of news?"

"One of the hands drifting the Shorthorn herd got sent back to the barn to pick up some stuff for Harley. He said he seen Lew Vara heading this way."

I was standing up near his horse. The animal had been worked pretty hard, and you could take the horse smell right up your nose off him. I said, "Well, okay. So the sheriff is coming. What you reckon we ought to do, get him a cake baked?"

He give me one of his sardonic looks. Ben and I were so much alike it was awful to contemplate. Only difference between us was that I was a good deal wiser and less hotheaded, and he was an even size smaller than me. He said, "I reckon he'd rather have whiskey."

I said, "I got some news for you but I ain't going to tell you now."

"What is it?"

I wasn't about to tell him he might be an uncle under such circumstances. I gave his horse a whack on the rump and said, as he went off, "Tell you this evening after work. Now get, and tell Ray Hays I want to see him later on."

He rode off, and I walked back to the ranch house thinking about Lew Vara. Lew, outside of my family, was about the best friend I'd ever had. We'd started off, however, in a kind of peculiar way to make friends. Some eight or nine years past Lew and I had had about the worst fistfight I'd ever been in. It occurred at Crook's Saloon and Café in Blessing, the closest town to our ranch, about seven miles away, of which we owned a good part. The fight took nearly a half an hour, and we both did our dead level best to beat the other to death. I won the fight, but unfairly. Lew had had me down on the saloon floor and was in the process of finishing me off when my groping hand found a beer mug. I smashed him over the head with it in a last-ditch effort to keep my own head on my shoulders. It sent Lew to the infirmary for quite a long stay; I'd fractured his skull. When he was partially recovered Lew sent word to me that as soon as he was able, he was coming to kill me.

But it never happened. When he was free from medical care Lew took off for the Oklahoma Territory, and I didn't hear another word from him for four years. Next time I saw him he came into that very same saloon. I was sitting at a back table when I saw him come through the door. I eased my right leg forward so as to clear my revolver for a quick draw from the holster. But Lew just came up, stuck out his hand in a friendly gesture, and said he wanted to let bygones be bygones. He offered to buy me a drink, but I had a bottle on the table so I just told him to get himself a glass and take advantage of my hospitality.

Which he did.

After that Lew became a friend of the family and was important in helping the Williams family in about three confrontations where his gun and his savvy did a good deal to turn the tide in our favor. After that we ran him against the incumbent sheriff who we'd come to dislike and no longer trust. Lew had been reluctant at first, but I'd told him that money couldn't buy poverty but it could damn well buy the sheriff's job in Matagorda County. As a result he got elected, and so far as I was concerned, he did an outstanding job of keeping the peace in his territory.

Which wasn't saying a great deal because most of the trouble he had to deal with, outside of helping us, was the occasional Saturday night drunk and the odd Main Street dogfight.

So I walked back to the main ranch house wondering what he wanted. But I also knew that if it was in my power to give, Lew could have it.

I was standing on the porch about five minutes later when he came riding up. I said, "You want to come inside or talk outside?"

He swung off his horse. He said, "Let's get inside."

"You want coffee?"

"I could stand it."

"This going to be serious?"

"Is to me."

"All right."

I led him through the house to the dining room, where we generally, as a family, sat around and talked things out. It was just off the big kitchen, and the table was a big slab affair that had served us well in all our growing-up years. There was a table in the kitchen, but the place was generally occupied by two female Mexican cooks—and Buttercup. Besides that the wood-burning stove made the place as hot as the hinges of Hades.

Lew and I got in there and sat down. I yelled for Buttercup to bring us some coffee. We put our boots up to add to the scars on the table that had been inflicted since my mother died. Prior to her demise wouldn't a one of us boys ever thought of throwing his boots up top of that table. But we'd got careless since that time, and even though Howard had made an issue out of it, we kept on doing it. Consequently that table looked like it had been put through a couple of wars.

I said, looking at Lew, "Get started on it."

He wouldn't face me. "Wait until the coffee comes. We can talk then."

About then Buttercup came staggering in with a couple of cups of coffee. It didn't much make any difference about what time of day or night it was, Buttercup might or might not be staggering. He was an old hand of our father's who'd helped to develop the Half-Moon. In his day he'd been about the best horse breaker around, but time and tumbles had taken their toll. But Howard wasn't a man to forget past loyalties so he'd kept Buttercup on as a cook. His real name was Butterfield, but me and my brothers had called him Buttercup, a name he clearly despised, for as long as I could remember. He was easily the best shot with a long-range rifle I'd ever seen. He had an old .50-caliber Sharps buffalo rifle, and even with his old eyes and seemingly unsteady hands he was deadly anywhere up to five hundred yards. On more than one occasion I'd had the benefit of that seemingly ageless ability. Now he set the coffee down for us and give all the indications of making himself at home. I said, "Buttercup, go on back out in the kitchen. This is a private conversation."

Naturally he got an injured look on his face and headed back for the kitchen mumbling something about "them as wants cawfee from now on kin damn well git it fer theyself."

Lew smiled, but I could see his heart wasn't in it. He was troubled, no mistake. I nodded toward his coffee. "What kind of sweetin' you want in that? Sugar or something longer?"

He said, "The kind that comes in a bottle."

So I knew it was going to be plenty serious. Lew ain't a man does much drinking before nightfall and damn little after that, not so long as he's got that badge on his chest. Without a word I got up and went into the office and came back with a bottle of whiskey. I put a good measure in Lew's cup and some in mine even though I didn't much want another drink. But it wasn't my style to let a friend, especially a friend who appeared to be a little down by the head, drink alone. Still trying to lighten the mood, I sniffed the air and said, "What month is it anyway?"

Lew looked up from his coffee. "March," he said. "Why?"

I said, still trying to get something out of Lew, "Oh, I was just wondering when Buttercup was going to take his yearly bath. I swear, I never smelled anything that walks upright that reeks like him."

He didn't even bother to smile. He said, "Justa, sit down, will you? I need to talk to you."

I sat. I picked up my coffee cup and blew on it and then took a sip. I said, "Let me have it, Lew."

He looked plain miserable. He said, "Justa, you and your family have done me a world of good. So has the town and the county. I used to be the trash of the alley and y'all helped bring me back from nothing." He looked away. He said, "That's why this is so damn hard."

"What's so damned hard?"

But instead of answering straight out he said, "They is going to be people that don't understand. That's why I want you to have the straight of it."

I said, with a little heat, "Goddammit, Lew, if you don't tell me what's going on I'm going to stretch you out over that kitchen stove in yonder."

He'd been looking away, but now he brought his gaze back to me and said, "I've got to resign, Justa. As sheriff. And not only that, I got to quit this part of the country."

Thoughts of his past life in the Oklahoma Territory flashed through my mind, when he'd been thought an outlaw and later proved innocent. I thought maybe that old business had come up again and he was going to have to flee for his life and his freedom. I said as much.

He give me a look and then made a short bark that I reckoned he took for a laugh. He said, "Naw, you got it about as backwards as can be. It's got to do with my days in the Oklahoma Territory all right, but it ain't the law. Pretty much the opposite of it. It's the outlaw part that's coming to plague me.''

It took some doing, but I finally got the whole story out of him. It seemed that the old gang he'd fallen in with in Oklahoma had got wind of his being the sheriff of Matagorda County. They thought that Lew was still the same young hellion and that they had them a bird nest on the ground, what with him being sheriff and all. They'd sent word that they'd be in town in a few days and they figured to ''pick the place clean.'' And they expected Lew's help.

''How'd you get word?''

Lew said, ''Right now they are raising hell in Galveston, but they sent the first robin of spring down to let me know to get the welcome mat rolled out. Some kid about eighteen or nineteen. Thinks he's tough.''

''Where's he?''

Lew jerked his head in the general direction of Blessing. ''I throwed him in jail.''

I said, ''You got me confused. How is you quitting going to help the situation? Looks like with no law it would be even worse.''

He said, ''If I ain't here maybe they won't come. I plan to send the robin back with the message I ain't the sheriff and ain't even in the country. Besides, there's plenty of good men in the county for the job that won't attract the riffraff I seem to have done.'' He looked down at his coffee as if he was ashamed.

I didn't know what to say for a minute. This didn't sound like the Lew Vara I knew. I understood he wasn't afraid and I understood he thought he was doing what he thought was the best for everyone concerned, but I didn't think he was thinking too straight. I said, ''Lew, how many of them is there?''

He said, tiredly, ''About eighteen all told. Counting the

robin in the jail. But they be a bunch of rough hombres. This town ain't equipped to handle such. Not without a whole lot of folks gettin' hurt. And I won't have that. I figured on an argument from you, Justa, but I ain't going to make no battlefield out of this town. I know this bunch. Or kinds like them." Then he raised his head and give me a hard look. "So I don't want no argument out of you. I come out to tell you what was what because I care about what you might think of me. Don't make me no mind about nobody else but I wanted you to know."

I got up. I said, "Finish your coffee. I got to ride over to my house. I'll be back inside of half an hour. Then we'll go into town and look into this matter."

He said, "Dammit, Justa, I done told you I—"

"Yeah, I know what you told me. I also know it ain't really what you want to do. Now we ain't going to argue and I ain't going to try to tell you what to do, but I am going to ask you to let us look into the situation a little before you light a shuck and go tearing out of here. Now will you wait until I ride over to the house and tell Nora I'm going into town?"

He looked uncomfortable, but, after a moment, he nodded. "All right," he said. "But it ain't going to change my mind none."

I said, "Just go in and visit with Howard until I get back. He don't get much company and even as sorry as you are you're better than nothing."

That at least did make him smile a bit. He sipped at his coffee, and I took out the back door to where my horse was waiting.

Nora met me at the front door when I came into the house. She said, "Well, how did the soon-to-be grandpa take it?"

She looked about as pretty as she ever had since I'd known her, and that was considerable pretty. She and I had had about as stormy a courtship as I reckoned it was possible to have. She was five years younger than I was, and for a time, she'd taught school there in Blessing. The biggest conflict that had come between us had been my work on the ranch. Too often it had kept us apart, and too often there had been dangers that came along that she didn't want me to be a part of but which I had no choice about. It had gotten so bad at one point that she'd nearly run off with a Kansas City drummer who traded in dry goods and called in at her daddy's mercantile store in Blessing. She'd left vowing she was through with what she called the wild Texas frontier. But she'd only got as far as Texarkana, Texas, where she got off the train and come home. We kind of slowly worked our way back together until we finally reached the point where she accepted my marriage proposal. But that very nearly didn't work out on account of me being ten days late for my own wedding when me and my brother Ben had to go down into Mexico and break our middle brother, Norris, out of a jail in Monterrey. But she'd been patient about it and she'd waited and she'd understood and, in the end, she'd taken me on as her spouse. I loved the woman as much as it was possible to love anything or anybody, and I loved her without reservations.

Except I was a little bit scared of her. Scared, maybe, of losing her. She appeared, I reckoned because of my size, to be a small woman, but I figured her to be around five foot six inches tall. She had light, wheat-colored hair and a bosom and hips that made my throat get thick every time I looked at her. She was loyal, she was brave, she was loving, she was my partner for life, and she could read me like a book. Wasn't any point in trying to lie to Nora. I'd tried it and every time she'd caught me out.

I said, "Howard? Like to have knocked the heels off his boots. I give him a straight shot of whiskey in celebration. He's so damned tickled I don't reckon he's settled down yet."

"What about the others?"

I said, kind of cautiously, "Well, wasn't nobody else around. Ben's out with the herd and Norris is in Blessing. Naturally Buttercup is drunk."

Meanwhile I was kind of edging my way back toward our bedroom. She followed me. I was at the point of strapping on my gunbelt when she came into the room. She said, "Why are you putting on that gun?"

For the last several years I had been promising Nora that the frontier days of Texas were over and that law and order would be the pledge of the day; that we would live in a peaceful community and that I would be a rancher who tended to home and business and that was all. I'd truly believed those days were just around the corner, but there always seemed to be something to come up to make a liar out of me.

"Why are you putting on that gun?"

It was my sidegun, a .42/40-caliber Colts revolver that I'd been carrying for several years. I had two of them, one that I wore and one that I carried in my saddlebags. The gun was a .40-caliber chambered weapon on a .42-caliber frame. The heavier frame gave it a nice feel in the hand with very little barrel deflection, and the .40-caliber slug was big enough to stop any thing you could hit solid. It had been good luck for me and the best proof of that was that I was alive.

I said, kind of looking away from her, "Well, I've got to go into town."

"Why do you need your gun to go into town?"

I said, "Hell, Nora, I never go into town without a gun. You know that."

"What are you going into town for?"

I said, "Norris has got some papers for me to sign."

"I thought Norris was already in town. What does he need you to sign anything for?"

I kind of blew up. I said, "Dammit, Nora, what is with all these questions? I've got business. Ain't that good enough for you?"

She gave me a cool look. "Yes," she said. "I don't mess in your business. It's only when you try and lie to me. Justa, you are the worst liar in the world."

"All right," I said. "All right. Lew Vara has got some trouble. Nothing serious. I'm going to give him a hand. God knows he's helped us out enough." I could hear her maid, Juanita, banging around in the kitchen. I said, "Look, why don't you get Juanita to hitch up the buggy and you and her go up to the big house and fix us a supper. I'll be back before dark and we'll all eat together and celebrate. What about that?"

She looked at me for a long moment. I could see her thinking about all the possibilities. Finally she said, "Are you going to run a risk on the day I've told you you're going to be a father?"

"Hell no!" I said. "What do you think? I'm going in to use a little influence for Lew's sake. I ain't going to be running any risks."

She made a little motion with her hand. "Then why the gun?"

"Hell, Nora, I don't even ride out into the pasture without a gun. Will you quit plaguing me?"

It took a second, but then her smooth, young face calmed down. She said, "I'm sorry, honey. Go and help Lew if you can. Juanita and I will go up to the big house and I'll personally see to supper. You better be back."

I gave her a good, loving kiss and then made my adieus, left the house, and mounted my horse and rode off.

But I rode off with a little guilt nagging at me. I swear, it is hell on a man to answer all the tugs he gets on his sleeve. He gets pulled first one way and then the other. A man damn near needs to be made out of India rubber to handle all of them. No, I wasn't riding into no danger that March day, but if we didn't do something about it, it wouldn't be long before I would be.

When I got to the big house, I pulled up in front and took

notice that Lew's horse was gone. I went clumping into Howard's room and asked after him. Howard said, "Why I don't know. We was having a little visit and I give him the good news about you and Nora and then he up and got the strangest look on his face and went out of here all of a sudden like he was shot out of a cannon. What in thunder is with the man?"

"Confusion," I said. Then I turned and went out of the room. Howard hollered after me something about what had gotten into me. I just yelled back, "Explain later. I got to git."

I could still hear him mumbling something about the "whole durn place has gone to hell and back" as I went down the hall and out the big front door. My bay colt was standing where I'd left him. I swung into the saddle and touched him with the spurs and set off at a good, high lope toward town. I didn't figure Lew could be much in front of me, and I figured to catch him well short of town.

I came up to him before the bay could work up much of a lather. He was going along at a slow canter, and I slowed my horse as I came alongside him to match his gait. He glanced over at me but didn't say anything. I said, "You didn't wait."

He still wouldn't look at me, but he said, "And you didn't tell me you was fixing to become a daddy."

"What's that got to do with it?"

He jerked his horse up at that, stopped him so hard that the animal jawed at the bit and jerked his head around. It took me a second more to stop, so that I had to turn my horse and come back. We sat there, a-horseback, facing each other. He said, "What's that got to do with it? My friend, you are funning me."

"Not so I've taken notice."

His face worked for a minute and I could see him trying to form the words. They were coming hard. He said, "I admit I kind of come to you for help. My mind wasn't completely made up when I got to your ranch. You've always been so damn good at figuring situations, I took it in my head you might help me out. Now I see you can't.''

"How come that?''

He give me a look like I'd just let my hat blow off. He said, "Hell! Yore daddy just done got through telling me the good news. I know you and I know Miss Nora. You reckon I'm the kind of son of a bitch would visit a new family with my troubles? Shit!''

It had come to be a fine early spring afternoon. The wind off the gulf was blowing in a gentle breeze that was swaying the newly growing grass. It would be good grass that would put a lot of weight on our cattle, cattle our family would profit by. We liked to think of ourselves as a lucky family, but deep down, each of us brothers knew the luck had come from the work and the hardships and dangers old Howard had faced when he'd first settled the place. I said, "What the hell has Nora going to have a kid got to do with what has to be done? You reckon this will be a better place for the kid to grow up in if you turn tail and run and eighteen or nineteen marauders come in and shoot the town up?''

"Aw, hell!'' he said. "You're talking bullshit and you know it. I ain't about to involve you in nothin' like this considering the circumstances.''

Then he tightened the reins in his hands and made to ride around me. I turned my mount at the same time and blocked him. I said, "Where you going, Lew?''

He said, "Get out of my way, Justa.''

I said, "And if I don't?''

He give me an eye. He said, "Now don't start getting stubborn. My mind is made up.''

"What? We going to get off our horses right here and have another famous fistfight? You'll probably win this one because ain't no beer mugs for me to hit you in the head with.''

"Don't talk foolish. You know me and you ain't ever going to fight again."

"Then what are you going to do?"

He looked miserable, but he said, "What I told you I was going to do. Get into town and turn my badge in. Then I'm going to send that messenger boy back to Galveston with word that they ain't got no bird nest on the ground and ride out. Maybe then them trash will leave this town alone."

"Fine," I said. I turned my horse out of his path and let him pass. But as soon as he'd gone by I touched my bay and fell in beside him. We went a few strides and then he looked over at me. He said, "Where the hell you going?"

I said, "Well, sounds to me like there's going to be an opening for sheriff. I figure to apply for the job."

That made him jerk his horse up short. I figured much more of that and he was going to take the jaw out of the animal or give him such a cold mouth he'd never again be good for riding stock. He said, "Have you gone crazy? Ain't I just told you what might be heading this way?"

"Yeah. But the circuit judge is in town and I've got some influence with him so I figured I could get appointed just about as fast as it will take you to jerk that badge off and light out of town."

He sat there staring down at the pommel of his saddle. He said, "Justa, don't play me like this. We been friends too long. You got to believe that I'm doing what I think is best."

I said, "And you got to believe I don't think you are. But if you do what you say you are going to do, you ain't leaving me no choice."

"What about Miss Nora and your baby that's a-coming?"

"That ain't got nothing to do with the business at hand. There might be some other women up there in that town expecting. If them hombres are as bad as you say they are, I don't reckon it will do them much good in their labors. Lew, you and I both know there ain't no good time for a fight. You fight when you have to. I don't like to fight but it sounds like we got one coming. You take off we're going to be short one good gun. Think on that.''

We sat there on the prairie while he studied on it. Finally he said, ''You don't figure they be coming because they think it'll be easy pickings because I was oncet one of them?''

I said, ''You were never one of them and they know it. They remember you as a young kid who wouldn't go along with their depredations. They think you're still the same. They picked this town because they thought they could ride roughshod over you. Any fool with half a mind could figure that one out. And you ain't a fool so I been having a hard time figuring out why you've come to such a course of action.''

We sat there a while longer while he mulled it over in his mind. Finally he said, ''Might be you are right. That being the case what do you reckon we ought to do about it?''

I said, ''Let's get on into town and let me talk to that robin as you call him and see what we're up against. Then we'll commence laying a course of action.''

For the first time that day he seemed to cheer up a bit. He said, ''Well, if that's what you reckon.''

''That's what I reckon,'' I said.

We put spurs to our horses and set off for town at a good gait.

═══*Chapter Two*

WHEN WE GOT into Blessing we went straight to Lew's office. I wanted to talk to the messenger boy first, but Lew went behind his desk and sat down so I took a seat in a swivel chair across from him. We hadn't said much on the ride in and now we just kind of sat there thinking. Finally I said, "Hell, Lew, there are three counties surrounding Matagorda County and there is a sheriff in every one of them. Seems likely to me we ought wire for some help. They'd expect the same of you."

For answer he opened his middle drawer and pitched me three telegrams. I looked at each one. They were all from the sheriffs of the three surrounding counties, and though the wording was different, they each said pretty much the same thing: SORRY CAN'T HELP STOP GOT MY OWN TROUBLES STOP GOOD LUCK.

I laid them back carefully on Lew's desk. I said, "Yeah, I reckon you would have thought of that without any advice from me. What about the Texas Rangers?"

He said, with a shrug, "There's one assigned down here but he's got a territory about a hundred miles square. I ain't even heard from him." He looked away. He said, "Besides, so what? A Texas Ranger? He'd just be one more gun. I've heard a lot of stories about them Rangers but they ain't bulletproof and I ain't never seen one walk on water."

We sat thinking. Finally I said, "You know the family

has got considerable influence up at the capital. What about we get a detachment of the state militia in here?''

He sat back in his chair and intertwined his fingers behind his head. He said, ''Fine. How long can they stay? A week? Two weeks? A month? Not much longer than that, if that. And all them desperadoes have to do is wait them out. We do that we might as well send that robin back with a message that we're scared to death.''

I got out a little cigarillo and lit it. Then I tossed the pack across to Lew. He took one and scratched a big-headed match on his desktop and lit his own. I said, ''Yeah, I reckon you got a point. Okay, how many men you reckon we can raise around here?''

''Good men? Men able to go up against them desperadoes?''

I looked down at the floor. It didn't need much of an answer. Our ranching community was made up mostly of hardworking men who tended to their cattle business and who occasionally fired a gun at a rattlesnake or shot a broken-legged horse or cow. They weren't gunmen; not only didn't they have the skill, but their time was badly needed in the everyday business of making a living. They would not have the time, let alone the risk they'd be taking to the detriment of their own lives and their families, to hang around town to confront a crowd of gun-happy ruffians who would think no more of shooting you than they would of ordering a drink of whiskey.

I said, ''You sure nobody here in town?''

Lew shrugged again. It was always his gesture when he didn't know what to do or say about a situation. Lew did a lot of shrugging sometimes. He said, ''Ain't nobody I'd trust to watch my back.''

I considered. I said, ''Then that just leaves me and you and Ben and Norris and Ray Hays for starters.''

Lew looked a little surprised. He said, ''Norris?''

Now it was my turn about to shrug. Norris was the

bookish brother in the family, the businessman. He'd been sent up to the university at Austin to get his learning, and he handled all our pretty extensive affairs outside of the Half-Moon ranch, which was, of course, the keystone to our business. Without the Half-Moon we wouldn't have ended up owning a bank and a hotel and a bunch of municipal bonds and various stocks and scattered parcels of land as well as notes on this ranch or that ranch where we'd advanced a hard-pressed owner the capital to keep him going.

Norris did run that part of our business, but with my okay. He couldn't sign a check for more than a thousand dollars without my cosignature, and he couldn't pull much of a deal without my okay.

Norris was a problem. Oh, not in his business dealings; at his worst he only made us a little more than you could draw on gilt-edged securities; on some deals he doubled what he went in with. The problem with Norris was that he was jealous of me and Ben. He wasn't content with his business acumen and his books and his suits with the foulard ties; he wanted to be a fighting man. But Norris wasn't really cut out for that. While me and Ben more or less took after our father with big hands and shoulders and arms, both of us dark complected, Norris strayed toward our mother's side. He was light and carried a little more of his bulk around his middle than he did in the upper part of his body. He was nearly as big as me but nowhere near as hard. Not that Norris was any pushover; he wasn't. Not for the average man. But Norris insisted on wanting to be with me and Ben, and sometimes Lew and Ray Hayes, when we were taking on the caliber of opponent he wasn't fit to handle. But that was Norris; he was sensitive and stubborn and proud. I could talk to him until I was blue in the face about the way he had it over me and Ben when it came to books and business deals, but it was just a waste of breath. For some reason he didn't seem to value that side of himself as much

as he did seeing himself in a fight. More than once I'd had
to send him home from some conflict because the business
simply couldn't afford to lose him, let alone my feelings for
him as a brother.

But I knew there'd be no way to keep him out of this
squabble, especially one so close to home and one that was
likely to take place in the town where he kept his office and
where we owned the bank and the hotel. So I just looked at
Lew and said, "Yeah, Norris. Maybe as sheriff you could
order him to stay out?"

Lew gave a short laugh. He knew Norris damn near as
well as I did. He said, "Not damn likely. You're his brother.
You're the boss. Why don't you order him out?"

I just give him a sour look and lit another cigarillo. I said,
"Might be I've got a couple of hired hands that have had a
little more gun experience then they've owned up to. I could
sound them out when I get back to the ranch and they get in
from work."

Lew still looked dispirited. He said, "Yeah, but that
would still make us only seven."

I said, "Then there's Brad Millen and Charlie Johnson."

I was speaking of a couple of ranchers who had small
spreads some five or six miles out of town. I knew them
both to be good, steady men and men who wouldn't back off
from a fight.

Lew said, "Charlie Johnson, maybe, but I can't see Brad
Millen taking a hand in the matter. He'd weigh it up and
figure they wasn't that much in it for him and turn us down
flat. This fight is going to take place in town. They ain't got
that much business that it affects them. Why should they
risk anything for Blessing? Hell, that's what I got hired
for."

Lew was right about Brad Millen; he did calculate
everything out down to the last cat's hair. I'd done a few
cattle trades with him, and I'd never seen a man as careful
in the way he kept score of a tally. But he wasn't a

mean-hearted person; I knew for a fact that he'd more than once donated the services of one of his stud bulls or loaned out a few of his hired hands to a less fortunate neighbor. He was just a man who liked to get his money's worth.

I said, "Might be a way to get them to throw in with us and lend a hand."

Lew said, "Yeah?"

"We hold notes on both of them and both of them is overdue."

Lew had been looking off toward a far wall, his hands still intertwined behind his head. He took them down slowly and swiveled his eyes back to me. "You wouldn't."

I took a drag off my cigarillo and said, "You got any whiskey?"

"Yeah." He pulled open a drawer. "Really?"

I said, "I generally will do anything I have to to win a fight."

Lew, who was part Mexican and part Cherokee Indian, could look several ways. Today he was looking like a gringo. He said, "Well, it's your business. If you feel all right about it I ain't going to be one to complain. But that would still only make us nine. We'd be on the bad side of two to one odds. At best."

I said, "Hell, Lew, what do you want—egg in your beer?"

He kind of hunched forward. He said, "I still think my way is best. We send that robin back with the news that I ain't the law around here anymore, they likely to change their line of thinking and head for greener pastures."

"Bullshit." I said. "What they're liable to do is figure there ain't any law around here at all and the pastures can't get any greener. Lew, I swear I can't figure this out. All you seem to be talking about is running. I know you ain't scared so what the hell is it? You ain't about to convince me that by pulling out that gang won't head on down here. Hell, you've throwed the robin in jail. Don't you reckon he'll report back that you was sheriff last time he looked? It ain't going to take no stretch for them to figure out they ain't a bit of trained law here? Now, will you tell me what the hell is going on?''

His face flamed, though it was hard to tell as dark as he was, and he said, ''Ain't a damn thing going on. I done told you everything I know.'' Then he suddenly got up and walked over to a back wall and made a big show out of inspecting a rack of carbine rifles that were there.

I said, ''All right. Don't you reckon it's about time we talked to the robin?''

''We better first figure out what we want to tell him.''

''What you reckon we ought to tell him?''

He shook his head. ''I don't know. Hell, Justa, you're the one that always does all the planning. What do you reckon?''

I said, ''It's different this time, Lew. This is law business and I ain't the sheriff. I'm here to help, but you are the boss.''

He made a little huffing sound in his throat that tried to pass for a laugh. He said, ''That'll be the day, Justa Williams. You ain't had a boss since you was about twelve years old. Naw, we'll work this deal together. I'm smart enough to know that you're smarter than me.'' He give me a look. ''I need your help, old friend.''

''You have that,'' I said. But I was still troubled that he wasn't telling me something about this gang coming down. He'd been exonerated of all charges against him in the past, and I couldn't help wondering if some members of this bunch of ruffians didn't know something about Lew that he didn't want the rest of us to know and that he'd figured the best way to avoid any shame was to cut and run. I knew the bullet or the fist hadn't been made that Lew was afraid of, but I also knew how much he valued the good opinion of the Williams family. But it was not an issue I was going to push. Lew was a proud man and I was willing he should play his hand the way he saw it.

I said, "Who you reckon is the boss of this bunch?"

He made a grimace. "I already know. Sam Sixkiller."

"Sixkiller?"

"Yeah, he's a low-down half-breed. His daddy was a poor-mouth Comanche and his mother was a white whore. He got the best out of both of them, which is about like saying he drug the best out of two piles of trash."

"He any good?"

Lew nodded. He said, "Oh, yes. He ain't never seen a scruple or a conscience. And he's a smooth mouth. Minute he starts talking friendly you better put one hand on your wallet and the other on the butt of your pistol."

"How old a man is he?"

Lew reflected for a minute. He said, "Maybe forty, maybe a little younger."

I whistled. That was pretty good going for a man in his line of work. I said, "I reckon we better take this man serious."

"Oh, yes," Lew said.

I said, "Let's go talk to the robin."

"Let's figure out what we're going to talk about first. Hell, Justa, we got to know that."

"And I got to know what the robin is like before I can figure out what to say. You *savvy*?"

He came back to his desk and sat down. He said, "Always got to be right."

"Ain't no chore around you."

He gave me a look, but he said, "Let's have a drink." He set the bottle of whiskey on the desk and then came out of his drawer with a couple of glasses. He poured us both out a good shot, and we give our toast, saying "Luck," and then knocked them back. I said, "He ain't going to get any smarter sitting back there."

"All right," he said. He wiped the back of his hand

across his mouth and took a ring of keys out of the middle drawer of his desk. He said, "You got any idea a-tall of how you're going to play it?"

I shook my head. "Just catch him on the fly. Go whichever way he wants to be driven."

"All right." He heaved himself out of the chair. "Let's go."

Lew had said the boy was about nineteen, but he didn't look anywhere near that. He still had them pustules on his face like boys just coming into their teens. He was slight and almighty nervous looking. I took him to be closer to sixteen. He was dressed in denim jeans and an old, double-lined wool coat that the stuffing was coming out of. I couldn't blame him for wearing the coat because the back of Lew's jail was cold and damp, even in the seventy-degree early spring weather. He was the only prisoner back in the cells, and he got up right smart when me and Lew came through the door from the front office. He came to the bars and gripped them and said, in a whining voice, "This ain't right, sher'ff. I ain't done nuthin' and you done clamped me here in this hoosegow. By gawd, it ain't right!"

Lew said, "Says his name is Axel. I don't know if that's his first name or his family name. I don't know a damn thing about him except what he's told me."

I studied him a little closer. If he hadn't come from a mixed breed of pups and been brought up on biscuits and bullshit, I didn't know anything about anything. I said, "Well, unlock the cell and let's go in and talk to the boy. Likely he's got a bunch of conversation he wants to make with us."

Lew went up to the cell door with a big key extended. He said, "Get away from the door, boy. Go set on your cot. We're coming in."

He did as he was told. Lew and I went into the cell, Lew making sure the door was locked behind him. It kind of amused me. The kid couldn't have weighed more than a hundred and thirty pounds. I said, "Yes, I reckon we better be careful. Though I do think that between us we can handle this maverick steer here."

There was an opposing bunk, and me and Lew sat down on it, side by side. I got out my package of the little cigarillos and offered one to Axel, but he just shook his head. He said, "I don't take tobaccer."

"A damn wise decision," I said. "Might stunt your growth."

For a minute or two we sat there looking at each other. I could tell the kid was scared though he was doing a pretty good job of acting bravado. Still, a strange jail in a strange town with strange people will generally break down your backbone. I said, "What's your whole name, boy?"

He said, "I was give to un'erstan' I was comin' in amongst friends. I ain't sayin' 'nother word 'bout myself. You kin ast till you turn blue in the face. I don't see no reason to he'p y'all out in the least notion."

I got up, dropping my cigarillo butt on the floor and blowing out a mouthful of smoke. I said, "Well, the hell with it, Lew. Hang the little bastard. I'll tell the carpenters to start building the scaffold. If the county won't pay for it then I will. Sack him up. I ought to be able to get the circuit judge to sign the papers today so we can hang him sometime tomorrow morning."

Lew picked up on the direction I was going in. He got up right behind me and said, "All right. Hate to see the kid hang so early. Couldn't you do it in the afternoon? Maybe even the late afternoon?"

I turned and give the kid a look. The process of real fear was starting across his face. I said, "Shit, no! I got a cattle ranch to run. I can't be wasting time on some little punk kid. Hang the bastard."

He'd come off the bunk, his face going kind of pale. He said, "You can't hang me, I ain't done nuthin'."

I pulled my revolver and pointed it at him. I said, "You

sit right back down there on your cot or I'm fixing to save the county the price of some rope. You understand me?''

He stared, gawk-eyed, for a second and then he slowly set back down on the cot. I said, ''Boy, you got a few things to learn. We hung a man last week for lathering up one of my horses and putting spur marks on him. I *own* this county, so if I say you are going to hang you are going to feel that death trap fall out from under your feet. It will cost me nearly a hundred dollars to have that scaffold built, but I will have it done, you can bet on that. In fact, you are betting your life.''

Lew said, ''Now, Justa, give the boy another chance. He's young. Maybe he'll learn.''

I holstered my revolver, shaking my head as I did so. ''Oh, that's the line all you do-gooders take. I say hang him now before he can do any more harm. I asked him a simple question and damn if he don't come smart aleck with me. No, hang the little bastard. Open that door, I need some fresh air. I don't reckon this soon-to-be-dead boy has had a bath in many a month. Hate to be the undertaker that has to deal with the body.''

The kid wanted to get up and plead his case, but I give him a hard look and he faded back down onto his cot. Lew unlocked the cell and we went into his office. He was in the lead, and he went straight to his desk and poured us both out a tumbler of whiskey. He was laughing so hard he had trouble with the pouring and damn near spilled some. He said, ''Justa, you ought to be ashamed.''

I said, ''Are we in a fight or not?''

He said, ''I reckon.''

''Then don't talk to me about being ashamed. Is Morris Carter still doing handiwork around town?''

''Near as I know. But your daddy-in-law would know better since he generally works out of the mercantile.''

''Fine,'' I said. I downed my whiskey without bothering with the toast. I said, ''I'm going to hunt him up and give him ten dollars to knock together something that looks like a scaffold. Let young Axel spend the night thinking on that. He might be a little more cooperative come the small hours of the morning.''

"You mean I got to stay here and nursemaid that little bastard?''

"Yeah,'' I said. "I mean exactly that.'' I got up. "And you better do a damn good job of it. We need some information off that boy. Only way to get it is to scare the liver out of him.''

Lew said, "How far you willing to go?''

I was heading for the door. I stopped and said, "That boy come in here talking about murder and robbing. You figure out from that how far I'm willing to go. And when you go back to talk to him you might remind him of that. It's a hanging offense. I'll go that far. Does that answer your question, Lew?''

He studied me for just a second, and then he said, "Yeah. I reckon it does. I guess I just thought only I was tough.''

I fiddled with the doorknob before turning it and opening the door. I said, "Lew, I ain't tough. I just ain't going to see what my family built up taken away by a bunch of ne'er-do-wells. And that includes really hanging the kid. You're the law, but the circuit judge is in town and I do have influence with him. Don't bet I won't do what I have to do.''

Then I went through the door and stepped out on the street, leaving Lew staring after me. Of course I wasn't going to have the boy hanged; in fact I had no such power, but Lew would be talking to the kid later, and it was important that he believe that I would indeed hang him. Otherwise, Lew might not be as convincing as he needed to be. It was a dirty trick to play on a friend, but I felt we were in a serious situation.

I walked down to Parker's Mercantile. Lonnie Parker, my father-in-law, was the proprietor. I had always been friendly with Lonnie, even when my courting of Nora hadn't been going as well as could be expected. But I'd always suspected that Lonnie had been extra nice to me more because of the trade he got off our ranch than just because he liked me. But now, of course, he didn't have to worry about that and he was just as friendly as ever. As I walked into his store I wondered if he knew that Nora was going to have a baby. She'd been into Dr. Jackson the day before, and it would be a woman's nature to tell her mother something so important in the female line; but I was kind of half-hoping I'd been the first she'd told. I'd soon know; Lonnie couldn't keep anything to himself.

He was behind his counter, and he give me a big smile and a hello when I came in. We visited for a few minutes and he didn't say anything about the baby so I reckoned he didn't know. That kind of pleased me. When I inquired about Morris Carter's whereabouts, Lonnie jerked his head toward the rear of the establishment. He said, "He's back there gettin' some paint. You want me to call him?"

"I'll go on back," I said. I strolled back through the dim store, past tables of ladies' hats and cloth goods and saddles and bridles and boots and high button shoes, all of them coming together to make that smell you can't get nowhere else but a mercantile store. I found Morris in the back mixing up a bucket of paint with a stick, lifting the lead from the bottom to mix in with the lighter stuff that was on top. I said, "Morris, I got a job for you. Needs doing this afternoon."

He scratched the back of his neck. He was an awful nervous man, but if you needed some handiwork done he was the party you wanted. I explained what I needed. I ended by saying, "Build it on that vacant lot so it's in full view of the windows of the cells at the jail."

He swallowed. He was a tall, skinny man with a prominent Adam's apple, and it bobbed up and down like a rubber ball. He said, "You, you, want me to build you a, a hang-hanging scaffold, Mr. Williams?"

On top of everything else he stuttered. I said, "No, Morris, don't *build* a regular hanging scaffold. Just make it look like you're building one."

He give me a blank look. "Huh?"

I said, "Morris, just go over there to that lot beside the jail and start nailing some lumber together. Make a lot of noise. Hell, you can build a chicken coop with some short stairs leading up to the top. Just go and do it. This afternoon."

His Adam's apple went bob-bob. He said, "Mistuh Williams, I done promised Mizz, Mizz Ar-Armbrister I'd git some paintin' done fer her, her this a'tternoon. En you know, know Mizz Armbrister."

I got out a ten dollar bill and gave it to him. I said, "Morris, you don't have to get it done this afternoon. Just take some old lumber over there and do a lot of hammering and nail some boards together. Do it for about an hour. Then go back in the morning and hammer some more."

"You ain't, ain't got no sort of plan fer me, me to work from?"

I was running out of patience. I said, "Just do what I'm telling you. Hammer and nail. You got it?"

"It be all right with the high shur'ff?"

"It's his idea."

He took the money reluctantly, still looking puzzled. Well, I didn't care if he understood or not. All I wanted was that robin to hear the hammering going on outside his cell window and let him do a spot of worrying.

Lonnie invited me to stay in town and take supper with them at his house, but I begged off, saying I needed to get on back home. After that I stopped in for a moment with Lew and told him what I'd arranged. He just kind of sighed and said he hoped I knew what I was doing.

I said, "You're the sheriff. And you can stop my plans anytime you want to."

He give me a kind of bleak smile. "No," he said, "I reckon I'll string along with you on this one. Lord knows, I ain't had no better ideas. But I still don't understand what you're going to do with that boy."

"Neither do I," I said. "But I figure if we rattle him enough we might either get some information or some cooperation. I got to go."

"Hey wait—"

But I'd already shut the door behind me and was mounting my horse. Lew came out just as I was about to rein away from the front of his office. He said, "You ain't going to leave me hanging, are you?"

That made me smile, his choice of words. I knew what he meant, but I said, "I thought that would concern Axel."

He said, "Aw, hell, Justa, you know what I mean."

I said, "I'll be by in the morning. Take a good night's sleep."

Then I wheeled my horse and set off for the ranch.

I got to the big house about the time Nora was starting to fret about me being way late for supper. I got washed up as quick as I could and sat down to the table. She'd cooked a pot roast with potatoes and onions and green beans on the side. The rest of the family had eaten, so it was just me and her.

Nora let me eat before she said, "Well?"

"Well what?"

"What's going on in town that you had to wear your gun?"

I debated whether to try and lie or to not tell her the whole truth. Finally I decided on a kind of neutral course. I said, tearing off a piece of bread and mopping it in the gravy, "Nora, honey, would you be willing if I didn't tell you all about this right now?"

"No," she said.

"It ain't really all that serious. It's just kind of confused. Kind of hard to explain."

She said, "Justa Williams, you've never had any trouble making yourself understood before. I don't see why now should be any different. I've put up with enough from you to last ten women a lifetime. What makes you think you've got anything to tell me now that will surprise me? Is it trouble?"

She was boxing me up. I tell you, I hated to give her any kind of news except the best, what with her condition. I said, "Look here, Nora, I ain't trying to hide anything, it's that the situation ain't real well formed up yet."

She said, "Well, why don't you tell me what you can?"

I shoved my plate away. I said, "I need to talk to my brothers. Why don't you and Juanita go back to the house and I'll be there as soon as I have a little talk with Ben and Norris."

"You want some pie?"

I shook my head and got out a cigarillo and lit it. "Naw, I'm full. I'll take a drink of whiskey in the office and then get on home."

She sat there resting her elbows on the table and framing her face with her open hands. She looked near heart-stopping pretty in the lamplight. She said, "Must be important if you've got to talk to your brothers about it."

I reached out a hand across the old scarred dining room table. At one time Nora had tried to insist on a dining cloth, but it kept getting things spilled on it so she'd finally given up. Kind of slowly she took a hand away from her head and covered mine with it. I said, "Nora, if I thought it was anything you needed to know I'd tell you quick as a whip. But it ain't nothing for you to bother your head about. I don't want you worrying yourself over nothing."

"I'll do it anyway," she said. "Why not just tell me? It can't be as bad as what I'm thinking."

I sighed and shook my head. I said, "You are a handful.

All right. You're going to feel foolish when I tell you." I readied up my mind and told her a pretty good half lie. I said, "You remember that Lew had a little trouble in his younger days up there in Oklahoma Territory. Well, he got word that some of his old running mates was coming to pay him a visit. He didn't know if he had the authority, not having had the proper schooling as a lawman, to clap them in the jail the minute they hit town and not wait until they got up to some mischief. Judge Kelhorn, the circuit judge, is in town and he wanted me to go over and use what little influence I had to see what could be done. I done it and that was all there was to it."

She searched my face. "Lew couldn't have asked the judge himself?"

"Lew's a little shy about his past," I said. "Especially when it comes to circuit judges. I reckon he figured I could ask it more delicately than he could without giving away a whole lot about what he done before."

She was still examining my face, looking for the lie. She said, "And that's all there is to it?"

"That's all," I said. "Now let me ask you a question— When you went into town to see Dr. Jackson did you stop off and tell your mother about the baby?"

She smiled kind of secretively and shook her head. "No."

"Why not?"

She squeezed my hand. She said, shyly, "Because I wanted you to be the first to know. I'll go into town tomorrow and tell them."

I looked at the empty plate sitting in front of her, untouched. I said, "Nora, did you eat?"

"I had a bite earlier with the others. I'd planned to eat with you but I just didn't feel like it."

I said, "Now, dammit, Nora, you've got to eat. You've got to keep your strength up."

She got up and began clearing the table. She said, "Damn

you, Justa Williams, you get pregnant and see how anxious you are to eat. Don't be preaching at me, a man like you."

Wasn't much I could say. I got up. I said, "See you at home in about an hour."

"Going to take you an hour to talk to your brothers about this business that isn't so important?"

I said, with a little heat, "Goddammit, Nora, we also run a ranch on the side in case you ain't noticed. I know you think I spend all my time thinking up schemes to worry you but that just ain't quite the case."

She was nearly to the kitchen door, carrying a dish in each hand. She stopped and turned. She said, "I had that coming. I'm sorry, honey. But you got to admit with your past history . . ."

Of course all that did was make me feel more guilty. I said gruffly, "Forget about it. I reckon women take on a little more at times like this."

"I wouldn't know," she said. Then she passed on into the kitchen.

I ambled along the hall and turned into the office. Ben was sitting in an easy chair against the wall having a glass of whiskey. Norris was at the big desk going over some papers. Howard was in his rocking chair with a well-watered whiskey in his hand. They glanced up when I come in. Ben said, "Well! Here comes the new papa."

I give Howard a look. I said, "Couldn't you have let me tell them myself?"

He played the innocent. He said, "I reckoned you already had. I was that surprised when they let on they hadn't heard."

"You old liar," I said. I got a glass and went over to the table by Ben's chair and poured myself out a pretty good bait of whiskey. I said, "You wouldn't tell the truth for spot cash." I took a sip of the good whiskey. It didn't have much effect falling in on top of all that pot roast I'd eaten. They say a man ought not to drink on an empty stomach, but if you want quick results that is the way to go.

Now Norris pushed his chair back and said, "Well, congratulations are in order I believe."

I nodded my head. "Thank you, sir. Thank you."

Ben said, "What you reckon it's going to be?"

I took another swig of whiskey. "Young," I said.

Ben said, "Ha, ha, big brother. Very funny."

"Not near as funny as that question or how tired I'm going to get of being asked it."

Norris was leaning back in his chair, contemplating me. He said, "I hear Lew Vara was out here this afternoon and that you followed him back into town. What's going on?"

I sat down and sipped at my whiskey before I answered. Finally, I told them the whole story. Ben whistled, lowly. Norris sat up straight in his chair and said, "By, God, we own considerable property in that town. The hotel, the bank, the auction barn. Not to mention several parcels of land and some rent houses."

I said, tiredly, because that was the way I was feeling, "I know, Norris. But that ain't why I'm so worried. They is people in that town. Friends of ours. And there's Lew."

Howard rumbled to life. He said, "How many from here, Justa?"

I shook my head. I said, "I don't know right off." We had twelve regular cowhands not counting Ray Hays or Harley, our foreman. But, for the spring work, we'd taken on four extra hands. It was out of them four extra that I was thinking there might be a couple that wanted to make a bonus. I turned to Ben, who was the expert on such matters and said, "Ben, what about Willy Boyd and James Kline?"

He knew what I meant, but he had to study on it for a minute. He said, "Maybe, but I'd have to see them and I'd have to talk to them. I reckon your instinct is right. I just can't say right now."

I said, "Well, get them off to the side tomorrow. If they

look like they can be of any help, offer them a hundred dollar bonus and we'll put them up in the hotel in town.''

Norris objected. He said, ''But that takes them off the spring work. That will make us two hands short.''

I give him a look but didn't say anything. It was Howard that observed, ''Well, Norris, what would you have them be, seven miles away from the trouble when it comes? We may not get no warning the way Justa tells it. Must it be Lew Vara by himself to hold them off until we get there?''

Norris looked down and didn't say anything.

I said, to Ben, ''Norris has got a point. If Willy and James do want to go into town and get sworn in as deputies for Lew, you might tell Harley he's got free rein to hire two more men in their places.''

He said, ''What about Ray Hays?''

That made me smile. Ray was a kind of special case. He might be considered, by others, as an employee of the ranch, but he wasn't in agreement with that. In some ways he was like Buttercup, almost one of the family. Some years back Ray had saved my life by changing sides from that of a man that was attempting to kill me. He had come to my aid and I reckoned I owed him plenty for that. That had been up in the hill country of Texas around Bandera. When it had all been over I'd hired him to come back to the Half-Moon. Supposedly he worked for Ben on the remuda, but he and Ben had become great friends and I didn't reckon I'd ever seen him do all that much work. But he was funny and he was brave and he was loyal and, outside of me and Ben and Lew Vara, I reckoned him to be the best gun hand in that part of the country. I could spook him with a look or a word, but hadn't anybody else try it.

I looked over at Ben. I said, ''What about Ray Hays?''

''He's gone off courting. Headed for Palacios.''

''What! Who give him off?''

Ben said, ''I did.''

I commenced to swear and I done a pretty good job of it.

I said, "By what right do you give my hired hands off without coming to me first?"

Ben said, "He works for me. Or have you forgot?"

I said, "Then you either get on a horse or you send somebody. I want him back here first thing in the morning."

Ben stared at me for a long moment. Then he said, "No."

I blinked. "What?"

"You ain't deaf. Ray's been cooped up on this ranch for a considerable time. He heard an old girl friend of his was in Palacios. He took off for there this morning. I ain't calling him back. He's due the time off."

I leaned toward him. I said, "Ben, have you lost your senses? We got us a serious situation on our hands. I'm all for a man getting all the pussy he can handle but this ain't got nothing to do with it. Now you go and do like I tell you."

Palacios was a hard twenty-mile ride away. If we got a rider started that night he might make it back with Hays by mid-morning. Meanwhile I had to go see the two ranchers, Brad Millen and Charlie Johnson, and to sweeten up Nora and to get myself into town and see how scared the robin was. I stared at Ben, waiting for him to get up.

But he just shook his head. He said, again, "No. I ain't that interested in Lew Vara's problems. I always reckoned there was something about his past he never come all that clean about." He give me a defiant look. "I ain't getting mixed up in it any more than I have to and I ain't calling Hays back."

I could feel Howard looking at me from where his rocking chair was along the far wall. More than once Ben had defied my authority, as had Norris, but never so blatantly, never so forcefully. I got to my feet. I said, "You're fired, Ben. Norris, take him off the payroll." Then I came back to Ben. I said, "I can't fire you from the family corporation or I would. So I reckon you'll still get your cut of that. But you ain't drawing wages no more. And I can't fire you from this house because it still belongs to Howard. But I can fire you from this range because I'm the boss of that. Don't let me catch you on it. You be wise you'll take what horse flesh you personally own and get the hell off my ranch until you figure out who is boss.''

The last thing I saw as I stalked out of the room was Norris looking at me with his mouth open. Dad just had his head slightly inclined, one hand holding his cane, staring at Ben. Howard had once told me that an army couldn't have but one general and a ranch couldn't have but one boss, and if I wanted to run a ranch the right way, I would have to be that boss. Well, it had just happened, right in front of his eyes. The shock to me had been that it had been Ben, the young foolisher that was always looking for a fight. I didn't know what had put the burr under his saddle blanket, but he'd picked a bad time to get a hump in his back with me. As I walked out the front door I wondered if he'd come around. And then I found myself thinking that I didn't give a damn. Maybe he was feeling his oats. Well, that was fine. Except he could have found a hell of a lot better a time to start feeling them.

Our foreman, Harley, had a little house just down the line past our two bunk houses and our two big barns. He'd been with us going on eighteen years and he deserved a good style of living and his own place. He lived there with his wife, a kind little lady who was much given to teaching Sunday school and growing vegetables in her own little plot. I went up to the door of his cabin and give it a pretty good pounding. It was going on for nine o'clock so I knew that Harley would already be asleep. But, finally, he come staggering to the door, an old weather-beaten man in his mid forties wearing mostly a pair of long handles but trying to pull a pair of jeans up as he opened the door. He was still about half-asleep, but he recognized me and said, ''Yes-sir?''

I said, ''Harley, I want you to go shake somebody out of

the bunkhouse and send them off to Palacios. Ray Hays is there and I want him back here by morning.''

He looked at me kind of blankly. "Huh?"

I said, "Harley, have you taken to being hard of hearing?"

"Nossir."

"Then I want you to send somebody to Palacios and fetch Ray Hays back here by morning."

"Where would he be? In Palacios?"

I said, "I don't know. That's your job. Just tend to it."

"Right now?"

I was turning away. I stopped and said, over my shoulder, "Yes, Harley, right now."

I left him staring after me and went back to the main house. I didn't go in. I just gathered up my horse, swung aboard, and set out for my own house. It had not been a pleasant day's work.

I got home just as Nora was preparing for bed. She was in her nightgown and I come up behind her and put my arms around her, but I could feel the coolness. I said, "What the hell's the matter, honey?"

She said, "You are an awful liar, Justa Williams."

I said, "In what way?"

"You know."

"Know what?"

She wheeled in my arms so that she was facing me. She said, "I've been thinking on this Lew Vara business. You make it seem so simple but I think there's a good deal more to it. I think you have been lying to me by omission."

I sat down on the side of the bed. I said, "Maybe you're right. Maybe it is a little more serious than I'm thinking it is. I just fired Ben."

She was brushing her hair in front of the bureau mirror. At my words she stopped in mid stroke and looked around at me. She said, "You *what*?"

I looked down at the floor. My impetuous words were

already coming back to haunt me. I said, "I said I fired Ben."

"But how can you fire Ben? He's family."

"He works on this ranch. I run this ranch and I can fire anyone on it."

She put the brush down on the bureau top. She said, "I do not believe I am hearing this. Whatever in the world possessed you to do such a thing?"

I shrugged. I said, "I give him an order. He refused to do it. I give it to him again. He still refused. Can't be but one boss and I got the job. So I told Norris to take him off the payroll."

"But whatever was it about? What kind of order did he refuse?"

"It doesn't matter," I said. I got up and started for the little office I had off the parlor, intent on having a drink. Nora followed me. She said, "Now just a minute, husband. There's more here than meets the eye. You and Ben have been arguing since you were both able to talk. Does this have anything to with this Lew Vara business?"

I kept going like I hadn't heard her, passing through the door of my office and taking a bottle of whiskey and a glass out of the cabinet on the wall. I poured myself out a drink and downed it. She was standing in the door, her hands on her hips, watching me. She looked mighty fetching in her little nightgown. She said, "Well? Are you going to answer me?"

I poured myself out another drink, corked the bottle, put it back in the cabinet, and then sat down in my desk chair. I said, "Nora, it don't really matter what was at issue. He defied me. Said he wouldn't do something I told him. He may be an heir to this ranch but he's also a hired hand. Just like I am, just like Norris. Hired hands do what their bosses tell them without back talk."

She took a couple of steps toward me. She said, "So it is about Lew Vara's trouble. That trouble you said didn't amount to anything. Well, it must amount to something if Ben's willing to fight you about it.'' She came still farther until she could kneel by my chair. She looked up into my face. She said, ''Justa, you are starting to worry me badly. You must tell me the whole of this business. I want to know just how dangerous it is.''

I did not want to upset her. But I knew that sooner or later the truth would have to come out. Finally I began, haltingly, to tell her about half the story. When I was finished she just sort of clutched her stomach and said, ''You'll have nothing to do with it.''

I took my face out of my hands and said, ''How do I do that?''

She said, kind of wildly, ''I don't care! But you have this child.''

I said, ''Nora, there are babies born all over this territory. If the men quit their jobs on account of that then nothing would be done. I'm asking you to understand me.''

She said, ''I understand you all right, Justa Williams. You care more for your friend Lew Vara than you do for me and your own unborn baby.''

I got up. I said, ''Oh, goddammit, that ain't got nothing to do with it. I owe Lew a bunch. But more than that I owe this town and this area much more.''

The flame got up in her face. She said, ''Who the hell elected you the protector of all? Justa Williams! The big hero! Well, I'm sick of it. You just leave me alone.''

I put it down to the way that women get when they are of their time to have babies. I went up and tried to put my arms around her. She shoved them away. There were tears running down her cheeks. She said, ''Oh, you! Oh, the hell with you!''

I did my best to try and get her to listen to me, but it was a lost cause. She was of a fixed opinion, and nothing I could say was going to change her or give her pause. I was just glad I hadn't told her any more than I had.

Finally I just gave up on it and went into my office and started in to nursing the bottle. Hell, it didn't seem like a man could do what he felt he ought to do without answering to half the folks in his life. Finally I got enough whiskey in me so I figured I could fall into bed and go to sleep. I didn't figure Nora was going to sleep close to me, but then sometimes that is the price you will have to pay. I went to sleep thinking how quick I was going to have to get out of bed the next morning to see my two hired hands and then ride the ten or twelve miles to see Millen and Johnson. I knew it wasn't going to be a good sleep. I was already flinching, and on top of everything else, I'd lost Ben, my top gun. Hell, didn't seem like anything was going right.

And then there was the robin and the judge I had to talk to. It sure would have been better if I'd had my wife's support. But she'd gone to bed, wanting no part of me. Just before I dropped off to sleep I figured I'd better leave the judge out of it for the time being. He might turn official on me and the situation was still too uncertain to be thrust under hard and fast rules.

═══Chapter Three

THERE COME A hell of a knocking on our front door just after dawn. I wasn't awake, as I normally would have been, on account of staying up so late worrying about Lew and his troubles, but mostly worrying about how Nora was taking matters. Nora got out of bed first and went to the door. I just laid there under the covers against the coolness of the March morning. Pretty soon she came back in her gown and robe and said, "It's Ben."

I got right out of bed. I said, "Put on some coffee and then leave us alone."

I dressed slowly. I knew that Nora had let Ben into the parlor, but I figured to keep him cooling his heels as long as possible. He either wanted more trouble or he was going to make an apology. I wasn't in the mood for either.

As I came out of the back bedroom I could see the glow of both the lantern from the kitchen and the one from the parlor. Nora had obviously lit only one in the front setting room, which generally took about four to make it out that people lived there. I walked slowly into the parlor. Ben was sitting on the big divan, twirling his hat in his hands. I come into the room, but I didn't say a word to him, just went around firing up the lanterns. Through the front window I could see the sun just getting above the horizon, but the lanterns give us the light where we could each see the other's face. I said, "Well, what do you want?"

He said, after a painful second, "I'd, uh, kind of like to apologize."

I said, harshly, "You can take your apologies to the grocery story and see how many turnips they'll buy you. You defied me, Ben, and that ain't going to be soon forgotten."

He looked down. He said, "I know it. And I'm ashamed of myself."

With no less harshness I said, "Well, that just won't get it. You been the spoiled pup of this litter for way too long and it's damn near time you learned yourself a lesson."

His head was still down. He said, "I been thinking on this all night. After you left, Dad and Norris give me a pretty good reading out. Then Harley come in, in some state of confusion about Hays." Ben made a motion with his hand, "Since Hays is supposed to work for me— But then it kind of come through to me that he actually works for you. We all do." He was still playing with the brim of his hat, but he looked up at me. He said, "I was just wondering— wondering, mind you—if you might not take me back. I understand you can fire me. It kind of stunned me at first and I didn't think you could until Dad and Norris said it was a fact."

I kind of looked at him. The sun was up good now and the light was flooding the room. I went around trimming lanterns, leaving only two on low wick. Before I could say anything Nora come up the hallway from the kitchen. She said, "What do you want for breakfast?"

It was a kind of foolish question because I ate about the same thing every morning. But I knew why she'd asked it. I said, "Biscuits and cream gravy. With coffee."

She said, "For both of y'all?"

I looked over at Ben. He was staring at the floor. Without turning my head I said, "Yeah. But don't rush."

Then I looked back at Ben. He was still staring at the

floor. It hurt my heart to see my little brother like that, but I hardened it and said, "So you've come to beg for your job back. Is that about it?"

"Yes," he said.

I said, "As far as I'm concerned you are just another hand. You have, in the past, taken it on yourself to act like you was something else just because you was my brother. Well, this time you overstepped yourself. You got anything to say to that?"

"No," he said.

"You was wrong, weren't you?"

"Yes."

"*What?*"

"Yes *Sir.*"

"How bad you want a job back?"

"You said *a* job."

"You heard me right."

"What do you mean by *a* job?"

"Beg and find out!"

He give me a look. He said, "I ain't going to beg."

I said, "Then you damn sure ain't going to get no job. To tell you the truth I've been about sick of your free and easy ways. You think just because you were born into this family that you can have things your own way. Well, let me tell you, buster, that ain't the way it works. When dad turned this ranch over to me he told me to run it. And that means running everybody on it, blood kin or not. You been testing me for a good number of years. Well, you just ran out of them little brother chips you been spending so freely. You want a job, it's going to take a little more than you're sorry. You want a job, you're going to have to ask for it same as any other out-of-work cowhand. Which is what you are. Otherwise you can take that hat you keep fiddling with and get the hell out of my house."

I stood there, in the middle of my setting room, my chest

kind of heaving. I was damn good and mad. I figured the reason I was so mad was that Ben, the man I thought I could count on beyond any other, had let me down.

He was a good long while in answering. Then he said, kind of lowly, "You know I can't make it without this ranch and this home. I'd be pretty lost without it. And I've always had you as my big brother that I could turn to no matter how bad I screwed up. Except I got to tell you something. . . . Seems here of late I've come to resent you and all that authority you carry around like it was nailed to you. I know, I know, that ain't your fault. You got to do it if you're going to be a boss. But Dad said something to me after you left that kept me awake all night. He said I'd betrayed you."

He looked up at me, then, and cut his hand through the air. He said, "Justa, I swear I never meant that. I guess I been getting too full of piss and vinegar here lately. I guess I was just looking for any issue to have a falling out with you over. Big brother, you make mighty large boot tracks. Sometimes they ain't that easy to follow in. I done wrong and I talked wrong. I'll take whatever you give me."

I stood there looking down at him. Finally I said, though my heart was against it, "All right. Report to Harley. We've got a calf crop coming in. You do whatever he tells you to do. You don't get your orders from me anymore; you get them from Harley."

There was startlement in his face. He said, "You mean I ain't bossing the remuda anymore?"

"No. Ray Hays now has your job."

"What will I be doing?"

I said, evenly, "You gone deaf? I told you. Whatever Harley tells you to do. And if I was the newest hired hand on this ranch, which is what you are right now, I wouldn't be sitting around here feeling sorry for myself. That sun is good up. Them hired hands, of which you are one, have had breakfast and they are saddling up for the day's work. Was

I you and I wanted to keep a job, I'd get the hell off of my divan and get to work.''

He got up, pretty smartly. He said, ''Yes. sir. I'm going.''

I watched, seeing him leaving a trail of pride behind. As he opened the front door I said, ''By the way, the job pays sixty dollars a month and room and board.''

He stopped with the doorknob in his hand. He said, ''But—''

I said, ''Yeah, I know. You was making three hundred dollars a month and getting your grub and roof off the family. But that was when you was boss of the horse herd. You ain't that no more. You are getting beginner's wages and you will sleep in the bunkhouse and you will eat with the crew. Ray Hays is now going to draw your wages. You savvy?''

He looked at me. I stared back. I could see his mind working. Finally he jammed on his hat, nodded, and went out the door.

It had come good light now. I watched him ride off and then I turned off all the lanterns and went back into the kitchen. Nora was sitting at the little breakfast table we had there. She said, reproachfully, ''You didn't have to be that hard on him.''

I sat down while she got me a cup of coffee. I said, ''Woman, them ears of yours are going to do you harm one of these days. The business between my brother and me was between us. You was supposed to have been back here fixing breakfast.''

She put cream and sugar in my cup and stirred it around and set it in front of me. She said, ''A person would have to be deaf in both ears not to be able to hear you yelling at Ben.''

I said, with some heat, ''Goddammit, I wasn't yelling at him!''

She said, ''Yes, goddammit, you were!''

I stared at her, shocked. I said, "Woman, clean your mouth up. You was raised in a Christian background. You know better than to talk like that."

She said, "Yes, and you graduated high school. Yet you ought to hear yourself talk. Your grammar is so bad I wouldn't have let you out of the third grade."

I said, "Get them biscuits and that gravy. I'm hungry."

Then she had the nerve to mimic me. She said, "'Git them biscuits!' My lord!"

I looked down at my plate. I said, "All right, if I'm such a dummy why in hell did you marry me? You must have had other choices. Men that spoke the kind of grammar you like."

She was in the process of stirring up the cream gravy in the skillet with a fork. She looked back at me and said, "Oh, Justa Williams, why don't you just shut up! You don't know half as much as you think you do."

And then she suddenly burst into tears.

I got up immediately from the table and went to the stove and put my arms around her from the back. I said, "Honey, what's the matter?"

She was trying to wipe the tears away with one hand. She said, "Oh you!"

I said, "What me? What have I done?"

She said, "If you don't know I can't tell you."

I said, "Is it about Ben?"

She wouldn't turn from the stove. She said, "It's just about everything. Don't you ever think about anything but this damn ranch? I swear, Mother cussed that mercantile store from ever since I can remember, but it was nothing to this ranch of yours. At least Daddy didn't have to go off shooting guns and causing trouble."

Well, I was dumbfounded. I'd never had no experience with it myself, but I'd heard men whose wives were having babies tell it that they just went slightly nuts and that the best way was just to pat 'em on the shoulder and not argue with them. They said they, the women, got all messed up inside and that it affected the way they thought. Said something changed inside of them when they was going to have a baby. Well, I reckoned Nora hadn't heard that same information I had. I went to put my arms around her and kind of cuddle up to her backside, but all she did was shrug me off and say, "Justa Williams, don't try that on me. Now get over to the table and eat your breakfast and then go to work. I'm sick of the way you're acting here lately."

Naturally I did what she told me. There are times you take on a woman and there are times you don't. This was one of them "don't" times. So I sat down and ate my biscuits and gravy and drank my coffee and never said a word. When I got ready to leave, Nora give me one of them prim, dry-mouthed, pursed-up kisses. I just let it go at that and went out and caught my young gelding and saddled him. I had two other riding horses there, but he needed the work. At first he didn't want the bit in his mouth, but we got that worked out. He decided he'd rather open his mouth to breath than have me pinch his nostrils closed the rest of his soon-to-be-short life.

It was a solid eight o'clock when I came riding up to the main ranch house. Ray Hays was sitting on the steps of the porch. He looked considerably the worse for wear from his night before, but he was on hand. I got off my horse, dropped the reins, and went up and sat by him. He said, kind of dolefully, "Mornin', boss."

"Same to you, Ray."

Ray Hays was a medium-sized man, a little on the thin side, with a face that you might first see as hard and then see in a different light as soft. He joked he was servile, but there were men still trying to get over gunshot wounds, some who never had, that had misread Ray as an easy target. You could see him at a dance and think you'd never seen a man having more fun; or you could see him as he was on our front porch, pulling his long face, and you'd figure him for a man who'd never had a friend in the world.

I said, "Ray, I'm putting you in charge of the horse herd."

A moment passed and he said, "Yeah, I heered about that."

"So?"

He put both his hands on his thighs and looked down. He said, "Well, I cain't do it. Ben's my friend. I cain't take his job."

"Pays three hundred dollars a month. Good deal more than you are earning now."

He shook his head. He said, "Ain't got anything to do with it. Ben's my pal."

I studied his profile for a second. I said, "You going to defy me too?"

He said, "Ain't doing that. Don't mean such. But I saw Ben ride out as a cattle herder this morning. A common ranch hand. And he owns part of this ranch."

He turned to me and said, "Boss, I'd just as soon draw what little wages I got coming and get it on down the line."

I stood up. I said, "That's your right. Come on in the house and I'll pay you off."

He looked startled. He said, "You mean just like that?"

I said, "Of course I mean just like that. Man asks me for his time I'll pay him in the middle of a stampede with a hurricane blowing."

He got that gumfuzzled look on his face that he sometimes got when he couldn't figure things out. He said, "Boss, what's going on here?"

I said, "What the hell do you care? You want to draw your time. Well, I'm ready to pay you. What the hell else you need to know?"

"What about Ben?"

I said, "Ben is a man who needs to learn a lesson. So are

you. But neither one of you seems particularly appreciative of the idea. So all I can do is demote Ben and let you go.''

He stood up beside me. He said, ''Now, wait a minute, wait a minute. I never said I wanted to be let go. I jest said I kind of wanted to understan' what was going on.''

I give him a hard look. I said, ''What's going on is that Ben has got a little growing up to do. You can run that remuda as well as he can. Let him come to his senses. Now, if you want to quit the place over this matter that is your business. But I got some bad trouble on my hands and I ain't got time to wet nurse either one of you. You understand me, Ray?''

He kind of stuttered around. He said, ''Why, yes sir, boss. First I'd heard about you having outside trouble, then some cowboy come riding up to my girl's house and tol' me to get my ass on home. But if we got outside trouble, well, you know I ain't gonna let you down.''

I just give him a kind of sour look. I said, ''What about Ben? What about all this talk about what a friend you was of his?''

He said, earnestly, ''I is, I is. But like you said, the boy has got to learn a lesson. You can't work at no job if you don't know who the boss is.''

I nearly smiled. Hays was so damn easy. He was dedicated to the Half-Moon and we both knew it. All he had to have was a little threat, some indication that his place of business was being threatened, and his whole attitude changed. I said, ''Well, then, you better go get you a fresh horse. We got about twenty miles of riding to do today.''

''You betcha, Boss,'' he said. He started away. I let him get about ten yards in the direction of the barns and then I said, ''Ray?''

He turned around. ''Yes, sir?''

I said, ''You ain't going to be drawing no three hundred dollars a month. You'll get your same wages.''

He stared at me, his mouth open. He said, "But you tol' me—"

I said, "Ray, you turned them wages down. Remember?"

He thought about it for a second and then put his head down and went to mumbling. I said, "What?"

"Nuthin'," he said.

"What?"

"I was jest thinkin' I was never much good as a businessman."

I said, "Ray, don't give me no ideas that you ain't much good or else I might take them to heart and act on them."

"But, Boss—"

"Get your goddam horse and get mounted. And be damn quick about it. I ain't got all day."

We went first to Charlie Johnson's, which was only about a four-mile ride away. We caught Charlie at his house just coming in from some business he'd had at his barn. Over a cup of coffee he heard me out. Charlie was a small, lean-boned man with a serious face. He was a deal older than I was, maybe working on fifty. He said, after I'd finished, "Justa, I'll help you. And I'll help Lew Vara."

I said, "How about any of your men?"

He shook his head. He said, "No. You know as well as I do that we've had an early spring. I've got cows dropping calves all over the place. I've got four hired hands all told. They be working about sixteen hours a day right now. I hear you and I know what happens in that town happens to me. But you better go out there and tell it to my mama cows. They don't know shit about it."

I got up and shook hands with him. I said, "Charlie, we're both cattlemen. And we know what's got to come first."

He stood up. He said, "Justa, I'm my own foreman. But the day you send for me I'll be there with a gun. And I won't back off. But you can understand I can't stand around in town waitin' for that bunch to show up. It just come at a bad time.''

I said, ''Don't worry, Charlie. I'll send a man when I need you.''

I wasn't looking forward to the next stop, which was about another four miles on. Me and Ray rode without saying much to each other. Brad Millen was a feisty little son of a bitch that you weren't about to tell his business to. If he warmed to you, he made a hell of a friend, but you'd better not threaten him or he'd tell you to go butt a stump. And I was, if he didn't agree to help, about to threaten him.

We caught him at his catch pen, leaning across the fence watching a newborn crop of calves catching the hot iron. He didn't even much want to give us his attention at first, but then he finally agreed, grudgingly, to go back in the house for a talk. We sat down at the kitchen table. He didn't offer us so much as a drink of water.

I reckoned him to be in his early thirties. He was redheaded and mottle-faced and stayed mad about half the time. I did the same as I'd done with Charlie Johnson, explaining the fix we were in. But, unlike Charlie, he throwed his head back and said, ''What the hell's that got to do with me? Trouble them town folks get in ain't got shit to do with me.''

It was going to have to come down to it sooner or later, so I figured sooner. I said, ''Brad, my bank holds paper on your ranch. You are six months behind payments. You need me to tell you any more?''

He said, ''You wouldn't.''

For the first time Hays spoke. He said, ''Don't bet on it.''

Millen looked at me. He said, ''You're a sorry son of a bitch.''

I said, ''That might quite possibly be. But if you don't think I won't call your note in and take over this ranch you better think again.''

We sat there staring at each other. Finally he kind of gulped. He said, "You would, wouldn't you?"

"Yep," I said. "That bank's in town. You've already give me your opinion of the town. Well, now you can take your chances as to how close you might be tied to that town."

"And if I don't help I'm gonna get my note called in?"

"You are going to lose your ranch."

He looked away and then he looked back. He said, "This is a hell of a note."

I said, "Take your choice, Millen."

He thought on it a minute. He said, "You don't give a man a hell of a lot of choice, do you?"

I just said, "No."

He debated a minute more. He was an amazingly hard-headed man. Finally he said, "What do you want?"

I said, "Your gun. And the gun of any hired hand you think might be useful. I'll pay a hundred-dollar price for help."

"What about me?"

I give him a steady look. I said, "You? I won't call your note. That's my best deal. Take it or leave it."

He got up and walked over to the sink in the kitchen and pumped himself out a glass of water. He drank it down and then he turned around and looked at me. He said, "You ain't give me no choice. I got to take your terms. But I want to tell you, Justa Williams, that you are one of the meanest men I've ever dealt with."

I got up. Ray Hays rose as I did. I said, "I don't much give a damn about what you think of me, Brad. All I want is your help and I'll get it any way I can."

He said, his face that red it got when he was angry, "Well, you got it. When am I supposed to know what I got to do?"

I said, "I'll send a man. You better drop what you're doing and get on the run."

"You're a bastard."

I shrugged. I said, "Everybody is entitled to their own opinion."

As we rode away, Ray Hays said, "Boss, you done pissed that man off."

I kicked my gelding into a long lope and said, "So what?"

Ray said, over the wind that had come rushing into our faces, "What if he don't take to it?"

I yelled back, "He's a good man. I just prodded his conscience a little. He'll be all right."

It was a six-mile ride into town, so we let the horses down a notch or two and give them a blow every once in a while. When we pulled up in front of the sheriff's office, Lew Vara was standing on the boardwalk looking like he'd been expecting us. In a kind of agitated way he said, "Where the hell you been?"

I swung off my horse and tied him and said, "Tending to business. What's all the upset about?"

He flung an arm in the general direction of the other side of the jail and said, "You've got that goddam Morris Carter out there building a damn gallows. Half this town thinks we're fixin' to have a hangin'. Hell, Justa, I ain't got no authority to hang a man. What the hell is going on here?"

I said, "How's the robin taking it?"

Lew said, "He's been flinging himself at them damn bars ever since that hammering started this morning. Tryin' to squeeze through. Justa, if he does himself a harm I'm responsible."

I said, "Let's go in. Sounds like he's getting pretty ripe."

Lew said, "Hell, he's so ripe he's starting to smell."

I said, "Then let's me and you and Hays go down to Crook's and drink a beer."

"What!"

I said, "We been on a long and thirsty trail this morning.

Right after we get a little alcohol on Hays's breath you'll need to arrest him and throw him in with the robin. Then meanwhile me and you can get us something to eat.''

Now it was Hays's turn to say, ''What?''

I said, ''Just part of the job, Ray. Just part of the job. You put the fear of God in him and convince him that we hang folks around here. Do a good enough job and Lew will let you out.''

He said, ''Aw, shit, boss. I never reckoned on this.''

But Lew was half-smiling. He said, ''You are a vicious son of a bitch, Justa.''

''Just trying to help,'' I said.

We went on down to Crook's. Hays had three beers faster than I could count them. On his third one I said, ''Hell, Ray, this is supposed to be a put-up job. You keep downing them things like you are doing and Lew really will have to put you in jail for public intoxication.''

He wiped his mouth with the back of his hand. He said, ''Boss, I know I got to do it but I can't stand them tight places like jail cells. I got to have one more beer. Reckon how long I got to be in there?''

I said, ''I guess until you sober up. But get you another beer.''

I saw him go to the bar with his mug. I also saw him get a shot of whiskey and down it without a backward look to see if I was watching. I figured, what the hell, he had it coming.

Right after that we left and went back to the jail. Walking down the boardwalk I wasn't altogether certain that some of Ray's staggering was part of the act I'd told him to put on. But, for my purposes, it didn't much matter. We went into the jail, and I waited in the office while Lew made a big show of taking Ray back into the jail part and putting him into the cell next to Axel. They would be separated only by bars. After that Lew came out. As we walked down to

Crook's he said, "I hope to hell you know what you're doin'. This is about as illegal as hell."

I said, mildly, "How's the scaffold coming?"

He gave me a horrified look. He said, "How's it coming? You never seen? It looks like you are fixing to hang a man!"

I said, "I'm hungry, ain't you?"

So we went on down and ate. I thought the beef stew was pretty good, but I could see that Lew's mind was somewhere else. Finally I finished my plate and shoved it away and said, "All right, let's go back and deal with what we've got."

He said, "I don't see what you figure to get out of this. Besides that, you ain't told me a word about any other guns you got coming in."

I said, "I don't reckon you want to hear it."

He just shook his head. He said, "That's mighty good news."

"Let's go see old Axel. He ought to be pretty soft by now."

Lew said, "If he ain't hung hisself by now."

I stopped him in his tracks right there. I said, "Did you come and ask for my help or didn't you?"

He said, "Guess I did."

"If you was to set out to borrow a mule from a man, wouldn't you expect that man to tell you how to handle that mule?"

He still looked uncertain. He said, "Well, yes, I reckon."

I said, "Then quit telling me how to work the mule you borrowed off me."

We walked the rest of the way to his office in silence. Once inside I said, "You and I are going back there. I'm going to kick up a fuss. You just go along with me."

"What are you going to do?"

"None of your business."

He give me a sour look. He said, "It ain't my business? Hell, this is only my jail."

I said, "Lew, just go along with it."

He shook his head, but then we walked back into the cells. I said, in a loud voice, "Sheriff, get that drunk out of that cell. You ain't got no right to put him next to a condemned man. And I want him out of there right now. He's nothing but a common drunk. I'll pay his fine if need be, but it ain't right to have him plaguing a boy that's going to be hung in the morning."

I couldn't tell which one of them was making the most noise. Hays to get out of the cell or Axel to get my attention. I paid Axel no mind. When Lew unlocked Ray's cell door and let him out I give him a cuff on the back of the head. I said, "And you one of my hired hands. I ought to fire you on the spot."

But as we walked by Axel's cell he reached his hand out through the bars as if to detain me. "Please, sir, kin I talk to you?"

I just give him a brief look. I said, "Boy, you got about sixteen more hours of breathing. I reckon the man you need to be talking to is a preacher."

Then we passed on out and settled into Lew's office. I looked at Ray. I said, "Well?"

Hays just started shaking his head like he did when he was nervous. He said, "Boss, that man is out there building one of them there things they hang you from. Hell, it nearly scared the liver out of me lookin' at the damn thing. Reckon what it's doing to that kid. Right now he'd sell his grandmother for soap. You want him, you got him."

I said, "Take yourself a five-dollar bonus, Ray."

He said, "I went through that for *five* dollars?"

I said, "Well, of course, you don't have to take the five dollars."

He kind of half rose out of his chair. He said, "You mean I done it for nuthin'?"

I said, "Sounds like it to me. Though I will give you some advice. I never seen a man go broke taking a profit. Even if it was just five dollars."

I left him there with his mouth hanging open and walked over to the window that faced out on the vacant lot. Morris was there hard at work. It appeared to me, in spite of my instructions, that he was hard at work building a hanging scaffold. I guessed he'd forgot all I'd told him that it could look like a chicken coop.

I come back and sat down. I said, "Well, Lew, it appears you are fixing to hang somebody."

He banged one of his big fists down on his desk. He said, "Justa, you have got to stop this. I'm a sworn peace officer of the state of Texas. I can't go on with this."

I stood up. I said, "For a few minutes you can. Where are them damn cell keys?"

He opened his desk drawer and took out the big ring of keys. I held out my hand, but he made no move to pass them over. I said, "Lew, strictly speaking this ain't exactly legal. So—"

He said, "You damn well got that part right."

"—so there ain't no reason for you to involve yourself. I can question the kid by myself."

He said, getting up. "This is my jail. Anything goes on in it is my business. So I just reckon I'll be at hand during this business. What the hell you expect to find out anyway?"

He headed for the door that led back to the cells. I said, "I told you, I don't know. Just all I can I reckon."

He followed me and said, "Nothin' is going to come of this. I can tell you that. Nothing. That kid don't know diddly squat and all you've done is had a structure built next to the jail, my jail, that's got half the town gawking. Won't be long before they'll be in here asking what's going on."

Just as I opened the big wooden door with the little barred window in it I said, "Lew, you are getting to be an old woman."

When we got back in the cells, we found Axel staring out the window at where Morris was hammering away. He turned when he heard our boots in the little concrete hallway. His face was dead white. He opened his mouth to say something, but no sound came out. I didn't believe I'd ever seen eyes so wide and staring. I said, "Well, Axel, got your house in order?"

He finally found his voice. It came out a croak. He said, "You cain't mean it. You cain't! I ain't done no hangin' offense crime!"

I shook my head. I said, "That ain't the way we look at it around here. You come in to town to talk to the sheriff about doing murder and robbery and pillaging. We take them to be hanging crimes."

He come over to the bars and gripped them so hard his knuckles went white. He said, in a high, whining voice, "Please, mister, I wadn't gonna do none of them thangs. They jest sent me in to pass the word along. I swear it."

Lew said, "I 'magine you'd swear to just about anything right now, boy, to save yore neck. You're going to swing an' ain't a thing you can do to talk your way out of it."

In spite of misgivings Lew was playing his part. I said, "Now, look here, Sheriff, this is a young boy. How old are you, son?"

"Eight— eighteen." He was close to blubbering.

I said to Lew, "How about letting me talk to the boy a minute. It's Axel, ain't it?"

"Yes, sir."

I said, "Just let me talk to the boy by myself a minute. Maybe we can make some sense out of all of this."

Lew looked like he was thinking the matter over. Finally, though, he said, "Well, all right. But just for a minute. Get away from that door, boy!"

While Axel backed to the other side of the cell, Lew unlocked the door. He said, to me, "But you better watch him. I don't trust none of his kind."

I looked at the scrawny little kid and wanted to laugh. But I kept a straight face and went into the cell. Lew clanged the door shut behind me with enough noise so that Axel nearly jumped a foot. I sat down on the cot. There was a little stool, but the kid just stayed with his back to the cell wall watching me with round, scared eyes. I didn't say anything for a moment, just got out a cigarillo and lit it and took a few puffs. I watched him get scareder. Finally I said, "You know I told you earlier I got considerable influence around this town and this county. In fact, in this part of the state. You recollect me saying that?"

He swallowed. He said, "Yes— yes, sir."

I studied him a minute more. He'd taken to trembling. I said, "Was I of a mind to, I could get them gallows taken down. Might even could get you your freedom. The sheriff has to do what the judge tells him to but the judge generally does what I say. You understand me, boy?"

He give me that same, choking, gulping "Yes."

I kept on studying him, trying to decide how much of this fear was play acting and how much was real. He'd been tough enough and brazen enough the first time I'd seen him, and Lew had said he'd been downright cocky when he'd first made his approach. Of course any man has his breaking point, especially a boy, but I also knew that his kind could be mighty cunning. I said, "How come they picked you for the job of coming in and sounding out the sheriff? You look a mite young for that kind of responsibility."

He looked down, kind of shamefaced. He said, "Reckon it's because I be the runt of the bunch. Reckon they figgered wouldn't be no loss if I didn't make it back."

"I see," I said. I rubbed my jaw. I needed a shave, but conditions being what they'd been between me and Nora when I left the house, I hadn't taken the bother. Well, right then I couldn't worry about how mad she was, though it was pretty steady at the back of my mind. I said, "So you just come braving your way in here, telling the sheriff you and a bunch of other murderers and thieves wanted to come into his town and run wild. That about the size of it?''

He got a sullen look on his face. He said, ''I wuz give to un'erstan' that the sh'ruff 'ud be friendly. Thet he used to run with our bunch.''

''Who told you that?''

''Sam.''

''Sam Sixkiller?''

He nodded.

''He claims to be friends with the sheriff?''

''He said they 'uz tight as kin.''

''Tight as kin?''

The kid nodded. I thought about it for a moment and also thought about the funny way Lew had acted about not wanting to be there when the gang arrived. That had been so unlike him that I had decided it was a line of questioning I didn't want to pursue. I didn't know a whole hell of a lot about Lew's background. When we'd been in our late teens, right before that fierce fight we had, he'd lived in Blessing with a mixed couple that nobody could tell if they were Mexican or Indian. He'd said they were his parents, but they kept so much to themselves that nobody ever knew much about them. Certainly I didn't. Most of my time was spent at the ranch, which I was already running; Lew and his folks were townspeople. I had the vague memory that the man, Lew's father, was a man of all work and his mother took in washing or cleaned houses or some such. But right then that didn't have anything to do with the matter at hand.

I said, ''What's your whole name, boy?''

He looked sullen, again, at that, but he finally said, ''Hammit, Axel Hammit.''

''Where you from? Where'd you grow up?''

That got me the same sullen head dropping, but old Morris was still hammering away. He said, ''Kansas.''

''How old was you when you run away from home?''

'' 'Bout twelve, I reckon. Me 'n' my older brother.''

"What happened to him?"

"He's up yonder with the rest of the bunch."

"I see," I said. Well, that kind of complicated matters. He might be willing to betray the gang, but him having a brother in with it kind of threw a whole new light on the matter. I said, "Well, tell me, Mr. Hammit—if it come down to you swinging or your brother getting kilt, what would be your druthers?"

He straightened up and said, with more force than he'd shown all day. "Why, that sumbitch! I'da kilt him myself 'fore now if I'da had the chancet! All that bastard does is beat up on me an' kick me 'round. Hell, I wisht it was him a-sittin' here. I'd be a-standin' outside this here jail laughin' my fool head off."

If he was lying, he was one of the best damn actors I'd ever seen. He'd gotten so excited by the idea that he'd come away from the wall of the cell, the wall that was separating him from the supposed hanging scaffold.

I said, "Just back up there. Or, better yet, take you a seat on that other cot. If I have to shoot you, you ain't likely to do me a bit of good. You drink whiskey?"

He ran his tongue over his lips. "Ever' chancet I gits."

I half smiled. It hadn't come as much of a surprise. I imagined there wasn't much he wouldn't get into every "chancet" he got. I said, "You want to save your hide, Axel?"

"Gawd, yes!" he said. And his eyes went back to wide and staring. "Iz they a chancet?"

"There might be a way," I said. I got up. I said, with a thin smile, "You wait right here until I get back."

He said, earnestly, "I shore will, sir, I shore will."

Little fool didn't even know a joke when he heard one. I went to the cell door and was on the point of calling Lew when I seen he'd left the keys on a little peg to the left of the door. I let myself out, relocked the cell, and went down to

Lew's office. He was sitting behind his desk. He looked around. "Well?"

Then I noticed that Hays was still there. I said, "What the hell are you doing here? How come you're not back at the ranch? You figure you're on vacation?"

He got that injured look on his face he could wear so well and said, "Ain't nobody told me to go back. You told me to come but you didn't tell me to go."

I said, "Well, I'm telling you now."

He was halfway to the door when a thought struck me. I said, "No, wait a minute. Sit back down."

He give me a look and mumbled something under his breath. I didn't ask him what he'd said, figuring it could only get him in trouble. Instead I turned to Lew and said, "Give me that bottle of whiskey."

He got it out of his desk drawer with a questioning look, but he went ahead and handed it over. It was about three-quarters full. I said, "No, this is too much. Got a big tin cup I can pour some of this in?"

"What are you up to?"

"Never mind. How about the cup?"

He opened his desk drawer again and come out with a pint of whiskey. He said, "Is this too much?"

"About right," I said. I exchanged bottles with him and then went back to the cell. I was glad to see that Axel was once again staring out the window at what he thought was going to be his destiny. I wanted him as worried as he could get. He turned when he heard me open the cell door, and his eyes lit up when he saw the pint of whiskey in my hand. But I just waved him toward the far cot and sat down where I'd been sitting. I pulled the cork out of the bottle with my teeth, took a long pull of the raw stuff, and then sat there watching him watching me. Or rather him watching that bottle of whiskey. Finally, I said, "Axel, this here whiskey is either going to be the last drink you ever have or the first of many. It's up to you."

"Hell," he said, "thet ain't no cherce. Gimme a chancet at that whiskey 'n' I'll show you." He put out his hand like he was reaching for the last biscuit on the plate. I pulled the bottle back just out of his reach.

"Not just yet," I said. "I want to know how long you been running with that bunch." Then, when I saw a look of guile come over his face, I said, "And you better not lie to me."

He looked down and settled back on the cot like he'd just lost his chance at the bottle. "Purty good while. Me 'n' my brother drifted down ta Oklahoma after we lit out from home. Wadn't long 'fore they taken us up. Reckon four or five year."

"So they been like a family to you?"

"Shit!" he said. He spit the word out like it was a bite of green persimmon. "Fam'ly, my ass! More like a buncha godawful sumbitches. I had jest thought my ol' pappy was mean. He wadn't shucks next to Sam. That sumbitch ain't happy 'less he's tormentin' a body or kickin' 'em around or cheatin' 'em."

"Here," I said. I suddenly reached forward and handed him the whiskey. He grabbed the bottle like it was life itself and flung it up to his mouth and went to sucking. Before he come up for air he'd downed near half a pint. I just watched in fascination. I didn't reckon I'd ever seen a grown man twice his size drink like that.

Then, before he could start upward with the whiskey again for another go, I reached over and jerked the bottle out of his hand. I said, "Just hold up! You can have it back in a minute but first me and you are going to have us a little talk. You savvy?"

"I savvy," he said. But his attention was all on the whiskey. I guess it was good for taking off the edge of fear that hammering had put in his belly.

I wasn't real sure how to put my proposition to the boy, so I finally decided to just go straight at him. He wasn't overly bright, but I figured he had enough animal cunning to look out for himself, else he wouldn't have lasted as long as he had. I said, "How'd you like to walk out of this jail, walk away from that hanging scaffold, get on your horse, and get out of here a free man?"

"Huh?" he said. "Does a hawg like slop?"

I said, "Be some things you'd have to do."

"You jest name 'em, Cap'n, and I'm yore man quicker'n a turkey kin spit."

I said, "Where's the gang now?"

He furrowed his brow while he thought. He said, "Likely, they be in Brazoria by now. When they finished up in Galvez they uz gonna drift south a-waitin' on me. I uz 'spose to meet 'em thar 'bout now. Tell 'em the lay of the land. Course they ain't no tellin' with that bunch. If they made enough trouble in ol' Galvez they mighta got throwed in the hoosegow."

It was chilling news. Brazoria was only about fifty miles away, no more than a two-day ride. I said, "Boy, do you know how to send a telegram?"

"A what?"

"A wire."

He furrowed his brow again. "I've heered of it but I ain't ever actually had cause to do the thing myself."

I said, "It doesn't matter. We can show you how."

He was giving me that cunning look again. He said, "Whata I need to know how to send one of them thar tell-e-graphers fer?"

I said, "Because I'm going to ask the sheriff to let you out of here and send you back to the gang. You're going to tell them exactly what we tell you to tell them and after that you're going to telegraph us their every move, where they are, what they're saying, what they're planning, even how drunk they are."

He stared at me. "You askin' me to tattle on my own bunch?"

I inclined my head toward the direction of the scaffold. I said, "You don't have to do it."

His eyes followed the tilt of my head. He swallowed, hard. He said, "How 'bout more of that whiskey?"

I handed him over the bottle. He didn't drink quite so hard this time, but still, he nearly killed the pint. He took the bottle away, wiped his chin where a little of the liquor had dribbled down, and sat pondering. Finally he heaved a long sigh. He said, "'At's mighty hard, Cap'n, mighty hard. I don't mind tattlin' on them sorry sumbitches, but they liable to ketch me at it. They do they'll skin me alive."

I said, "And if you don't do it, I'll hang you."

That caused him to finish the bottle. When it was empty he looked at it longingly and then up at me. I shook my head. I said, "Nope. That's all you'll get in this place. Like I told you, that could be your last drink or the first of many. It's up to you."

I could see the whiskey working in him. I'd calculated his size and his drinking experience and figured it would take just a little under a pint to get him calmed down and thinking. Of course I hadn't wanted him drunk, just mellow enough to see both sides of the question at hand.

He was thinking about something. It was almost like I could see the wheels turning in his head. Finally, he said, "Puzzle me out som'thin'. Yesterday you wuz all fer hangin' me, 'n' that shur'ff feller kind of hung back. Today it's the shur'ff wants me to swing 'n' you is back here tryin' ta save my neck. How come that be?"

I said, "I don't care what happens to your worthless skin. But if you can help us with information I'm willing to trade you that for your life. I reckon the sheriff feels the same way. Though I can't say for sure."

Still with that cunning look on his face, he said, "What if I's to jest go on back to the bunch 'n' tell 'em what happened 'n' never send you none of them tell-e-graph things at all? Or send you some lies?"

I said, "Then when y'all came riding in here and we opened up with about thirty rifles, you'd be the first to get it. Maybe a belly shot so you'd have time to think it over."

He said, "What if I's to jest hightail it out of here 'n' never go near the bunch? Jest go to ground 'n' hide out?"

I put both boots on the floor and leaned toward him. Lord, he needed a bath! I said, "We've thought of that. When you leave here there'll be a man tracking you. One of my men. He's half-Indian, half-wildcat, and all mean. You don't head for your bunch, he will kill you. You'll never see him. Just one minute you'll be alive and the next you won't. And if you don't get information to us over the, as you call it, 'tell-e-graph,' he will kill you. You do anything except what we tell you to do and you are a dead man." Then I sat back and let him digest the information and his options,.

He thought about it, and then he said, sort of miserably, "I cain't figger out how I's supposed to git near one of them tell-e-gram places. They see me doin' it they gonna know I's into somethin'."

I said, "That's a risk. Out that window is a certainty. Was I you I'd rather take a chance than have no chance. And, believe me, you ain't got a chance with us. One way or the other you will not see the sun go down in this town."

For the first time I could see in his face that he realized he was in a box canyon. Up until that point I think his little coyote mind had reckoned he could figure some way around his predicament. But I'd kept shutting every door he'd walked up to.

He said, "Kin I think on it?"

I got up. I said, "Sure. Take all the time you want. You got five minutes." I stepped over to the window. Morris was just putting the finishing touches on the gallows. He'd done an admirable job. Even though he'd been told to build just anything, he'd built something that would have scared me if I'd been in Axel's place. I said, "Well, no, maybe you ain't got even five minutes. Looks like that bronc out there is about ready to go.''

He caved in then. I didn't see where he had much choice. He said, ''Ar'right, Cap'n, I'm yore man. But I reckon you ought to know I'm a mite scairt. Kin I have 'nother drank?''

''We'll see,'' I said. I let myself out of the cell, relocked it, and headed for the front office.

=====Chapter Four

LEW HEARD ME out without doing much more than puff nervously at a cigarillo. He was behind his desk; Hays was tipped back in a chair against the far wall. When I'd finished, Lew thought a moment and then frowned and said, "Hang it, Justa, it sounds fine. Sounds good."

Hays said, "Sounds *too* good."

I just turned and give him a look that shut his mouth. Then, to Lew, I said, "What is bothering you? What's the hang back?"

He said, "Why, it's them words that came out of his very own mouth. What if he goes back to that gang and tells Sam Sixkiller what he's supposed to be doin'? He might send us a bunch of bogus information. I tell you I know Sam Sixkiller and he's a mighty slick hombre."

I said, "And I tell you I got this kid to believing there will be a man on his trail all the way. When he leaves here I'm going to have Hays riding behind him, just barely in sight."

I heard Hays's chair hit the floor with a thump.

I said, "Oh, relax, Ray. I ain't really going to have you track him all the way. Just a couple of miles. I've already told him he'd never see the man on his trail."

Lew said, "That aside, I don't, for the life of me, see how we can depend on anything this boy sends us."

I put my boot up on the desk. I said, "Hell, Lew, in the first place I don't think this boy much cares for that gang and especially for Sam Sixkiller. I got the feeling off him he hopes they get their ass kicked. He said he'd been trying to get away from them for years except he had no place else to go and he figured he'd starve without the gang.''

Lew shrugged. He finally said, ''Well, I guess we ain't got a hell of a lot to lose.''

''Nor a hell of a lot of time to lose it in. If they are in Brazoria and working their way in this direction, we ain't got much time at all. Say it takes Axel two days to reach them, a day for them to mull it over, and then two more days coming our way. That's less than a week. And they could already be moving this way, for all we know.''

''Not that bunch,'' Lew said, and there was something in his voice that bothered me, something I couldn't quite put my finger on. He said, ''Sam will take his own sweet time, stopping off to raise hell wherever he thinks he can get away with it. And there's plenty of small, unprotected towns and little ranches between here and Brazoria. If, indeed, that is where he is.''

I said, ''Well, make up your mind, Sheriff. You was going to turn him loose in the first place. I got a man out there putting the finishing touches on a gallows. I got to go out there and tell him something.''

Lew said, ''You sure this boy has got brains enough to send a telegram?''

I said, ''Hell, even Ray Hays can do that.''

Hays made some kind of noise, but it didn't exactly come out in words. However I didn't figure it was too complimentary.

I said, ''We'll just have him send simple messages. Number of men, location, that kind of stuff. All he has to do is go in and tell the telegrapher. We'll give him some silver dollars to pay for the wires.''

Lew shrugged and said, ''Well, why not.'' He got up. ''I'll bring him out.''

While he was gone I took occasion to step outside and walk around the jail to where Morris was still busy. I said,

"Mighty good job, Morris. Where'd you learn to build a gallows?"

"Seen a pi-pitcher of one in a new-newspaper oncet. 'Membered it."

I got out my roll and peeled off a ten dollar bill and handed it to him. I said, "Morris, you done fine. Now you can take it down and haul it off."

He looked at me speechlessly. Finally he said, "Huh?"

I said, "Take it down. Haul it off. You can have the lumber."

He said, "You mean y-you ain't g-gonna hang nobody?"

I shook my head. "Not right now."

Hays had followed me out of the jail and come up beside me. He said, "Whyn't you leave it standin', Boss? Kind of as a warnin' to troublemakers."

I give him a look. It wasn't a bad idea. But I didn't have general troublemakers in mind. Not, I figured, that we'd ever have occasion to use it, but it might come in handy. I wasn't aware I was still staring at Hays until he said, "Whata you lookin' at me for, Boss? I never meant *me*."

"I was just thinking, Ray." I said. "Sometimes you amaze me with a halfway decent idea." I said, "Morris, just let her stand. You done good."

Now he was really befuddled. He stood there turning the ten spot over and over in his hand. "Leave it be?"

"For the time being."

Then he looked down at the money. "W-What'll I do with this?"

"Keep it," I said. "I'll take it out in work one of these days."

We walked away. Hays was mumbling something. I said, "What?"

He said, "Aw, nothin'."

Then he said, "You give Morris ten dollars fer doin' nothin' and all I get for going to jail is a fiver. And I ain't even got that yet."

"Job ain't over," I said.

He said, "When do I get to eat? My belly thinks my throat's been cut."

"You had beer and whiskey."

"An' that's all I git?"

"For the time being. I got something else I need you to do first."

"Like what?" He was giving me a leery look.

I stopped us just outside the jail. I said, "The sheriff will have Axel out by now. I want you to take him down to the telegraph office and get him shown how to send a telegram."

"Send a—" He gave me an incredulous look. "A child can send a telegram."

"Just do it, Hays."

He shrugged. He said, "I thought I was supposed to be out at the ranch handling the horse herd."

I said, "And when you get that done I want you to bring him back here. Me and the sheriff are going to give him a little talking to and then I want you to ride him three or four miles out of town. To the north, toward Brazoria."

"That far?" he said. "You said trail him a couple miles. Damn!"

I didn't pay him any attention. I said, "We're going to give him his gun back but you hold the cartridges until you leave off him. While you're riding I want you to impress on him that the meanest Meskin God ever made will be trailing him. I'm depending on you to work this boy, Ray."

He looked disgusted. "Four miles out and four miles back and me still with no lunch."

I said, "When you get back you can go to Crook's and get you the biggest steak he's got." I started toward the door, then said, over my shoulder, "That is if you've got the money to pay for it."

He made some awful sound behind me, but I didn't pay him no mind, just opened the door to the office and stepped in. Hays followed me, still mumbling about the unfairness of it all.

Lew was behind his desk, and the robin was sitting huddled up on a bench to my right. I motioned him to his feet. I said, indicating Hays, "This man is going to take you down and show you how to send a telegram. You listen to everything and learn it good. If you don't that rope is still waiting."

I turned around to Hays. I said, "Ray, I know he can't write so he's just going to have to tell the telegrapher what he wants to send. Make him keep it simple. Location, what town they're close to. Direction. How fast they're traveling. Are they moseying along or are they moving. Reckon you can explain that to him?"

Ray gave Axel a sour look. "It'll be a chore but I guess I can do it."

When they were gone I sat down and Lew poured us both out a tumbler of whiskey. He said, "I ain't got a great deal of faith in this information method of yours."

"You got a better idea?"

"Yeah. My first one."

I studied him. I said, "Lew, you got any other reason not to want to face that bunch except your flimsy idea they'll bypass us if they think a friendly sheriff ain't here?"

He looked up at me. "What do you mean by that?"

I sipped at my whiskey. "Just what I said. No more, no less."

He looked away. After a moment he said, "I hate to remember that part of my life. I thought I'd left it far behind and now it has come back."

"To haunt you?"

"Haunt me? Hell, that's a right funny way of putting it."

"I meant it was just that—the remembering."

He didn't say anything, just took a meditative sip of his whiskey. Finally he said, "It's a hard thing to explain, Justa. I'd as soon you wouldn't ask me right now."

"All right," I said. "I respect that. I know you got the safety of this town in mind and if it was anything that might be threatenin', I know you'd tell me."

"Yes," he said.

We were silent for a moment and then he said, "Which way you reckon they'll come?"

I'd been giving it some thought. I said, "Well, if they are in Brazoria there's only one good ford of the Colorado River coming from there. That's up near Wadsworth. That would put them either coming down alongside the railroad tracks or taking the Wadsworth Road. If they come through Van Vleck they can cross on the wagon bridge this side of Bay City. That would put them down near Sergeant. But that would be pretty marshy going this time of the year. All I can say is I hope our robin can be of some help. As the time grows near I've planned to put out a couple of men a few miles up the road to give us some early warning. But I ain't got enough men I can spare off the ranch to cover all routes."

He shook his head. He said, "Onliest thing I know, Justa, is that we can't have no fight in this town. Not with as many guns as will be involved. If they got to be stopped it's got to be north of here."

"I know. That's why I'm betting so heavy on that robin. We can't just wake up one morning and find some right in amongst us."

"But hell," he said, "flat as this land is around here they ain't even any good cover for an ambush."

"Except high grass."

"Except high grass," he said, and smiled. He was thinking of the time he and I had successfully ambushed six bad hombres with nothing but a lariat rope and high grass. As well as I recollected Lew had taken a bullet in the skirmish but he hadn't said nothing about it until later.

I said, "Where's Axel's horse?"

Lew jerked his head. "In the hotel stables."

"He well mounted?"

"Better than you would think, by looking at him."

Of course that didn't surprise me. Folks in Axel's line of work generally did have a good animal between their legs. Their very lives very often depended on the speed and stamina of their horses. Besides, it was just as easy to steal a good horse as a poor one.

About that time Ray came back with Axel. Hays had a fagged-out look on his face. I asked him if Axel had learned what he was supposed to do. Ray said, "Yeah, I reckon, Boss. But that boy is dumber than a boot heel. I hope you ain't puttin' no great stock in him."

Axel just stood there. I'd always had the feeling he understood more than he let on, but I didn't say anything. I sent Ray around to the hotel livery to fetch Axel's horse and then told Lew to give the boy his revolver. The kid didn't have a proper gun rig, just carried the big Navy Colt stuck in his pants belt. Lew took the cartridges out, handed them to me, and then gave Axel his weapon. He looked at it a minute, then looked at me, and said, "Ain't no good, 'thout no bullets."

"You'll get 'em," I said.

After that Lew and I put some hard words on the boy. Lew ended by saying, "Axel, you got a chance now to get straight with the law. You do this right and I'll see that your slate is wiped clean. I imagine you're wanted in about sixteen counties, but we may can do something about that."

I said, "He got any money?"

Lew looked in his desk and came out with a little knotted bandana. It clinked with the few coins it contained. "Couple of dollars," he said.

Ray came back through the door just as I went into my pocket and came out with five silver dollars. I handed them to Axel. Ray said, "Huh! Gives money to ever'body but me."

"Hush, Ray," I said. Then, to Axel, I said, "Those are

for the telegraph. You understand? You are not to spend them for anything else. If you do, that man tailing you will surely be roasting your guts over a fire before the night is out. Lew, give me that piece of bottle we got left.''

Lew handed over the half-full bottle and I gave it to Axel. I said, ''Make it last, boy. Now this man,'' I pointed at Hays, ''is going to ride a piece with you just to make sure you get started on the right road. Ray, y'all go ahead. I'll be either here or down at Crook's when you get back. Just go with him like I told you.'' I handed Ray the cartridges for Axel's revolver.

Then they were gone and Lew and I were left looking at each other. He said, ''I taken notice of Morris leaving with his tools. You figure to leave that gallows up?''

''Thought I might,'' I said.

''Why?''

I yawned. It had been a long day. I said, ''No good reason. Figured it might come in handy later.''

He laughed. He said, ''You are a piece of work, Justa Williams. You are leaving that gallows to stir this town up, let them know trouble is coming and that they can't sit on their dead ass and expect somebody else to tend to it.''

''Maybe,'' I said. ''You want to go down to Crook's and get a beer?''

He got up. ''Might as well.''

We walked out into the waning afternoon. All up and down the street we could see people sneaking peeks at Morris's handiwork. It was hard to tell what they were thinking because those that passed us did little more than nod. It was like we'd suddenly got us a bad case of something or other and they didn't want to get too close for fear they might catch it.

After about an hour Hays got back and we started for the ranch. He put up a squabble about eating a steak at Crook's, but I convinced him we'd be at the ranch right at suppertime and wasn't no use in wasting good money on town food.

That early in the spring it came good dark around six o'clock, and I saw we were going to be hard-pressed to make it by then. I knew Nora liked to put supper on the table at six on the dot because that was the way her mother had always done it, and I figured, mood she was in, I could count on it getting colder by the minute every minute I was late. And her right along with it.

As we rode, quick-paced, I filled Hays in on what Lew and I had planned and asked him what he thought. He just looked doleful. He said, "Boss, 'pears to me you puttin' all yore eggs in that boy's basket."

I said, "What do you think of him?"

He shook his head. "Pretty hard to say. He looks to have a bunch of bird dog in him and then the next time you take a look you see a bunch of fox. I'll say the one thing: I don't think he's near as dumb as he lets on."

"He talk much on the ride out?"

"Not so's you'd notice. Mainly wanted to know if I taken you serious about hangin' him. I give him strong assurance that you was steady in yore mind about that. Was you gonna hang him?"

I ignored that and said, "Did you impress on his mind I had a man trailing him?"

"Oh, yeah. I near beat him to death with that one. Tried to act like I was friendly toward him an' that I didn't like my boss any better than he did." He give me a hasty look. "'Course you un'erstand, Boss, that was jest play actin'."

"Of course," I said. "Did he seem to buy it? About the tracker I mean."

"Well, he looked over his shoulder a lot. Wanted to know what the hombre looked like. I told him you'd have me skinned if I tol' him."

"About right, too," I said. Then I put spurs to my horse. I said, "We better raise some dust. Can't be late for supper tonight."

I rode into my little corral just as half of the sun

commenced to dip below the horizon. As fast as I could I stripped the saddle and bridle off the gelding, gave him a quick rubdown with a feed sack, and poured him out a bait of oats in his trough. The other two ponies I kept at my place came running at the sound of the feed being poured, but they weren't getting any. The little gelding had done a hard day's work and deserved a little extra. The others had just been lazing around all day.

There was a pump in the backyard, up near the house. Quick as I could I stripped off my shirt and give myself a washing. It was mighty cold work. The days were warm enough, but come evening, March let you know it wasn't summer yet. I dried off as quick as I could and then, carrying my dirty shirt, went into the house. Nora wasn't in the kitchen, just Juanita, stirring up a pan of something. I sailed on past her and went into the bedroom and got a shirt out of the bureau. It wasn't until I turned around to put it on that I realized Nora was lying on the bed. I didn't bother to button the shirt, just went and sat down beside her. Her eyes were closed, but they fluttered open as I put my weight on the bed. "Honey," I said, "what's the matter?"

She made as if to sit up, but I pushed her back down. She said, "I'm all right. Just a little tired."

I said, "Then you just lay there and rest." It had me plenty alarmed. Nora just wasn't the kind of woman to take to her bed in what for her was the middle of the day. I said, kind of worried, "You reckon I better send for Dr. Jackson?"

She did sit up then. She said, "Oh, good heavens, Justa Williams, don't be so silly. I told you I just got a little tired. I've had a rest and I feel fine. Now get out of my way. I've got to go in and keep an eye on Juanita or she'll make a mess of everything."

In spite of my arguing, she insisted on getting up. She'd loosened her bodice, and now she stood by the side of the bed while she did it back up. She didn't look all that steady on her pins to me.

I said, "Did you get faint or anything?"

"Have you washed up?"

"Yes. Done it before I come in the house."

"Then button up your shirt and go in your office and have your drink and supper will be ready by then. We're having fried chicken and biscuits and gravy and mashed potatoes."

"Sounds fine," I said. But I watched her as she left the room. She didn't seem to be walking with her ordinary bounce. But she'd give me to understand she didn't want to hear any more about the matter, so I taken it as good politics to keep my mouth shut. I went in my office and had the drink, but the whiskey didn't keep me from worrying.

Supper was as good as it always was, but, in the lantern light, Nora looked more drawn and pale than I reckoned I'd ever seen her. We finished the main body of the meal and then Juanita brought us in some coffee and apple pie. I'd done a good job of packing away the grub, but Nora had just picked at her food. Finally I couldn't take it no more. I said, "Nora, you are worrying me to death. You got to tell me what's wrong."

She fiddled with her pie for a second and then said, "Well, for one thing, Justa, I'm pregnant. That isn't a joy ride right there. I'm sick every morning. That's why they call it morning sickness. But that's just the way the body works. What's really ailing me is you."

"Me?"

"Yes. I know something serious is going on and that you are very much involved and yet you won't tell me the whole truth. You go from one cock and bull story to another and I'm sitting out here by myself imagining all sorts of things. You ride off and I don't know where you're going or what condition you'll be coming back in." Her eyes almost filled with tears. "I hate to sound like some weak woman but it wears a body down."

Well, it left me dumbfounded. Nora had always been so strong, so sure of herself, so, hell, bossy, that it left me floundering to see her nearly break down. Of course I knew that women did some changing when they was going to have a baby, but nobody had ever told me to what degree. I ain't by nature a demonstrative man, but I got up from my seat and went around the table and sat down by her and put my arm around her shoulders and drew her close. At first she made as if to resist, but her heart wasn't in it and she let me pull her head up into the hollow of my neck. I said, "Honey, I swear I ain't set out to worry you. Just the opposite. I ain't told you everything because I figured that would worry you. It wasn't that I didn't think you could handle it. I ain't never treated you like no weak woman. It's just I ain't been sure, you fixing to have a baby and all." I tried to make a little joke. I said, "You got to remember you're the first pregnant wife I ever had."

She made a little sniffle, but it didn't pass for a laugh. Finally she pulled away. She said, "Juanita will come in here any minute and see us."

I said, "To hell with Juanita."

She said, "No, you got to keep up your standards. Justa, if you don't want me to know what's going on, then that's fine. I'll make out as best I can. It'll worry me, not knowing, but I'll handle it somehow."

If I hadn't known Nora better I'd have sworn she was playing me. But that just wasn't my wife's style. No, she was sincere. I said, "Oh, good Lord, let's go into the setting room and I'll tell you everything you want to know. I warn you in advance it is going to scare you."

She got up, smoothing the front of her dress. She said, "Nothing could be as bad as what I've been imagining."

We went into the setting room, and while she went around lighting lanterns I took the occasion to step into my office and pour myself out a pretty good tumbler of whiskey. I figured to be in for a pretty long and difficult haul. It was going to be especially difficult on account of her condition and the need for me to have regard for it. But when we got settled, her on the settee and me in my big chair, she said, "Justa, you forget I'm pregnant. I can handle anything right now I could before. Just don't you try to lie to me." She fixed me with an eye. "Like you did last night. I admit you told me some, but you didn't tell me the whole of it, now did you?"

I said, kind of awkwardly, "Hell, Nora, it all hadn't happened last night. Been a bunch gone on since then. I couldn't tell you what hadn't happened, now could I?"

"Will you please quit crawfishing."

I sighed. I said, "Dammit, woman, have I got nine more months of this to look forward to?"

"Seven," she said.

"What?"

"I'm two months along. And you quit stalling."

I got out a cigarillo and lit it. I said, "Let me get this drawing."

She said, "Mind your ashes on the floor."

Well, I was glad to see her back acting like herself. Laying down and getting down in the mind were not Nora's way. I even preferred her fussing at me once in a while. She had schoolteacherish ways, and no mistake but I generally didn't pay them any mind. I said, "Well, to begin with, I ain't really been telling you the whole truth, not even the truth as I knew it last night. I know considerably more today. Or I think I know considerably more. But don't you get mad like you done last night. I just give you a little taste and you got angry and went to pouting. Now if you want the truth you got to promise me you'll take it like it is."

She nodded. She said, "Maybe I did act a little over-wrought last night. But I can promise you it won't happen again."

I didn't believe her. Nora had always talked tougher than she was. The day wasn't ever going to come when she wasn't going to be deeply affected by some of the tight places I continually got myself into. I was used to it because I'd grown up in that kind of a life when the Texas range country was an even rougher place than it was today. But Nora had always been kind of hid behind the log, protected and safe and not exposed, firsthand, to the dangers I pretty well took for granted. That is until I'd come into her life and especially since we'd been married. She might make a brave face out of it, but she wasn't any more ready for the hard and fast truth of what still went on around her than she was ready to find a bull loose in her kitchen.

So it was with some reluctance that I set out to satisfy her wishes. I didn't leave out much; just pretty well picked it up from the moment Lew and I sat in the dining room and he told me what was headed our way, on through my first meeting with the robin, through my recruiting Johnson and Millen and how I done it.

She stopped me at that point. She said, "You really didn't do that, Justa?"

"The hell I didn't."

Maybe it was the lantern light but she seemed to go pale. She said, "You'd really have gone that far? Called their notes in?"

"Yes."

"Then it is bad."

I went on and told her the rest of it, told her the gamble Lew and I were playing by depending on Axel for information. In short I told her the whole thing. About all I did leave out was my suspicions that Lew was hiding something from me. But those were just my suspicions and nothing I could put my finger on. I finished up by saying, "So that's where it sits right now. We got to somehow stop them outside of town or there is going to be hell to pay."

She said, almost in a whisper, "My momma and daddy are in that town."

"I know," I said. I looked closer at her. It wasn't the lamplight; she was getting paler. I got up and hustled the few feet to her side and held my tumbler of whiskey to her lips. I said, "Quick, take a pull on this."

Normally she couldn't abide what she called that "vile brew," but she sucked down half that big whiskey johnny quick. She coughed, but then a little color came back in her face. She said, "Damn that Lew Vara. And damn him for getting you mixed up in this."

I said, "Well, I wouldn't go so far as to say that. He's got hisself mixed up in our business enough times. And on a few occasions he's kept you from being a widow."

She grimaced. She said, "Oh, I didn't mean that. It's just that this whole business makes me so angry. When is this country going to be rid of hooligans? How can they ride around so free and easy taking what they want and frightening honest folks!"

I said, "Because there is a hell of a lot more desperados right now than there is law. When the law finally catches up, and it will, then some order will come to this country. Meanwhile, the average citizen has got to look out for his and himself."

"But why does it always have to be you? There's a hundred ranchers in this county."

I shook my head. I said, "Not quite. But most of them are small spreads and they don't have the luxury, like I do, of leaving their business in other men's hands. They don't have an Ed Harley and they don't have twelve full-time hired hands. We're rich and we're powerful, and there's a responsibility goes along with that."

She turned her head. She said, "Oh, hell! I'm tired. I don't want to hear any more about it. I made up my mind when I married you I'd probably be a widow before the year was out. Well, I've had more than a year so I guess I should be thankful.''

I was glad I'd told her. She was different in bed that night, cozying up to me, either being protective or feeling protected. She said, ''Did you really leave that gallows up?''

''Yes.''

''What do the people in town think?''

''They haven't said.''

She said, ''Well, darn it, you ought to tell them what's happening. They should help.''

I said, ''And I might panic them. Nora, these people aren't fighters. If the word were to get around that a gang of murderers and thieves was bearing down on this place half the people in town would load their wagons and leave.''

''Are you going to tell Daddy?''

''You think I should?''

''I don't know,'' she said, after a moment. ''But I would like Mother to come stay out here.''

She was laying with her breasts up against my back. I rolled over so our faces were together. I said, ''Nora, I ain't got any intentions of letting that gang get into town. It'd be like letting a fox in with the chickens. We got to stop 'em somewhere up the road. Now I said I would tell you about it; I didn't say I'd let you give me advice. Now shut your eyes and your mouth and go to sleep.''

Next morning I rode out early, hoping to catch Willy Boyd and James Kline, the two extra hands that Harley had put on for the calving, and sound them out about being gun hands.

But as I rode I was concerned about Nora. Her moods seemed to go up and down. That morning, at breakfast, she'd been low and dispirited. The whole time she'd carried a little worried frown on her face, and she hadn't eaten enough to keep a bird alive, just nibbled at a piece of biscuit and drank some coffee. She said she expected that I would be spending considerable time in town. I told her that, no, I didn't expect to be doing so right off. I said, "Hell, Nora, they ain't just up the coast. They're a good fifty miles from here. Ain't nothing going to happen right away."

She said, "I know Daddy won't come because of the store, but I want you to make Mother come out here and stay."

I said, "And how am I supposed to do that without telling her and scaring the daylights out of her?"

She said, "Just tell her I need her. She'll understand."

Looking at her I was more inclined to think of the reason as the truth rather than an excuse. I reckoned she did need her mother; I reckoned that first childbirth could be mighty frightening.

She also said she wished I'd make up with Ben. I told her that I had no quarrel with Ben my brother, only the Ben that was an employee of the ranch. But she insisted that they couldn't be separated. She asked me to reinstate him to his job of running the remuda. She said, "You've made your point. Justa, it doesn't look right for one of the owners of the ranch to be working as a common drover."

"Why not?" I said. "I did."

"Did you sleep in the bunkhouse and eat with the crew?"

"I've eaten with the crew a thousand times," I said. "And I reckon I've slept in the bunkhouse my share."

"As punishment?"

"Yes, as punishment. When I was about seventeen I figured I knew more than Howard. I was bossing a crew of men and I went against his orders. Next thing I knew I was *working* on that crew. And it was the haying crew on top of everything else. *He* give me a full two weeks of that and would have given me more if the hay hadn't played out. So don't tell me, my girl, how to manage this ranch. Ben ain't learned nothing yet. I let up on him now and he'll just think he can get away with something else."

"But you're going to need him. For the fight."

I laughed. I said, "Well, I reckon he'll show up for that. Ben is a Williams. And the Williams are being threatened. If I'd made him a cook's helper he'd still pick up his gun when the time came."

But I hadn't left her in a very good mood. I gave Juanita a quiet word to keep an eye on her mistress and to send for me or one of my brothers if she went to feeling bad. Juanita had made light of it telling me that the *señora* was acting very normal. She said, "*La primera es muy dificil por soy mujers.*"

Well, the first time was also very difficult for some fathers as well. At least, though, I wasn't throwing up as a regular thing.

I got to the big house a few minutes too late to catch the crews as they rode out. I'd have to hunt them up out on the prairie. There being no hurry I decided to go in and visit with Howard for a spell. I found him sitting with Norris and Buttercup at the big dining room table, drinking coffee. Buttercup yelled for one of the Mexican women cooks to bring me in a cup and then himself settled back with his own cup of highly flavored java. It was so highly flavored you could damn near see the whiskey fumes rising off it.

Howard said, "Well, what news, son?"

I grimaced. I said, "Ain't a lot. Me and Lew is trying something. Don't know if it will work or not."

Norris was dressed in his town clothes—sack suit and foulard tie. I imagined he was just waiting for someone to bring his buggy up to the house. He said, "Justa, you have got to keep those desperados out of town. They could wreck the place."

I just gave him a look. I said, "Thanks for the information, Norris. It had never occurred to me before."

He said, "Have you always got to be sarcastic?"

I said, "Have you always got to make damn fool statements? What the hell you think Lew and I are worrying about right now, the price of beer?"

"Cut 'em down!" Buttercup said. "Bushwhack the sonsabitches! Shoot 'em off their horses."

I said, "Buttercup, do you have any idea who we're talking about?"

He said, in that slightly slurred way he generally talked, be it night or be it day, "Doan make a damn. Bushwhack the sonsabitches! Don' give 'em ary chance."

Howard laughed. He said to Buttercup, "Have you taken notice of the country around here? Ain't many places to hide."

"High grass," I said, and grimaced.

Howard said, "How many men you got so far, son?"

"Seven," I said. Then I jerked my head at Norris. "No, make that six and a half."

Norris got red in the face. He said, "You just go to hell, Justa. Just go straight to hell."

I said, "I'm going to talk to a couple of those temporary hands that Harley put on. Offer them a pretty good piece of change to take part. The two I'm thinking of look like they might know their way around a six-gun."

"None of our regular folk?"

I shook my head. I said, "Howard, this could be the worst kind of a fight. Just out there on that bald-ass prairie with no cover. I've got Johnson and Millen and I feel guilty about them."

Buttercup said, "By gawd you kin count me in! An' 'at's a fact."

I said to Howard, "Dad, how does he manage to get drunk this early in the morning?"

Norris answered. He said, "Simple. He doesn't ever sober up."

I took a last sip of my coffee and got up. I said, "Anybody know which way they headed when they left out this morning?"

It was Buttercup that answered. He said, "Them two wild ones, that Kline and Boyd, they taken out east with a crew.

Harley says they is cows droppin' calves faster'n rain in a thunderstorm. It's this blamed weather an' you kin thank them damn politicians in Wash'n'ton fer that!''

We all looked at him blankly. I said, ''What?''

''Infernal pol'ticians. They got 'em a weather-makin' machine up thar'. They makin' it warmer so's to have a early calf crop so's to drive down the price of beef. Any damn fool knows that.''

I said, ''I got to get kicking. Norris, I wish you'd look in on Mrs. Parker when you get to town. I think Nora is kind of needing a little reassurance right now. See when it might be convenient for her to come out and stay a few days. I reckon I won't be home much.''

He nodded and I went out and got on my horse and headed toward our eastern range, which was down near the gulf and one of the warmer spots on the ranch. Consequently we were doing a brisk business in calves there, more so than other places on the range.

As I rode I could see the faint smoke from scattered little fires around the prairie. The men usually worked in four-man teams. Two men would rope and bring in the new calves to the fire, and there the other two would inspect the calf, brand it, and, if it was a bull calf, castrate it. Then the castration wound would be treated with worm medicine and the calf released to go bawling back to its mama cow complaining about the indignities it had suffered. In the past we'd waited until a calf was six weeks old or older before turning it into a steer, thinking, wrongly, that a few-days-old calf was too young for the knife. But experience had shown us that the younger animals healed faster and got over the experience easier.

Harley was working at the first fire I came to. I asked after Boyd and Kline. He pointed off toward a location about a half mile away. I could see in his face he was mighty interested in what I wanted with two of his hands, but he held his tongue.

As bad luck would have it, Ben was working on the same crew with Kline and Boyd. Well, that would just have to be. I give him good morning and told him to hold up while I talked to the two men I'd come to see.

Kline was at the fire, but Boyd was catching up calves and we had to wait until he brought one in. In the interval neither Ben nor I said a word to each other. I spent my time looking at the stock grazing around me, and he found some interest in knocking the rust off a set of unused irons.

When Boyd was dismounted and standing by Kline I motioned them to walk a few feet away. I didn't care about Ben hearing, but I didn't want the fourth man to know what we were talking about. But then, after we had walked a ways from the fire, I suddenly realized the insult I was paying Ben. I might have taken away his job, but I hadn't taken away his membership in the family or my need for his gun and his support. I called to him and he came ambling over, almost reluctantly. He came up just behind me and stopped. I looked around at him but didn't say anything. He knew what I was up to.

Boyd was a short, kind of square-built man. I reckoned him to be in his early twenties. Kline, it was clear, was older. There was nothing much to distinguish him from any other cowhand of ordinary build except a knife scar that ran down his cheek to the corner of his mouth. The scar had kind of drawn that side of his face up so that it made him look like he was constantly sneering. But that was just in looks. In the few conversations I'd had with him he'd been polite and fairly well spoken, and Harley said he did his work well and without complaint.

I didn't try to explain the circumstances, first because it wouldn't have mattered and, second, because it was none of their business. I said, "I've sized you two men up and I figure you can take care of yourselves in a scuffle. I've seen you both target shooting with your sidearms. You look like fair hands with a gun. That about the size of it?"

Boyd scuffed a boot in the dirt. Finally Kline said, "If you're a-thinkin' we be the kind to make trouble that ain't the size of it at all. We jest lookin' to work. You ast Harley. We ain't chousted nobody."

I said, "I never said you had. And that ain't the point of this inquiry at all."

"Then what you astin' 'bout our guns for?"

"Yeah," Boyd said. "What's the in'erest, Mr. Williams?"

I said, "Likely we're going to have a little trouble here pretty soon. Won't take place on the ranch, more so north of the town of Blessing. If you ain't familiar that's that little town about six or seven miles from here. I want to hire your guns. The job will pay a hundred apiece on top of your regular wages. I'd rate it fairly dangerous, and I'd say we'd be outmanned and outgunned. What do you say?"

For a second they looked away. Finally Kline spit on the ground. Then he said, in his drawl, "Wa'l, I can't speak fer Boyd here, but I ain't lookin' to git no hideful of lead fer no hunnert bucks."

Boyd said, "Me neither."

From behind me Ben all of a sudden said, "How about two hundred apiece? That make it worthwhile?"

Kline looked at him, startled. I'm sure they hadn't known what to make of Ben's sudden appearance on their crew. They hadn't been around long enough to really know who he was. Now they were getting an indication. Kline said, "You mean that, Ben?"

"Yes, he does," I said. "And it's Mr. Williams. Same as me."

They cut their eyes at each other at that one. But then Kline said, "Two hunnert, eh? An' regular wages?"

"Yes."

Kline shrugged. "All right with me." He spit on the ground again. "When we start?"

But I was looking at Boyd. "Well?"

He shrugged. "I'll string along with Jim."

"Fine," I said. "Now just get on back to work. Don't say nothing to the others about this. You'll be called when you're needed."

They started back toward the fire and I turned to thank Ben for his words. He just said, "Take the extra out of my profit dividends." Then he followed the other two, leaving me standing there. It appeared we had a ways to go before anything was going to get patched up.

I rode back to where Harley was working and got off my horse to talk with him a minute. I said, "How's it going?"

He wiped the sweat off his brow. He was working the branding iron and that was hot work. It was amazing how much heat dried cow dung could put off. It could turn an iron cherry red in a matter of minutes. He said, "Wa'l, we ain't fallin' behind no faster'n we was expectin' so I reckon we be doin' all right."

I said, "Harley, I'm going to be in and out of pocket for a time. Maybe a week. But you don't need me. You know what to do."

He said, "Mistuh Williams, onliest thing is them purebreds are gonna start droppin' calves might quick. An' you was always the one decided which bull calves you wanted to leave fer breedin'. You ain't astin' me to take on that chore of decidin' which ones to cut, be you?"

Well, that was a problem. We'd built up a beautiful herd of Hereford cattle and, by carefully keeping them fenced off from our main bunch, had kept improving the line by selective breeding of the better animals. We were getting bigger cattle and cattle that carried a lot more beef. The decision of which animals to leave as bulls for further breeding and which to turn into steers for slaughter was an important one. I said, "Hell, Harley, I don't know. I'll try to be on hand. But if I can't you'll have to use your best judgment."

He didn't look happy about that and neither was I. I rode away cursing the bunch of ruffians that were interfering with my life. They'd caused me a row with my brother, they were worrying my wife sick, and now they were starting to seriously get into my pocketbook. A wrong decision on a bull calf could literally cost thousands of dollars. That's why I'd always made the decisions. It had been my idea some years back to begin upgrading our basic herd of Longhorns. To do that I'd imported Shorthorn cattle from Kansas and Iowa and the Dakotas, Whiteface and Herefords, cattle that all my rancher neighbors had said couldn't survive in the heat of the Texas coastal country. But they'd not only survived, they'd thrived, and we'd gradually crossbred them with the horse-killing, wild-headed, all-bone-and-gristle Longhorns until we'd developed a strain of crossbreeds that brought considerably more money at the market and were ever so much easier to work and manage. After that I'd set out to build a purebred herd that I could not only market, but could sell to other ranchers to start their own crossbreeding operation. It had been immensely successful financially, not to mention the satisfaction I'd personally taken in proving all the doubters wrong.

But the headache in all of that was that I was the only man on the place who really understood the breeding. I kept the breeding records in my herd book, and I was the only one who could look at a week-old calf and see the configuration that would improve the herd. The difference was a bull I could sell to another rancher for a thousand dollars against a steer that might bring three to four hundred dollars. It made me angry to think about it, but I choked it down and rode on toward home.

==Chapter Five

I TOOK LUNCH at home. Even without looking at her I could
tell Nora was feeling poorly, because it was obvious that
Juanita had fixed the meal, and it had always been Nora's
pride that she did most of the cooking for me, a pride, by the
way, that I took great pleasure in because Nora was near as
good a cook as her mother, and that was going some.

She sat at the table with me, but she didn't eat. Juanita
had made some kind of stew which seemed to have about as
much garlic in it as it did meat. But I ate it, along with some
big chunks of bread, without comment. I did say, to Nora,
"You ever plan on eating again?"

She was fiddling with the tablecloth. Even with my rough
eye I could see she was still looking drawn and wan. She
was as pretty as ever, but I could see little signs of neglect
such as the way her hair hadn't had its usual vigorous
brushing that put such a sheen on it, and the powder she
sometimes put on her cheeks was uneven. She said, "I had
a late breakfast. After you left."

"Oh, yeah?" I just eyed her. She was lying and I knew
it, though I didn't know how good a brand of politics it
would be to call her hand on it. I said, "What'd you have?"

She hesitated. Nora wasn't accustomed to lying. She said,
"Egg on toast."

"Did you eat it?"

It flustered her. She said, "What a question!"

I said, "The question is, did you eat it?"

"Oh, la te da!" she said. "You must think I've picked up your habit of lying about everything." She bounced up. "Do you want some more coffee?"

I shook my head. I got a good look at her standing up. I said, "You been laying down again?"

She said, "You are just full of questions, aren't you? Why would you take it into your head that I've been laying down?"

"Your dress is wrinkled."

She said, "Justa, if you are going to subject me to some sort of inquisition every time you come home for lunch, I'd as soon you didn't."

I said, "Honey, I'm worried about you. Norris went into town this morning and I told him to go by your mother's and see if she couldn't come out and visit for a few days."

Her face clouded up. She said, "What made you do a fool thing like that? My heavens! You'll scare her to death! She'll think something is wrong and come flying out here leaving Daddy to look out for himself. Whatever were you thinking of?"

I said, mildly, "Well, you'd done told me you didn't want your mother in town in case of this trouble we might be having."

She turned away and looked out the window. She said, "You just won't let me forget about that for a moment, will you? You are just not happy unless you are scaring me out of my wits! Oh, why didn't I marry a dentist or a shopkeeper or something."

Then she burst into tears and ran out of the room and into our bedroom. I heard, but didn't see, her slam the door. It was a definite invitation not to follow her.

Juanita came out of the kitchen, wiping her hands on her apron. She shook her head and said to me, in Spanish, not to worry.

Hell, how was I supposed to not worry? I was wishing mightily that her mother was there. I knew when I was in over my head. I just hadn't drawn the cards to play in this particular game.

I spent the balance of the day looking over the Hereford herd. We had it on the northwest part of the range where it was supposedly a little cooler. The Herefords were calving later than the crossbreeds because that's the nature of blooded cattle. I didn't know the why of it, even though I'd asked everyone that I thought might know. I figured it was like Nora; she appeared to be having a mighty hard time of it, but I'd heard there were women who could be doing a washing or cooking supper right up until the time it came to lay down and throw out a baby. It was just the way of things.

Much of my mind, though, was in town, wondering if there'd been any news. I knew it was too soon and I knew Lew would notify me at the first sign, but still, one did speculate.

I still held on to one hope—that the wild bunch would fall afoul of some law well up the road and either get jailed or killed off. I'd mentioned that to Lew, but he'd just shook his head. He said that Axel had told him that the bunch had split up into small groups of three and four men, and while they was taking their fun, they were also minding their P's and Q's. He said that Axel had said they was all going to bunch up again somewhere north of Blessing, just where Axel hadn't been able to say. Well, I figured it was too bad we couldn't catch them little packets of men off by themselves before they all got back together again. But that would be impossible.

I got in in plenty of time for supper, so early that I decided to give myself a good washing. I had a little wooden boxlike thing rigged up in the back with a big water tank over it. You could go in there and pull on a rope and it would release a valve that turned a steady stream of water down on you so long as you kept the valve open. Nora never much liked to use it, except in the warmest weather, because the water came from a windmill we had on the place, and the windmill pipe went down into an artesian spring, and that water was mighty cold any time of the year. Of course I'd built the stall part for Nora's sake, or for the sake of her privacy. If it had just been me, I'd have just as soon stood out there naked.

I went into the house and got some clean jeans and a shirt and some clean socks. I saw that Nora was in the parlor, but I never let on, just went on about my business. I didn't know what her mood was likely to be, and I wasn't all that anxious to find out.

The shower bath was mighty stimulating. By the time I got done, my teeth were chattering and I had goose bumps all over. I got on my clean clothes as quick as I could and stepped out into what remained of the sunlight. When I went back into the house, Nora had come into the kitchen and was busying herself peeling potatoes. I didn't see any sign of Juanita. I said, "Where's your help?"

She said, "I gave her some time off. She's gone home to her family."

Juanita lived in a little cabin just beyond our small barn. She was the unmarried daughter of a Mexican man that had too many kids and too few cattle. They lived about four miles over from us.

I said, "She be back in the morning?"

Nora shook her head. "Probably not. Her mother is down with something and she's needed at home to help."

That kind of worried me. I said, "Honey, I don't like you here by yourself all day. And I sure as hell don't want you doing any heavy work."

She wiped her hands on a cloth and then turned around and reached up and kissed me lightly. She said, "Justa, I'm not all that fragile. And I'm sorry if it seemed like I got upset at lunch."

"Aw," I said, "why, that's all right. I never thought a thing of it." Of course I'd thought plenty of it and I hadn't thought that she *seemed* to get upset. She'd got upset and that was the plain truth of it. But now she was acting like the old Nora, so that a little of the worry began to drain out of me.

She said, "You smell good, all crisp and new. Though how you could stand to take a shower bath in this cold weather is beyond me. Now go get your drink and I'll finish fixing supper."

After we'd taken the evening meal, I rode over to the big house like I usually did, to sit around with Howard and my brothers and talk business and have a few drinks. They'd finished supper and were sitting around the big office when I came in. I was glad to see that Howard was up. On his bad days he usually took to his bed right after supper and sometimes didn't get up to eat it. Norris was at the desk he used. Mine faced his. His was all concerned with bank business and stock and bond deals. Mine was all about cattle. Ben was sitting against the wall by the table where the bottle of whiskey and glasses were set. I walked up and poured myself out a drink; Ben gave no sign I was even in the room. But from his desk Norris said, "Justa, I got to have your signature on something."

"What?"

"We've got a hundred thousand dollars' worth of New Orleans Municipal bonds maturing. I'd like to move them into their equivalent in Houston. The rate is a half a point higher than if we renew the New Orleans bonds."

"Are they as safe?"

"Is Houston safe?"

"Go ahead and do it."

I went over to his desk and signed where he showed me. Then I went and sat down in one of the big chairs and lit a cigarillo. Ben looked over at me. He said, "Just wanted to let you know, *Boss*, that I eat supper with the crew and I'll be sleeping in the bunkhouse. But I figured it'd be all right with you, *Boss*, if I came in and visited with my family."

Howard suddenly said, harshly for him, "Now I want you two boys to stop this. It has gone far enough. You're brothers, damnit, now act like it!"

Ben put his drink down and got up. He said, "Talk to the *boss*. I'm just one of the hired hands." Then he walked out of the room. A few minutes later I heard the front door slam. Norris wheeled around his swivel chair and said, "This is just what Dad needs, to get upset over some silly quarrel between you two."

I said, to Howard, "Take it easy, old man, it'll work out. Ain't no use he and I trying to talk right now. He's still on the prod and nothing I could say would do any good. Give it a little time and don't fluster yourself."

Howard grumbled, but he knew I was right. Ben could be awfully stubborn at times, and I knew it would take time for his feathers to get unruffled. The only thing I was still puzzled by was why he'd taken such an occasion to disobey me. Was it so important that Hays go look up some old girl friend and get his ashes hauled? Was his friend's mule more important than his job? Or was he just looking for any reason to defy me? It could have been any reason. Ben, more than any man I'd ever known, could be counted on to do the unpredictable. I asked Howard and Norris what they thought.

Howard just shook his head. He said, "I don't know, I'm just mighty sorry it happened. But I do reckon you come down on him too hard. I know you had to come down on him. Man can't run a place if the help don't mind him. But I think you done him mighty hard, especially after he come to you and said he was sorry. Makin' him sleep in the bunkhouse and eat with the crew. Justa, that was hard."

I said, "I was deliberately harder on him that I would have been on anyone else. Ben and Norris are the two people I have to be able to depend on more than anyone else in the world. When it comes to business, I got to make damn sure there ain't ever no question about who's in the saddle."

Norris said, "It could have been because it was Lew Vara."

I looked at him, puzzled. I said, "Lew Vara? What the hell has Lew got to do with it? Lew is about the best friend this ranch has got."

Norris just shrugged. He said, "It was just a thought. Leave me out of it, this is between you and Ben."

Next day I went along pretty much as I had except I stuck a little closer to home and found excuse, on several occasions, to stop by my house. Nora didn't look a whole lot better, but she seemed more cheerful. She'd rested well the night before, and I was hopeful she'd just had a little spasm of being pregnant. Norris had dutifully gone by her mother's, and Mrs. Parker had said she would arrange to be out in a couple of days. Norris swore he hadn't alarmed her and that Mrs. Parker had been planning the trip anyway.

But it was a good thing I stopped by the house extra often. On one trip home in the afternoon I found Nora setting out to do a washing. She'd got a fire going in the backyard and had water bubbling in the big wash kettle. I caught her just dumping a load of clothes and soap into the boiling water. I guess she'd figured to go lugging arm loads of wet wash over to the clothesline to hang them out to dry. Naturally it was me ended up doing that because you can't convince a woman, once they get a wash started, to just up and walk away from it. So I ended up with a load of wet clothes and sheets and whatnot, following along beside Nora while she hung the goods on the line. I said, "Have you taken leave of your senses? What do you reckon I pay Juanita for? Hell, she'll likely be back tomorrow and we had plenty of clean clothes."

She said, "I got to feeling restless. I wanted something to do."

"Then why didn't you stroll up and see Howard? Honey, I know it's lonely around here for you, but your mother will be along shortly and you'll feel a lot better then."

She just said, "What do you want for supper?"

I sighed. I said, "They just butchered a beef up at the big house. I'll bring home some steaks this evening."

When I finally got back to my own work, the front of my shirt was soaked from carrying around the damned laundry.

I was starting to get a little antsy about Lew. Still it was only the second day, and Axel shouldn't have had time to reach Sixkiller and his bunch, let alone slip off and send us a telegram. I was just anxious to get the matter settled. It had been hanging over my head like a black cloud ever since Lew first made me aware of the situation.

We had steak and potatoes and green beans, the beans being winter beans that had struggled along and lived into spring. It was a good feed and I got up from the table with that pleasant satisfied feeling, got myself a tumbler of whiskey, and sat down in the parlor. I could hear Nora busying herself with the dishes. Juanita had sure picked one hell of a time to go off nursing. As many sisters as she had, I didn't see why it had to be her. Maybe the fattest one always got the job.

But I didn't like to see Nora doing so much. I'd noticed how tired she looked at supper, but I knew there was no good trying to get her to leave the kitchen for Juanita. It would have been easier to get a bull to give milk.

She wasn't showing much, but it seemed like that evening I'd been more aware of her belly kind of taking on new and bigger dimensions. It wasn't anything startling, but you'd have said, "Yes, this is a pregnant woman," if somebody had asked you.

Finally she finished up and came in and sat with me. For a time she sewed and then looked at a Sears & Roebuck catalogue while I studied some Houston newspapers we had mailed to us for cattle prices. They were never current by the time we received them, but they were handy for spotting trends.

After a time we both got to yawning and Nora went off to

wash her teeth and do them hundred other things women got to do before they can go to bed. I had one more drink and studied a while longer, then went and got myself ready for bed. By the time I got to the bedroom Nora was already curled up under a sheet and a light blanket and was just drowsing off. I kissed her good night and told her I loved her. She mumbled something back, and I got under the covers as easy as I could so as not to disturb her and then settled down to relax myself and drift off.

It was hours later, somewhere around two in the morning, that I come awake with the feeling something wasn't right. I was sleeping with my back to Nora and I could hear little moans coming from her side of the bed. I whirled around on my side. She was laying on her back, the covers flung off, her knees up, and both hands clutching at the little round mound of her belly. "Nora!" I said. "What's wrong?"

For answer she just moaned again. Quick as I could I leapt out of bed and lit the lamp that stood on the table by my bedside. By its light I could see the pain on Nora's face. Her forehead was so damp with perspiration that some of her hair was matted flat on it. She'd hiked her gown up the better to comfort herself, and she kept raising and lowering her bent knees. I didn't know what to do; I didn't know what to say. I had never been so scared in all my life. I said, "For God's sake, Nora, what is happening?"

She moaned, "Oooooh, I don't know. I just hurt. I hurt, I hurt."

I said, "I got to get some help. I won't be gone but a second."

I grabbed my revolver out of its holster where it hung over the bedpost and ran through the house and out the front door. Standing there in the crisp early morning air, without a stitch on, I fired three shots in the air. It was the signal to those at ranch headquarters to come to me with all possible speed. Leaving the front door open, I ran back into the bedroom to see about Nora. She wasn't doing any worse, but she wasn't doing any better either. I jerked on a pair of jeans and then found a towel and wet it off the kitchen pump and come back in and bathed her face. It didn't help her pain any, but it give me something to do.

"Honey," I said, "I got to check outside. I've got to see if anyone is coming yet. I've got to send for Dr. Jackson."

She just moaned and clutched herself harder. I tell you the sight was just tearing me apart. I had never felt so helpless in all my life.

I knew it had only been about five minutes since I'd fired the three shots, but I was hoping, praying, for quick help. I ran through the silent house, damning Juanita and her sick mother, though I didn't know what she could have done even if she had been there. But at least she was a woman, and God knows, she'd have had to know more about such matters than I did.

I ran out the front door and stood still and listened. At first I thought I heard faint hoofbeats and then I decided I didn't and turned toward the door. I hadn't taken a step when I could distinctly hear the sound of a horse running hard. There was a little swale a few hundred yards from my house, and when the horse had gone down in that, the sound was cut off. I stood there, waiting. All of a sudden a rider come bursting out of the night and skidded to a stop in front of me. It was Ray Hays. He was riding bareback; he was shirtless and barefoot and was carrying a revolver in his waistband. "Boss?" he yelled.

I didn't want to delay him. I said, "It's Nora! Go for Dr. Jackson. Saddle the fastest horse you can find and take him with you. Put the doctor on that horse. Don't let him fiddle with that damn slow old buggy of his. Get him started, then go by the Parkers and tell Mrs. Parker that she's needed. Then catch up with the doctor and bring him here as fast as you can."

He said, trying to hold his prancing horse, "Ben's right

behind me on a saddled horse that ought to work for the doc.
I'll take it and Ben can come on ahead afoot.''

"Do it fast!''

"I'm gone.'' Then he kicked his horse into a hard gallop
and quickly disappeared into the black of the night.

But in a few moments I heard an exchange of voices
come through the still air, and I figured Ben had surrendered
his horse and was heading for the house. I hurried back
inside. Nora was still writhing around in some god-awful
kind of pain. I took the towel and wiped her face off and,
against Ben's coming, gently lifted her hands and pulled her
gown down. She didn't even seem to take notice, just
screwed her face up a little tighter and kept on moaning. I
held her hand by the back of it, putting mine over the two
of hers that she was holding herself with. I said, "Hang on,
honey, I've sent for the doctor. Help is on the way.''

For just an instant she took one of her hands away to
squeeze mine. She said, very lowly, "Oh, the baby. The
baby.''

"The baby's going to be fine, honey. I promise. Don't
fret yourself. The doctor will be here quick's possible.''

Then Ben was at the bedroom door. He took in the scene
and said, "My God, Justa, what is it?''

"I don't know,'' I said. "Something to do with the
baby.''

He said, "She acts like she's having hallacious cramps.
Look how she jerks her knees up when it hits her.''

I watched Nora for a second. She was doing what he'd
said. "What do you reckon?'' I asked him.

He said, "Maybe we ought to try a little damp heat. I
done it on horses had muscle cramps.''

I said, "Hell, let's try anything. Go build a fire in the
stove and get a kettle of water on. I'll gather up all the
towels and such I can find.''

Even though I didn't know if it was going to be any help
or not, it was good to have something to do. Just sitting and

watching Nora suffer was near more than I could bear. I gathered up what few towels I could find and then thought of the washing on the line, the washing I'd help do myself. It about halfway convinced me that it was the heavy work that had brought on this attack. I ran through the kitchen and out into the backyard, hopping one-footed every so often when my bare foot come across a rock or a cocklebur. It was still plenty dark, but I felt my way along the clothesline, grabbing up everything that felt like a towel. Then I ran back inside. Ben had the fire going good and a big copper kettle full of water set over the hottest part of the stove. He said, "Don't worry, big brother, it's going to be all right. Lay them towels down and get on back to Nora. I'll bring some in when they're ready. And take yourself a drink of whiskey. You're pale as a ghost."

I did as he suggested, and it calmed my nerves down to where I near about could stand them. I went in to Nora, and pretty soon Ben showed up with the first batch of damp towels. I felt one and judged it to be too hot, but Ben said, "Justa, it can't be just warm. It might feel a little hot to her at first, but she'll get used to it."

She didn't want the towel at first because it seemed to interfere with her clutching at the pain. But I persisted with the idea, and she gradually let me slip the first two towels in under her hands. She gasped a little at the heat, but then she seemed to kind of give in to it.

We kept at it for an hour, Ben running the cooling towels back to the kitchen and bringing back fresh hot ones. By now she was used to the heat, and Ben was bringing them in so hot he damn near couldn't hold them with his bare hands. I had no idea how he was wringing them out, coming, as they did, straight out of boiling water.

The towels didn't seem to do all that much good at first, but then, after nearly an hour, it appeared she was beginning to relax and wasn't having near so many spasms.

I said, "Ben, I believe it's working."

"It takes a while. We got to keep it up, though."

I said, "I hope to hell we ain't burned her stomach."

He said, "Way she was hurting, I don't reckon she would have taken notice."

Then, finally, the doctor was there. He shooed us out of the room, looking himself like he could stand some tending to. He had his nightshirt on under a big heavy coat and tweed trousers and some kind of shoes that looked to be about half slippers. He said, "You two wait in the parlor. Don't ask me any questions right now because I don't know anything yet."

Ben and I got a bottle of whiskey and a couple of glasses and went and sat in the parlor as we'd been told. We took the first one down in pretty quick time and then poured out again and settled down to take a blow. I didn't much know what to say to Ben. I was mighty grateful to him both for his idea with the hot towels and his company. I wasn't sure how I'd have handled the time it took the doctor to come if I'd been by my lonesome. Finally I said, "Where's Norris?"

Ben said, "He stayed with Dad. Howard got all excited when he heard your shots and we figured somebody ought to be there. I told him I'd give him three more shots if he was to come and bring help. But he'd have just been in the way."

"I reckon you're right," I said. I took a swig of my whiskey and glanced toward the front door, which was still wide open. I said, "I reckon Hays is walking the horses out."

"Likely," Ben said. "I imagine both of them had a pretty good workout tonight."

I cleared my throat. I said, "I'm much obliged to you."

He said, "Don't thank me, Justa. I'm your brother."

I looked down. I said, "Yeah, seems like I forgot that the other night."

He shook his head. He said, "No, you done right. I was

the one was in the wrong. Either you are the boss or you ain't. Brother or no brother.''

I said, ''Well, what say we forget about it?''

We was too far apart to shake hands, him on the divan on the far side of the room and me in a chair against the other. So he just raised his glass and said, ''Luck.'' I done likewise and the matter was settled. I said, ''You want to tell Ray he's out of another job or you want me?''

He leaned forward. He said, ''Tell you the truth, Justa, it's been so long since I've worked around cattle that I'm kind of enjoying it. And I'm learning about all these new ideas you've introduced. Besides, Harley can use the help. Let Ray go on playin' boss for a while longer. Even though he ain't got much to boss except a couple of part-time vaqueros. The remuda is in good shape and they ain't getting much hard work right now.''

I shrugged. The whiskey and the fright I'd got off Nora had me just about worn down. I said, ''Suit yourself. I've always wanted you to be a little more closer to the cattle operation. If something was to happen to me, you'd have to be the man to run it. As a matter of fact I've been meaning to give you a lesson in the breeding lines. Just never seemed to have got around to it.''

But all the time we were talking my mind was around the corner and down the hall to the end where our bedroom was.

Like he could read my mind Ben said, ''Take it easy, Justa. You done all you could. The doc's here. Let him worry.''

About then Ray Hays came through the door. He'd found himself a heavy wool coat somewhere, but he still wasn't wearing a shirt. I figured he'd had a mighty brisk ride to town shirtless and riding bareback. He had managed to get his boots on, though. He sat down, walking quiet, and said, almost in a whisper, ''How's Miss Nora?''

I said, ''Don't know yet, Ray. But I appreciate what you done.''

He kind of shrugged that off and said, "I walked the horses back to the main house. They be pretty tuckered but they'll be all right."

Ben said, "How come you didn't get you a shirt?"

Ray looked down at his bare chest where he'd left the coat unbuttoned. He said, "Couldn't find one in the dark 'n' you know how cranky them bunkhouse boys get if you go to making a light or rattling around. So I just grabbed up this coat and my boots."

"You get cold going to town?"

"It was worse comin' back," he said. "I got warm at the Parkers' 'n' then it was kind of a shock to my system to take to that air again."

I looked at him in some amazement. I said, "Why didn't you ask Lonnie Parker for a shirt or a coat? Y'all are about of a size."

He got up and got the bottle of whiskey and then looked around for another glass. He said, "Well, I didn't want to bother them. They was kind of flustered."

I crossed over to my office and got him a tumbler. While he poured himself out a drink I said, "You mean they never taken no notice you wasn't wearing a shirt and offered you some covering?"

He took down half a tumbler of whiskey and let it settle before he answered. He said, "Whew! That's the first time I been warm all night. But like I said, Boss, they was kind of flustered. Mizz Parker was ginnin' around gatherin' up this 'n' that 'n' Mr. Parker run out to hitch up his buggy. I had to catch the doc so I just kind of slipped out."

I said, "How'd Dr. Jackson make out a-horseback?"

Hays cut his eyes around. He said, carefully, "Well, I don't reckon he wants to enter any rodeos anyways soon. Fact of the business is he didn't want to git on the horse at all. I had to persuade him."

Ben said, "Hays, you damn fool, you didn't pull a gun on him, did you?"

Hays looked disgusted. He said, "Hell, Ben, who do you take me fer? Some wild injun? Naw, I jest kind of throwed him on the horse and got him moving."

Dr. Jackson was from the East. He'd gone to some hallaciously high-powered doctor's school in some place like Boston. It was said that the reason we got such a purebred medico was that he'd fallen in love with a girl from the Blessing area and she'd told him it was her and Texas or nothing at all. It sounded to me like the kind of story women like to believe is true. I figured he'd come our way because Norris had made him a damn good financial proposition and the fact that he had a Texas wife was just a coincidence.

However we'd gotten him, I was glad to have him on the scene.

About then he came swinging around out of the hall. We all jumped up. He put up a hand. He said, "Nothing to worry about." To me he said, "Justa, your wife is fine. The baby is safe. I've given her some laudanum and she's resting comfortably. The contractions have ceased."

I said, sort of getting shaky now that I could finally relax, "What was it all about, Doc?"

He shook his head. "I've seen this sort of thing before but not out here. It's what we call a hysterical miscarriage. False labor. Either one."

"Hysterical? Nora's never been hysterical in her life."

He said, patiently, "It's a medical term. Call it a nervous miscarriage if you want to. But the fact is, Justa, that something has been weighing mighty heavily on your wife's mind. Whatever it is has got to be taken care of."

I glanced at Ben. He grimaced. I said, "I'll do what I can, Doc. But Nora is a willful woman and sometimes she insists on knowing about matters that ain't good for her."

He said, "Staying out here by herself isn't good for her either. I want you to take her into town and let her stay with her mother until whatever is bothering her is resolved."

I thought about just how safe town might be if those marauders got by us. I said, "Well, Doc, that ain't a real good idea right now. But her mother's on her way out here now. She'll stay with Nora. Won't that be just as good?"

He give me a kind of sardonic look. Dr. Jackson was a slightly-built man with sandy hair and delicate features. He said, looking at Hays, "She would be seven miles closer to me in town. And I *know* it would be a lot safer for me."

Hays said, innocently, "Didn't you enjoy your ride, Doc? That horse I put you on is Ben's horse. Probably the best one on the place."

Dr. Jackson said dryly, "Well I'm certainly glad to hear that if I were to be killed it would have been on the best horse on the place. Now, how am I to get back to town? I can assure you I am not going back aboard another wild beast."

Through the window I could see it was just coming dawn. I said, "Well, Doc, Lonnie Parker and Mizz Parker ought to be along anytime. When they find out that Nora's all right I reckon ol' Lonnie will head right on back to that store of his. Or I can send Hays here over to the main house to hitch up a buggy and he can take you back in. Your pleasure."

He looked at Hays. He said, "I'll wait for Lonnie. I've had all the experience with Mr. Hays I can stand for one night."

Hays said, "Aw, Doc, now don't be sayin' that. You'll git me in a peck of trouble."

Dr. Jackson give me a grim look. "I'll say this for him. He's loyal and he's a man of single-minded purpose."

Ben said, "I'll go make a pot of coffee."

A little later on Dr. Jackson took me back to look in on Nora. She was sleeping peacefully. It did my heart good to see the pain gone from her face. I said, "But, Doc, I still ain't got the straight of this here hysterical business. You mean it wasn't no real miscarriage?"

"Not really. Oh, the contractions were real enough and the pain was real but it wasn't a uterine spasm."

"What?"

"Never mind that. Just figure it was all in her head. But I can't have her getting upset like this anymore. The next one might be real. By the way, the idea for the warm towels was a good one. You might have scalded her slightly but it went a great way toward relaxing her muscles."

I said, "That was Ben's idea. He's real good with horses."

Dr. Jackson smiled slightly. He said, "Well, I guess a muscle cramp is a muscle cramp and heat's the best thing, especially wet heat. Now I could use a cup of coffee."

It wasn't long before the Parkers arrived. Mrs. Parker came bustling in all full of worry and energy. Only after Dr. Jackson had shown her that Nora was all right and explained what had happened did she settle down. She didn't say anything, but some of the glances she shot me while he was explaining left no doubt in my mind that she held me accountable. She finally found a way of using up some of her worry by fixing breakfast for us all. I could see that Lonnie was anxious to get back and get his store opened on time, but she wouldn't hear of it before he'd had a good breakfast. Naturally she insisted that Dr. Jackson eat also, even though he protested he never cared for anything in the morning.

Finally everybody was gone. While Mrs. Parker was cleaning up in the kitchen I looked in on Nora. She was still sleeping peacefully. I figured she was plenty worn out. Pain can do that to you as I well knew and she'd had her fair share of it the night before. Dr. Jackson had left some laudanum, and she was to have another dose in the afternoon and one that night. On no account was she to get up and busy herself about.

Mrs. Parker finished up in the kitchen and found me sitting in my big chair by the parlor front windows. She sat down on the divan and said, "Now then, Justa, I want you to tell me what got my little girl so upset."

Well, naturally I couldn't tell her, not unless I wanted to worry her also or to maybe have the news get around town. I said, "Beats me, Mom. The only thing I been up to is that Lew Vara asked me for some help on a matter of small consequence. I told Nora about it and it seemed to upset her, though not unduly. But she's been gettin' upset about things more than usual here lately, matters she wouldn't have give a second thought to before."

She thought on that and then sighed. She said, "Yes, that's what I was afraid of. Some women have an easy time of it and some don't. I never did with Nora or her sister. I guess it runs in the family. Justa, you're going to have to be very patient with her. It's hard for a man to understand but this is a very trying time for a woman, even this early on."

I assured her that I understood about such matters and that I would do my dead level best to keep Nora as calm as possible. I said, "But, Mom, you've got to give her a talking to about trying to do too much." Then I told her about catching Nora trying to do a wash. I said, "If I hadn't caught her she'd have been lugging a bushel basket of wet wash around the yard."

"Oh, that girl," she said, and shook her head. "She can be so willful. She's got a delicate constitution you know, Justa. She just won't give in to it. I swear that girl will be the death of me yet."

Dr. Jackson had told me that Nora would sleep until about noon. I made my excuses to Mrs. Parker and saddled my bay colt and ambled up to the big house. Norris had gone to town and Ben was out working cattle, so it was just me and Howard. He was up and looking chipper. He'd already had an accounting of the night's activities from Ben, so I didn't have to go into that. I got us both cups of coffee from the kitchen, and we sat around the office discussing this and that. Finally he said, "Ben never come out and said it in so many words but I take it that little matter is patched up between the two of you."

"Yeah," I said. "I don't know what I'd have done without him last night. He was a power of help."

"Well, that's what brothers are for."

"That's what he nearly said." I sipped my coffee. "When it comes right down to it they ain't nobody like family."

Howard said dryly, "I'm glad to hear you say that."

I glanced at him, but there was nothing on his face. I said, "Only thing we didn't get settled was why it come up at the time. I wanted to ask him but it just didn't seem right. I know Ben has got to go on the prod every now and again and rebel but it didn't seem like such a big issue to make such a fuss over."

Howard said, "You want me to tell you? Because I don't think Benjamin ever will. It's got to do with what you said about there being nothing like family."

"So?"

"So Ben taken it into his head that you was treating Lew Vara more like family than your own family."

"Bullshit!" I said.

He shook his head. "Naw, it ain't bullshit. Ben never told me straight out but from this word and that word and a few other things I picked up from him it become pretty clear that you was acting like you thought more of Lew than of him."

"Well, I'll be a son of a bitch," I said. I got out a cigarillo and lit it. It was the only explanation that made any sense. And I could see Ben's point. Lew was my mighty good friend and one did tend to take one's family for granted, sometimes without noticing. I said, "I reckon I better speak to him about this."

Howard said, quickly, "I wouldn't do that if I was you. This matter is closed. Let it lay. Just don't be so quick to sing Lew's praises in the wrong company."

I said, "Hell, I wouldn't take a half a dozen Lew Varas for one Ben Williams. Not in any kind of trouble. And not that Lew isn't my good friend. He just ain't Ben and he ain't my brother."

"Might be you could sort of leak that out. Wouldn't be too obvious about it, mind, but a few hints wouldn't hurt the situation none."

"I got you."

Howard jerked his head in the general direction of Blessing. "I take it you ain't had any word on that other matter?"

I shook my head. "No, and it's getting about time. This waiting around is killing me. I'd damn sure like some information."

"You figured out any kind of plan?"

I shook my head. "Ain't got enough information to go on. All I know is I got to keep them out of the town. And that means a fight out on the bald-ass prairie with them holding two guns to our one. It ain't an inviting prospect."

"Ain't no way to get the men of the town involved? That way you'd at least be firing from cover if you let them come in."

I shook my head. I said, "It's my judgment that you'd have an awful lot of panic. Who you got in town, Dad? Men like Lonnie Parker. Storekeepers and clerks and barbers and cooks and such. We let them marauders get into town and let them amateurs start firing guns and we would likely see the biggest funeral ever held. No, it's better to keep them in the dark and handle it ourselves. Besides, if they come into town we got to wait until they do something. We can't just put men in upstairs windows and let them start firing the minute the gang comes in. If they got any sense, they'll come stringing in two and three men at a time."

Howard sighed. "Likely you are right," he said. "You've always had a head for this. I just ain't hankering to see my three sons in an open gunfight against bad odds."

"Neither am I," I said gloomily. I got up. "Maybe I'll get some helpful information today or tomorrow and figure something out. Right now I guess I better act like a ranch boss."

"And a soon-to-be father."

"Yeah," I said. "Though I ain't sure I ain't more scared of that part than I am of them desperados."

Chapter Six

I GOT HOME for a late lunch, not worrying about the time because I figured Mrs. Parker wouldn't have known to fix anything. But she'd brought a ham out from town with her that morning—though it was beyond me how a woman could think to take a ham with her when she was rushing to her daughter's sickbed. But I was pretty well convinced that Mrs. Parker figured a good meal could fix anything.

So she give me a lunch of ham and potato salad and pinto beans. Near as I could figure the world was still running second to Mrs. Parker as a cook.

After lunch I went in to see Nora. She raised her arms when I come in the room and scootched up to a sitting position. I went over and hugged her and gave her a kiss. She said, "That's wasn't much of a hug. I'm not going to break, you know."

I said, "I don't know about that. I do know about you doing washing and whatnot."

She sighed and said, "Oh, not you too. You had to tell Mother, didn't you? She brought me in some soup when I woke up and that's all I've heard about, that damned wash. Justa, you are a tattletale."

"Listen," I said, "don't start in on me. You give me a turn last night that will last a good long while."

She looked down and fiddled with her gown. She said, "I'm sorry about that. I guess I let my mind run away with itself. Mother give me a pretty good quizzing."

I straightened up. I said, "You didn't say anything, did you?"

She shook her head. "No. And I'm trying to put it out of my mind."

I lied, saying, "It's just as well. I don't honestly think anything is going to happen. I would have had word by now if it was."

She give me that suspicious look she was the mistress of. She said, "Honestly?"

"Honestly. But I thought you was going to put it out of your mind."

"All right." She laughed. "It feels so good not to be hurting that I'm not worrying about anything. Except this." She pulled her gown up to her waist so that her swelling belly was exposed. She said, "Were y'all trying to cook me?"

The little rounded mound was beet red. I said, "Good Lord! Does it hurt? We only done what we thought was best."

She leaned over and kissed me. "I know, honey. And it did a world of good. And, no, it doesn't hurt. Thank you."

I examined her closely. She looked tired, but the strain and worry was gone from her face. I knew the laudanum had something to do with that, but I was hoping it was also because of her intentions to quit worrying.

She said, "I'd like to get up but Mother says I can't."

"So did the doctor," I said. I patted her belly. "So you stay right there. I've got to get out and tend to a few things, but you stay right there. I'll be in early this evening."

I spent the balance of the day wandering around the range with half an eye to the work going on there and the other half directed toward Blessing and the serious trouble that might be coming our way. About mid-afternoon I considered making a fast trip to the town but gave it up as pointless. If there was anything to know or anything important happening, Lew would, I knew, get word to me as fast as possible. Besides, it would throw me late getting home and might give Nora a turn, a situation I couldn't risk.

Her mother fixed supper even though Juanita was back, a situation I was glad of because I figured Mrs. Parker would not be so gentle on Juanita as Nora was and might teach her the business of being a maid. We wouldn't let Nora get up for supper even though she put up a fuss. I took her a tray back and then sat with her while she ate some stew and bread and a piece of apple cobbler her mother had baked. We didn't talk about anything serious, and she seemed in much better spirits, though she was irked about being kept in bed. For my own part I had to act casual and nonchalant even though I was boiling with impatience for some information. I didn't go to the main house that night but talked with her mother, laying the groundwork for a lie that would cover my absence in case I had to leave suddenly and be gone. I spoke of negotiations that Norris had going on to buy a ranch north of the little town of Boling. I said, "If word comes I'll have to go along to sign the papers. Might be gone a couple of days. They ain't no train service to the little town so I'd have to go cross-country."

And Mrs. Parker, all unsuspecting, said, "Why of course you've got to go on with your work, Justa. I'm here. You go on and do what you have to do and don't worry about Nora."

But Nora, when I casually mentioned it that night, wasn't quite so easily taken in. She give me a hard eye and said, "Are you telling the truth, Justa Williams? Do you really have a ranch purchase in prospect?"

"Hell, yes!" I said. "Dammit, Nora, will you get this other business out of your mind? I've still got a land and cattle business to run and one has nothing to do with the other."

"Do you swear it?"

That made me uncomfortable, but I thought, what the

hell, in for a penny in for a pound. I said, ''All right, though I think this is silly, I swear it. Now, are you happy?''

It was well that I laid the lie because next morning the messenger boy from the telegraph office hunted me up on the range. He didn't have a wire for me but a message from Lew requesting I come to town as soon as possible. I sent the boy away with word for Lew that I was on my way. Then I rode to my house and told Nora I'd just got word from Norris about the purchase and had to go into town. I said, ''Anything I can bring you back? A sweet or some cloth or thread?''

She ignored that sally and said, ''You will be home tonight, won't you?''

I didn't figure it could be the real thing, because not enough time had passed, so I took a chance and said, ''Why, of course. I imagine it's just some little detail Norris wants to confer on. Likely he is getting them up a final offer and he wants my approval before he sends them an earnest money check.''

But I still left with a suspicious eye turned my way. I took a moment to speak quietly with Mrs. Parker and tell her that her daughter was working herself up again. I said, ''Mom, you've got to get her to quit worrying about me. She's scared if I get out of her sight, or leave this ranch, that I'm going looking for trouble. Dr. Jackson said specifically she was not to exercise herself or stir up her mind and that is exactly what she's setting out to do.''

Mrs. Parker sighed. She said, ''That girl. Sometimes I swear.''

I said, ''She's got a mighty good imagination.''

''Yes. Always has. Well, I'll just have to have a good long talk with her. But you go along now and tend to your business. A man has to do that if a woman is to cook food for the table.''

''Just get her mind on other things, Mom. I'll be home quick as I can.''

I left with her telling me to "be sure and look in on Lonnie" and rode for town at a good clip, letting the horse I was riding that day, the three-year-old gelding, have a good stretch of his legs.

When I walked into Lew's office I wasn't surprised to find him behind his desk, but I was considerably taken aback to see Axel huddled up in a chair against the side wall. I stopped and stared. I said, "What the hell!"

Lew give me a sour look. "He come back."

"I can see that. But why?"

Lew said, "He got scairt they was on to him. Said they was asking him too many questions and they was watching him. He said he tried to go to the telegraph office but he thought somebody was following him."

I gave Axel a severe look. I said, "Boy, have you lost your mind?"

He give me a blank look. "Naw, sir. Least I doan thank so."

"You seen that gallows is still out there, didn't you?"

"I taken notice, yes, sir."

"You think I was joshing you about that hanging business? I'm out a hundred dollars on that gallows already. You reckon I ain't planning on using it for that kind of money?"

He looked down and didn't say anything.

A thought come to me. I said, "Here! Turn out your pockets. I want to see them silver dollars I gave you."

But Lew shook his head and said, tiredly, "Save your time. I've already been through that. He says on food, but he come in here early this morning smelling like a saloon and drunk as ol' Billy hell. You reckon he come back because he spent the money first and couldn't send a telegram? He says he spent it running from the gang. They are gathering up, by the way."

I said, "Axel, when did you spend that money? Coming or going?"

"Comin'," he said.

Lew said, "We need to talk in private before we go on with the boy. Axel, go back and put yourself in a cell."

The boy got up. He said, "What 'bout my re-vol-ver?"

Lew said, "I'll just hold that for the time being, Axel. Now go on. I'll call you when you're wanted."

"Kin I have a drank of whuskey?"

Lew said, "No, you can't have a drink of 'whuskey.' Now go on before I kick you back there."

When he was gone and we'd heard a cell door clang, Lew got up and poured us each out a tin cup of coffee. He said, "It's pretty fresh. I had to make a fresh pot to get enough down that boy to sober him up so's I could understand him."

I sipped at my cup. It might be fresh, but it was still jail house coffee, strong enough to clean a cast-iron stove. I said, "He tell you anything we can use?"

"I don't know. He says they are gathering up. He says there be seventeen of them all told now. Says one of the lot got in a gunfight with another one and was kilt. Wish they'd all do the same."

"Are they in Brazoria?"

Lew said, "According to Axel they are. Justa, do we believe that kid or not? For all I know he just might have rode up the road to the first saloon somewhere up the line and drunk up what money he had. He might never have gone near that bunch."

I shrugged. Wasn't much answer to a question like that. Finally I said, "Maybe we can talk to him, scare him some more, and find out what the truth is. I tend to believe he did rejoin the bunch and that he did get scared. Why else would he come back here?"

Lew said, disgustedly, "To get more drinking money. Hell, Justa, I don't know. This thing has got me all sixes and sevens."

I said, "I think we got to start out not believing him and make him convince us he's telling the truth."

"And how do you propose to do that?"

"Details," I said. "He ain't smart enough to make up details. We keep asking for the smallest little item, and if he doesn't know it, we tell him we don't believe him. And we keep on telling him we don't believe him until he either tells us the unvarnished truth or makes up a story good enough for us to believe. And I don't think he can do that last."

Lew said, "I guess."

I said, "But the thing that is worrying me the most is where to tackle this bunch, even if there ain't but seventeen of them now. I keep visualizing that northern road in my mind, and even though I've seen it a thousand times, I can't get the feel of it. I can't think of a single good defensive position."

Lew said, "Reason you can't do that is because they ain't any."

I said, "Well, let's have him out here. It's an hour to the noon meal and we might as well spend it making Axel squirm."

Lew went back and brought the kid out to the office. We made him stand in the middle of the room with me on one side of him and Lew, at his desk, on the other. I said, "Axel, we think you are lying. And if you are lying to us, you are going to be the loser for it. You've made me damn mad. I went out of my way to give you another chance and this is the way you repay me. The sheriff is about halfway convinced that you came down here to spy on us. I'm not so sure but what he ain't right."

Axel turned his head and looked at me. The fear was back in his eyes. He said, "Naw, sir."

I said, "Don't be looking at me. And don't look at the sheriff. Look at that far wall. And get your hand off the sheriff's desk. Stand up there on your own two feet and stand straight."

Lew said, "Where's the gang stayin'?"

Axel swallowed. He said, "They be all over."

"Where's Sam Sixkiller staying?"

"Bowdin' house."

"Whose boarding house?"

"Mizz Phelps."

"Where did you stay when you went back?"

"Charlie Bird 'n' Mike wuz camped outside o' town. I bedded down wid them."

"Where'd you eat?"

"Eat wid Mike 'n' Charlie. They'd kilt a calf 'n' they wuz willin' fer me to eat with 'em 'cause the meat was turnin'."

"Where'd you buy yore whiskey?"

He turned his face toward Lew. "Never bought none till I wuz runnin' back ta here."

"What'd you drink?"

"Stole some offen Charlie 'n' Mike. An' Sam bought me some dranks when I first git back."

"What kind of questions did he ask you?"

"Jest how you wuz an' what you said."

"And what did you tell him?"

"Tol' him what y'all tol' me to tell 'im. Jes' said you'uz away an' nobody knowed when you'd be back."

I said, "You didn't tell him anything about me or about being thrown in jail? Or threatened with a hanging?"

He didn't look at me, but I could see his eyes roll around in his head at the mention of the hanging. He said, "Ah never said nuthin' 'cept what y'all tol' me to say."

Lew said, "What did Sam say?"

"He done him some laughin'. Said you wuz gonna git you a surprise when you got back into town an' found him settin' in yore chair."

"What did you tell him about the town?"

"Never said nuthin' 'bout the town. Wadn't suppose ta. Ol' Sam jest sent me down here to tell the shur'ff thet he was a-comin' like it 'er not. He ain't figured I's smart enough to tell nuthin' 'bout the town. An' he's right too.''

We kept on like that for the better part of an hour, boring in on Axel, going back over the same questions, asking them different ways, challenging him, threatening him, bullying him. Finally I said to Lew, ''It's near lunchtime. Put him in a cell and let's go eat.''

Axel said, ''Kin I git me somethin' ta eat?''

Lew was getting down his keys. He said, ''Maybe we'll just starve the truth out of you. I know one thing, you ain't gettin' no whiskey until you start telling us the straight of it.''

Axel went through the door to the cells protesting he was telling the truth. He said, ''Hones' shur'ff, I ain't been fibbin'. I done like you tol' me except fer sendin' them tell-e-graphs.''

''Get on back there,'' Lew said.

We went down to Crook's and had a meal. While we each ate a steak, we didn't do much talking, both of us busy with the business of eating and running over and over in our minds what Axel had said. Finally I pushed my plate away and lit a cigarillo. I said, ''I think the boy is telling the truth.''

Lew chewed for a moment and then swallowed. He said, ''Supposin' he is. What help is that to us?''

I shrugged. I said, ''Not a hell of a lot. About all I can take from it is that Sam Sixkiller is planning on starting this way damn quick. He's got his whole bunch gathered up so there ain't no reason for him to hold up.''

Lew said, ''Might be he's waiting to make sure I'm back in town.''

I give him a close look. I said, ''Lew, you sure there ain't anything you've forgot to tell me? Any little thing I ought to know?''

He said, shortly, ''I done told you no. What do you want me to do, swear on a Bible?''

It reminded me of Nora making me swear. I'd been lucky she hadn't insisted on the good book because I wouldn't have been able to lie with my hand on that. I wasn't known to be particularly religious, but I did set pretty good store by my soul and my maker. I said, "Hell, I was just asking. Don't get on your high horse. I was just curious if there might be something in Sixkiller's mind, something like he might think you owed him."

He said, "Well I don't."

We were drinking beer and I took a sip of mine. I said, "It strikes me as passing strange that Axel would come back here. If he was going to run off from the bunch why didn't he just take off and keep running? For all he knew we'd hang him coming back here."

Lew gave me an amazed look. He said, "You forgot the selling job you put on that boy? He still thinks he was followed there and back by your half-Indian half-wildcat man. First thang he said to me when he come in the door was to quick tell the man right behind him that he was comin' in to report. His horse was all lathered up and he was about as scared as he was drunk. I reckon he seen a horseman behind him and took him to be this man of yours. Hell, Justa, he couldn't go anyplace else."

I said, "You didn't tell me that. If that's the case then he did go back. He'd of been too scared not to. Listen, I'm going to ride out the Wadsworth Road and have a look around. There's got to be some concealment out there where we could ambush them."

Lew said, "All right. I'll take the boy back something to eat. But you're wasting your time lookin' that road over. Ain't no cover, an' besides, if I know Sam Sixkiller like I used to, he ain't going to be coming in one direction in one bunch. He'll split his people up outside of town some distance and come in with about three gangs from as many directions."

I got up. I said, "Maybe so. But I want to look anyway. I'll be back at the jail in an hour."

I walked out of the place ahead of Lew, went down to the jail, got on my horse, and set out up the north road. I didn't know what I was looking for so I looked at everything. Town ended just beyond the railroad depot, and from then on it was just empty, flat plains uninterrupted except by the narrow dirt road that was just about one wagon wide. About two miles out of town I passed by the auction barn. Our family owned it. Every first and third Saturday of each month farmers and little ranchers in the area would bring odd lots of livestock, horses and mules and cattle and milk cows, to the auction barn to sell and trade and buy. A surprising amount of money changed hands on those auction days. We took a brokerage of course for supplying the auctioneer and the place and guranteeing every sale.

I kept riding. I was about two or three miles on farther down the road, still looking at the same flat pasture land, when a thought began to work in my head. I stopped my horse and looked back. In the distance, toward town, I could make out the outline of the auction barn. I turned and rode slowly back toward it, my mind turning over and over the beginning of an idea. It would take some doing, but it was something that just might work.

When I got to the barn I stopped. It was set just off the road, and from the way the grass had all been ground down to bare earth, you could tell a good number of hoofs, cattle and horses, had been about the place. The barn itself was round and near about two stories high. It had a line of windows around the bottom part. Inside, there were benches all around that rose right on up like the balcony in a church. In the middle was a big ring where they run the livestock in for the crowd to look over while the auctioneer went through his spiel. The buyers and sellers and kibitzers sat on the benches. The place, I estimated, could hold a crowd of fifty or sixty, and sometimes there was that many in attendance.

I sat my horse in front of the barn, thinking. The windows would make good firing stations, but we couldn't just open up on them as they passed by. Lew was insistent that they had to make the first move, either break the law or give reason to make us think they were going to break the law. And just riding by an auction barn wasn't reason enough to open up on a party of men, no matter how certain you were of their intentions. Besides, I had no sure way of knowing that they'd be coming in on the Wadsworth Road. Logic contended that they would be, given their present location in Brazoria, but I had long ago learned that the quickest way to get yourself a surprise was to figure an enemy for doing something for certain.

Still, I sat there staring at the barn. It was the only structure for miles around and the only thing that offered anything in the way of cover for further than that. I didn't have a plan, but I had a hope. I turned my horse and headed back for town.

Lew was behind his desk with his feet up when I came in. He said, "Axel is hollering his head off for a drink. Reckon I ought to let him have a snort?"

"Naw," I said. I sat down. "Hold off on it. I might want to hold it over his head a little later. I'm kind of getting an idea, though it ain't real well thought out yet."

He took his boots off the desk and dropped them to the floor with a clump. He said, "Tell me about it."

I said, "It involves our auction barn. But, Lew, it's one hell of a long shot."

He readjusted his hat. He said, "Well, at least it's in the right place. Or the right direction anyway."

As briefly as I could, I laid out my thoughts. They hardly connected into a plan. I said, "So the trick would be to get them to come by the auction barn. Of course that's just one of the tricks. I think we've got to get a lot of rabbits into a hat. Or was it gettin' a lot of them *out* of the hat? Been so long since I seen that magician feller that came to town.''

Lew leaned back in his chair, pushed his hat back, and sat gazing up at the ceiling, scratching at his chin. He said, ''I can see where it might could work. But thar's still the problem of drawin' him in. That could miscalculate a bunch of ways. You thinkin' Axel to carry the word?''

I nodded.

He whistled. He said, ''Talk about puttin' all yore eggs in one basket. That boy doubles us over we'll all be out thar' and all they got to do is come in from a different direction to take the town wide open. By the time we got word they could have carried off any damn thang they wanted.'' He was chewing tobacco for a change and he took a moment to lean over and spit. He said, ''I don't like that part at all. No, sir, I don't like it.''

I said, unhappily, ''Neither do I. Think of something better.''

He spit again. ''Shit,'' he said, ''I can't. Or I already would have.''

I said, ''Axel's very presence back here indicates he's certain I'm having him followed and can have him killed at any time. Unless the little bastard is one hell of a lot better a liar than I think he is, he is making me believe that he is more afraid of us than he is of Sam Sixkiller. I can't think of any other way to get the message across to Sixkiller.''

Lew sat staring at the wall, thinking. I was doing the same thing except I was resting my elbows on my knees and staring at the floor. After a moment I said, ''Maybe we could switch him.''

''How so?''

''Let him overhear us talking about what a plum the auction barn is. Then send him off.''

''Tell him not to tell Sixkiller?''

''Well, no, not exactly. If we do it that way it sounds like we're trusting him not to be trusted. The other way we're trusting him to be trusted. Hell, either way it's a coin flip. The whole thing was just an idea I had on account of the auction barn being the only cover. The hell with it.''

Lew said, "Wait a minute. Let's don't give up so damn easy. Without that plan we ain't got no plan a-tall. Let's think on it a little longer."

I said, "If it just didn't depend all on that damn Axel. That boy is either dumb as hell or slippery as a greased pig. Either way he ain't no post to be leaning against."

Lew opened up his desk drawer and came out with a new bottle of whiskey and two glasses. He broke the seal on the bottle, unscrewed the cap, and poured us out a shot of whiskey each. We lifted our glasses, said, "Luck," and then knocked them back as befits the toast. From the back there came a long, drawn-out "Shurrrr'fff! Hey thar', Shurr'ff!''

I looked at Lew. He just shook his head. I said, "I swear to God, that boy can smell whiskey through a solid wall."

Lew yelled over his shoulder. "Shut up, Axel. You ain't gettin' none. Not yet. I'll let you know when you got some coming."

"Shurr'fff! I need a drank of whuskey!"

"Shut up, Axel, or I'll gag you."

I wasn't paying any attention to the byplay. A thought was working around in my head. I said, "Hell, Lew, let's sound about halfway straight on this. Let's send Axel back with the message that you're willing to go along to a certain point. That you'll let him have the auction barn on auction day and all the money and livestock that's there but you want him to stay out of town."

Lew looked thoughtful. He poured us both out another tumbler of whiskey before he said anything. He finally said, "It's still risky."

I said, "Why? You and Sixkiller are supposed to be old saddle mates. You're the sheriff here now. You're willing he should have some pie but not the whole thing because that would run you the risk of getting taken down as sheriff.

So you say he can have what's in the auction barn, which is considerable, but he is to stay out of town to protect your job. That would make sense to me.''

Lew stirred his glass around on the desktop. ''Yeah, it would make sense to you. You'd stop with the auction barn. But that's because you ain't the most low-down, murderin', thievin' scoundrel ever walked the face of the earth. Besides, don't get the idea that me and Sixkiller was such old chums. Could be it's old trouble between us that has drawn him my way.''

I said, ''That ain't the way you put it at first, Lew.''

He said, defensively, ''Yeah, maybe I didn't. Truth be told I don't know what he's after.''

I said, ''We get him after that auction barn, he won't ever be after anything else. I can promise that.''

He glanced up, surprised. ''You'd play him false? Mislead him?''

''Why hell yes,'' I said, surprised. ''You don't think I'd use that auction barn for anything more than to trap that mad dog, do you?''

Lew shook his head, sort of as if to clear it. ''Yeah,'' he said, ''I see your point. I don't know what got to going through my head. For a minute there I thought you really was fixing to offer it up to him.''

I said, ''You just keep on thinking that way. When you propose it to Axel it'll come through more sincere if you believe it yourself.''

Lew said, ''I ain't much of a hand at play actin'.''

I got up and walked over to the front window. Out on the street I could see people going about their business, little aware of the threat hanging over their heads. I said, ''Well, whatever we do we better decide on it today. Time is running out. If we're going to get Axel on his way we better do it no later than in the morning.''

''You want to start in on him today?''

I looked out again. Far off in the distance I could see the

dark clouds of a summer storm building. It was pushing three o'clock in the afternoon. I said, "Yeah, I guess so. But let's make it short. I got to be home early this evening. Nora is mighty suspicious of me."

"How's the missus doing?"

"Fine," I said. I didn't lie because I didn't want to tell Lew about Nora's trouble; I just didn't want to get into it.

Lew stood up, jangling his ring of keys. "You want him out here?"

"Might as well," I said. "Leave the bottle of whiskey on the desk where he can see it. Might make him more agreeable."

"Yeah," Lew said.

In a few minutes he was back with the kid. I didn't make him stand in the middle of the room this time. Instead I set him down in the chair by the wall and poured out a tumbler of whiskey. But I didn't hand him the whiskey even though he was eyeing it like a dying man. I just left it setting on Lew's desk and then sat down in my own chair. I leaned forward. I said, "Axel, we want you to go back, to Sixkiller's bunch."

He wasn't even looking at me. His eyes were on the whiskey. I said, "Axel, pay attention to me. If you don't, you ain't ever going to get a drink."

He finally, reluctantly, turned his eyes toward me. He said, "Wha'?"

I said, "We want you to go back. To Brazoria. Or wherever you catch up with Sixkiller and his bunch on the trail."

He couldn't have made up the fear and fright that come over his face. He started off saying, "Naw, sir. Naw, sir." And he kept on saying it and shaking his head at the same time.

I finally got him slowed down enough to say, "Just to take him a message. A message he'll be glad to get. It ain't going to be any danger to you."

"Uh uh," he said. "Uh uh, uh, uh." And went back to shaking his head. "Iffen I wanted to be skint alive I'd go back, but Ah ain't plumb loco. What I tell the man after I ran off 'thout a word? Huh! Naw, sir. Thankee, no."

I said, "Look, you go back and tell him you thought he meant for you to keep trying until the sheriff was back in town. He'll believe that. Make you look good, like you was trying to do your job. All you got to do is go back and tell him you talked with the sheriff. He'll be glad to hear that."

Axel rolled his eyes around. He looked far from convinced, but at least he was listening. His attention was starting to stray back to the tumbler of whiskey on the table. Lew said, "Axel, dammit, forget that whiskey for the time. You ain't gettin' it. If need be I'll put you back in that cell and you'll have a long gray beard before you get another drink of whiskey. Now, dammit, it makes perfect sense to me for you to have ridden back down here to finish yore job. Tell Sam you looked for him to tell him but couldn't find him. Tell him it just come in your head. Hell, as sappy as you are, he'd likely believe anything might come in yore head."

Axel thought about that for a moment. He said, "Yeah, he jus' might. He thanks Ah'm pretty sappy. He's allus astin' me iffen Ah been at the loco weed agin."

"There," I said. I reached over and got the glass of whiskey and held it just out of Axel's reach. I said, "See? He ain't going to think anything. Now you just take a message back to him for us and I'll let you have this drink. And maybe a few more."

He put out a shaky hand, groping eagerly in the empty air. I pulled the tumbler back. I said, "Just one thing, Axel— You take this drink, you are agreeing to do the job, to carry the message we give you. If you don't, well, that man I got following you is going to catch you and roast you over a slow fire. And I ain't joshing you about that."

He swallowed. He said, ''Ah be hearin' you, sir. I reckon I'll do 'er.''

''You sure?''

He swallowed again. He said, ''You be gonna write the message down, ain'tcha? My head ain't much fer holdin' stuff.''

I nodded. That was an even better idea. I said, ''Yeah. Now you understand? You are to go straight to Sam Sixkiller as fast as you can. Give him the message.''

He said, ''What Ah do then?''

I shrugged. ''Whatever you want to.''

''Ar'right.''

I gave him the whiskey, or rather he jerked it out of my hand. He took it down in one quick gulp and then held out the empty tumbler. I poured it full again from the bottle. I said, ''You better take it easy. You can't get drunk.'' I looked over at Lew. I said, ''You want to write the message?''

He got up abruptly. He said, ''Let's me and you step outside for a minute. A thought has come to me.''

''Now?''

''Yeah.''

I shrugged and got up. As Lew circled the desk he grabbed the bottle by the neck and took it with him. Wasn't no need of leaving temptation in Axel's way. We went to the door and stepped out on the boardwalk.

''What?'' I said to Lew.

Chapter Seven

LEW STARED OUT at the street for a moment, then he turned back to me and said, "I think I ought to be the one to tell Sam about the auction barn. I think it will sound more like I'm trying to make a deal if it comes straight from me."

I frowned. I said, "You ain't talking about going to Brazoria, are you?"

He shook his head and spit tobacco juice in the dust of the street. He said, "Naw. I figure to send a message to Sam by Axel saying I'll meet him on the road up a ways. I figure about halfway between Wadsworth and the Colorado River. That's about twenty miles off and would give me plenty of time to get back for the party if he takes the bait."

I said, "Are you seriously talking about meeting seventeen renegade bastards out on the broad-ass nowhere? Hell, Lew, that's plain crazy."

He chewed his cud of tobacco for a moment and then spit it in the street. He said, "It's the only way I know to properly bait this trap. If I go out to see him and meet him on his own ground it will make it seem like I ain't got anything up my sleeve."

"Yeah," I said, "especially if we get back with a sleeve with an arm in it."

He shot me a look. "You ain't going."

"Hell yes I'm going. Somebody has got to watch your back."

He said, "Justa, I'm much obliged for the offer, but I

can't let you. You got to think about Nora and that kid you got on the way.''

I said, "Look, ain't any part of this not going to be dangerous. They are a hell of a lot less likely to jump two men than one. Sixkiller would have to figure we could cut a pretty good swath through his bunch before we went down. Besides, I'll go as your deputy and that will make the story about hitting the auction barn and leaving the town alone all that much more believable.''

"Justa, I say no.''

"You can say no all you want to, Lew, but I'm going. That's a public road you're talking about. You can't keep me off of it. Besides, I can lie better than you can.''

"What about Nora?''

I shrugged. I said, "In the first place I don't think they'll start anything. Remember, you and Sam used to be old saddle mates.''

"Not exactly.''

I looked at him. I said, "You ain't enemies, are you?''

He wouldn't answer, just stared out into the street.

I said, "Lew, I've got to know about this. Something about the way you've acted from the very first has made me think there's more between you and Sam Sixkiller than you've told me.''

He still wouldn't say anything or look at me.

"Lew!'' I said. "Dammit, I ain't putting my life in danger without the truth. Now out with it. You ain't fooling nobody choking up your mouth like that.''

"Dammit!'' he suddenly swore. "The son of a bitch and I are related. Blood related!''

All I could do was stare at him. The news had come as quite a shock and left me fumbling around in my mind as to what it could mean. I never doubted Lew's loyalty or honesty or his intentions to protect Blessing and those in and around it, but this business of Sixkiller's being a blood relation hit me like a stump. Finally I said, "How close?''

He said, "I think the no-good son of a bitch is my half uncle."

"Your what?"

"My half uncle."

I stared at him a moment, trying to think. I said, "I don't think I ever heard of one of those. How does that work out?"

He said, angrily, "The bastard's grandpa got at my mother when she and my daddy lived up in Oklahoma. My daddy kilt the old man, but they went ahead and had the kid. He come out as my older brother, my half brother Frank. You never knowed him. He's about five years older than me. Lives up in Arkansas. Then they had me. Sam got born about ten years before me so I reckon that makes him my half uncle, or quarter uncle. Anyways, they is some Sixkiller blood in me somewheres an' every time I get shot or cut I always say that it's Sixkiller blood I'm bleeding an' I'm well shut of it."

I stared at him in some amazement. I said, "Why, you ain't no more kin to him than you are to a horse and buggy. Where'd you get such a crazy idea?"

He said, stubbornly, "It's what ever'body said. An' I heard it from more than one party."

I said, "But you're not blood kin."

He said, "Ain't I kin to my half brother? Blood kin to Frank?"

"Yes," I said.

"An' ain't my half brother blood kin to Sixkiller? On account of Sixkiller's grandpa bein' my half brother's daddy?"

"Just barely."

He said, "Well, barely counts when it comes to blood." He swung around on me. "Look here, Justa, I never been so ashamed of anything in my life. Not that that old man got to my mother; she couldn't he'p that. My daddy explained all that to me. She was just a young girl on the reservation.

Naw, I'm ashamed that I'd be kin to such trash. It's hurt me to tell you, Justa, but I feel like I didn't have no selection. Not an' still be fair to you. But, there it is and if you think the less of me I wouldn't blame you. I'd shore appreciate it, though, if you wouldn't put it about.''

I laughed out loud. I said, "Half uncle, huh?"

He nodded, frowning. He said, "That's about the way I worked it out. Daddy never would talk about it over much."

I said, "Lew, you are as dumb as a wagon load of river rocks. You ain't blood kin to Sixkiller."

Lew said, "He told me I was when I was on the owl hoot trail in Oklahoma."

"That's bullshit. Look here, your blood comes from your mother and daddy, right? And they get theirs from their mothers and daddies, right?"

He nodded slowly. "Yes," he said, "I reckon so."

"And so on back, right?"

He nodded again, his brow furrowed.

I said, "Then you tell me when Sixkiller's grandpa got any blood in that mix that come down to you? Shore he got some in your half brother. That's why he's your half brother. But he didn't get none of his blood in you."

He stood there, wrinkling his brow, trying to work it out. I could almost see his mind turning it over and over. After a moment he said, "Yeah, but—" Then he stopped and thought some more. After another moment he said, "But look here, me an' Sixkiller is—" Then he stopped again. Finally he blinked his eyes and said, "Why I ain't no more kin to that trashy bastard than I am a jackrabbit."

"Of course not."

He said, "But it made so much sense. Hell, I been believing that for years. I guess what throwed me was that I was blood kin to my half brother an' my half brother was blood kin to Sixkiller."

"Which you thought made you blood kin to Sixkiller. Well, that ain't the way it works. Sixkiller ain't got none of your momma or daddy's blood in him and you ain't got none of his family line in you.''

"Why, that son of a bitch!'' he said. "I nearly went outlaw because Sixkiller said it was in my blood. Can you beat that? Lord, what a chump I been. Worse, that son of a bitch had me convinced I had Comanche blood from his side. I don't know which makes me madder; the idea he nearly turned me outlaw, or the idea that I been thinking I was part Comanche, which is about the worst renegade Indian there is. Son of a bitch!'' His brow was starting to clear. After another second or two the slightest evidence of a smile worked at one side of his face. "Hell, I ain't got nothing to be ashamed of.''

"You never did,'' I said. "The misfortune that befell your mother was none of your doing.''

"The Indian side of me is Cherokee, straight Cherokee.''

"What's the rest, ignorant?''

He rounded on me for that one. He said, hotly, "All right, Justa, you better promise me you won't tell anybody about this. An' I mean not even your own family.''

I said, "I don't know, Lew. Information like that is likely worth a pretty good piece of change.''

He give me a sour look. He said, "Don't lollygag around with me, Justa. I'm mad as hell I been carrying this load around with me as long as I have.''

I said, "Well, nobody made you. If you'd have told me in the first place. . . .''

He looked down. He said, "I was scairt to. I thought it might make a difference. That is if it had been true.''

I shook my head. "No,'' I said, "it wouldn't have.''

"Yeah, but that's now. When I ain't blood kin to that lowlife.''

I said, "It would have been then, too, even if your worst fears had been realized. Man don't pick his family, but he can pick his friends.''

For a second he fumbled around in his pocket. Then he

finally come out with a cigarillo. He lit it, got it drawing, and then gave a short nod. He said, "Much obliged."

I said, "Now we better get to figuring this thing out."

Lew thought a moment. He said, "Today's Tuesday. We can get Axel out this afternoon or in the morning. Either way he'll easy come up on Sixkiller early Thursday morning. He can make it to halfway between Wadsworth and the Colorado easy by Friday afternoon. From there he can make it easy to the auction barn by Saturday afternoon."

I said, "Saturday won't do, Lew."

"Why not?"

I said, "Because this Saturday really is auction day."

He stared at me for a second. He said, "But it's got to be Saturday. This Saturday. Hell, Sixkiller ain't going to wait around for another week. He'd go for the bank, the merchants."

I said, "Let's tell him Friday. Or Sunday."

He said, "Who the hell ever heard of an auction day being on any other day than Saturday? Auction Friday? Auction Sunday? Hell, Justa, Sam ain't no schoolteacher, but he ain't *that* ignorant."

People were passing by us on the boardwalk. Every so often, even in the midst of that intense conversation, we'd have to break off to nod hello to a man or raise our hats to a lady. I said, "Lew, I ain't about to bring my friends and customers under that kind of danger. You been worried about Sixkiller and his bunch getting loose in town. Well, now you are proposing to take a load of citizens out to them. Howdy, Mrs. Bradly."

He frowned. He could see that I was right, but I could see his point also. He rubbed his jaw. He said, "What time does the last cow get sold?"

"About two in the afternoon. Usually. If there's a lot of stock it can run later."

"Then what happens?"

I shrugged. I said, "Some of 'em take off for home, some stand around and talk a bit."

"What time does the last soul leave the place?"

"About three. Usually."

"Then what?"

"Then the manager, Edgar Marsh, counts up the take and carries it to the bank. They open up to let him in."

"And what time is that?"

"Little after four."

"How much money?"

"Hello, Shanks. Oh, somewhere's between seven and nine thousand, usually."

He scratched his jaw and nodded to someone. He said, "Well, hell, Justa, all we do is advance the times. Tell sixkiller the auction is over with a little after three and that the money is getting counted around four o'clock. Money ought to draw him. And by then the crowd will be gone. Any stragglers we'll run out. Besides, he ain't gonna want to go in there when the place is full. He don't know what kind of trouble he might run into."

I said, "Yeah, but what if the auction runs real late? Been a good year. Hell of a lot of cattle and horses. What if Sixkiller comes early for some reason?"

Lew said, "Ain't there a hay barn behind the auction barn? And a couple of little sheds?"

"Yeah."

He said, "One good thing about that prairie is that we can spot Sixkiller's bunch five miles off. Maybe more if they're raising dust. We'll just herd the paying customers out to the safety of them buildings. Then we'll take on Sixkiller. Our first volley we ought to drop five or six of them at least."

"Including Sixkiller?"

Lew said, "That's where I'll be aiming."

I said, "Who's going to decide when they've broke the law or look like they're about to?"

"That'd be my job," he said. "Com'on, let's go back

inside 'fore folks begin to think we've taken root on this blamed sidewalk.''

We went back in. Only then did we realize that the whole time we'd been out on the boardwalk Lew had had the bottle of whiskey stuck in the pocket of the light jacket he was wearing. The top half had been plainly visible. As he took it out and set it on the desk he said, ''Gawd a'mighty! Now what will folks think?''

Axel was sitting right where we'd left him. As soon as he saw the bottle he held his tumbler out eagerly. Almost absentmindedly Lew poured him a full measure. Then he said, ''When you reckon we ought to send Axel? Now or in the morning?''

I said, ''It ain't a hard ride. Get a little food in him and let him get a good night's sleep and sling him out in the morning.''

Lew sat down at his desk. He said, ''I better write that note while you're here. What do you reckon I ought to say?''

''Just that you'll meet him Friday afternoon between the Colorado and Wadsworth on the Wadsworth Road. That you got a proposition for him.''

''Yeah,'' he said. He got out a blank sheet of paper and a lead pencil and began laboriously writing out the words. Lew was an awful lot better with a gun than he was with a pencil. Axel said, ''Sam kin read, don'tchaknow.''

Lew said, in exasperation, ''I know he can read, you ninny. Why you think I'm writing this damn note?''

Axel looked hurt. He said, ''Wuz jest tryin' to he'p.''

Finally Lew was through. I looked the message over and pronounced it first class. I said, ''I reckon I better get on along. If I'm late for supper Nora will have me drug behind a horse. Not to mention what her mother will do. Walk outside with me, Lew. Axel, you damn well better carry that note to Sixkiller.''

Being busy with taking a drink of whiskey, all he did was

bob his head. Lew and I went outside. I took a minute to tighten the girth on my saddle. I said, "Lew, make sure he doesn't have any money. Give him some food and a bottle of hooch. I don't want him to have enough money to get in a saloon and forget where he's supposed to be going."

"What about his gun?"

"He come in here with it." I swung into the saddle. I said, "I reckon unless I hear otherwise I'll see you here sometime Friday morning."

He said, "Going to be a hell of a hard ride there and back in one day."

I said, "We ain't riding all the way. We'll load ourselves and our horses on that eight AM northbound train and take them off in Wadsworth. Hell, we'll have time to kill. Then, if we're lucky, we can catch that southbound freight that gets in here to Blessing at six. I got to get kicking." I give him a wave and put spurs to my horse. I was scared to look at my watch, but I knew I was going to have to push like hell to make it home for supper. And I was going to be damned hard-pressed to explain what I'd been doing out so late.

I didn't make it home by six. In fact it was going on for seven by the time I got my horse put away, washed up, and went into the house. Nora was up, wearing a robe, which indicated she'd spent considerable time resting during the day. I didn't know if that had been her choice or some of her mother's work. They'd kept my supper warm in the oven, and Nora got it and laid it out for me. Then she sat down across. I was eating in the kitchen so she was right close. I said, "My, this looks fine."

Which was a kind of weak sally on my part because supper was liver and onions, and Nora knew I hated liver. She said, dryly, "I'm glad you're pleased. I asked Mother to fix it especially for you. Which kind of surprised her since she remembered you not liking liver and onions."

I said, "Oh, I like onions fine."

She was giving me that eye of hers. She said, "Well, you were at it long enough. How did your land deal go?"

I was trying to eat the damned liver. It was all I could do to chew the hateful stuff let alone swallow it. I said, "Oh, it's coming along fine. Little slow. Had to wait on a late telegram."

She said, "That's funny. I swear I saw Norris's buggy coming in to the main house right around five o'clock."

I put my knife and fork down. I said, "All right, Nora. You are determined to make something out of nothing, even though the doctor ordered you not to fret yourself. All of my time was present in town today, just in different places. The only time I was out of a crowd was when I rode out to the auction barn."

She pushed her hair back. It was starting to take on that sheen again that it did when she'd give it a good brushing. She said, "What did you go out to the auction barn for?"

I tried to sound exasperated. I said, "Dammit, Nora, does this having a baby business make all women go crazy? Or just you? We *own* the damn auction barn and I'm the boss of this damn outfit. It's part of my job to keep up with this business and all its parts. Yes, I stayed later than Norris. I also went down to Crook's Saloon with Lew and had quite a number of beers while I waited around for a telegram. How much more of this do I have to put up with?"

She looked down at her folded hands on the table. Then she sighed and looked away. Finally she said, "Am I acting crazy?"

"You are giving it a damn good impersonation if you ain't."

She rustled her hair with her hands and then swung her head back and forth so that the hair went flying around her head. It was something she did when she was agitated. She said, "Honey, I'm sorry. I know I'm acting silly. It's just that I get such ideas in my head." She put her hand halfway across the table, palm up. ''What are you going to do with me?''

I put my hand in hers. ''Make you eat this liver, I guess.''

She laughed and got up. ''Give it to me and I'll get you something else.''

I fended her off. I said, ''Naw, I'm going to eat it. Your mother is always telling me how good it's supposed to be for a body. Well, if I'm going to have to put up with you acting like this I reckon I better get my strength up.''

She leaned down and kissed me lightly. She said, ''I'll go see Mother in the parlor. You eat your liver and then come in and tell us all about everything.''

She left and I looked down at the liver. It was just about what I deserved for getting to be a more and more accomplished liar to my wife.

But I didn't feel bad about it. The truth would have been a hell of a lot harder on her.

When I finally finished the damn liver I got myself a drink of whiskey out of the office and then joined Nora and her mother in the parlor. The whiskey did wonders to get the taste of the liver out of my mouth, but I could still smell it. I figured when all this was over I'd slyly find out what Nora really hated and then make her eat a quart of it. Trouble was she seemed to like everything, even rhubarb. I said, ''Well, y'all have a pleasant day?''

Mrs. Parker was knitting and Nora was doing something she called tatting. Mrs. Parker said, ''We passed it pleasantly enough. Though Nora did try my patience about getting her rest.''

I muttered, ''You ain't the only one gets their patience tried.''

Nora said, ''What was that, Justa?''

''Nothing,'' I said. ''Looks like we're going to close that deal in Wadsworth Friday.''

Nora looked up from her work. She said, ''Wadsworth? I thought you told me that ranch proposition was in Boling.''

"It is," I said. Hell, I'd told so many lies I was about to get twisted around in my own web. I said, "We're going to meet in the middle. Wadsworth is halfway between."

"So you're going on the train and they're riding all that way. They couldn't just catch the train in Wadsworth and do it in Norris's office?"

Well, I was at a loss to explain that. I'd forgot that I'd told her there was no train service to or from Boling. So it didn't sound like such a halfway deal, us going on the train and them coming horseback. I was about to think up another lie, but Mrs. Parker came to my rescue. She said, "Now, Nora, men have their own reasons for doing business the way they do. Just be thankful you have a husband that makes you a good living and isn't a drunk or a wastrel."

Nora said, "All right, Mother." But I still felt like she was giving me a dimly suspicious look. Though it could have just been my own guilty conscience.

When I reasonably could I excused myself and walked down to the big house. I had to tell my brothers what was going to happen and I especially had to tell Norris that we were negotiating for a ranch in Boling in case Nora got to questioning him.

Surprisingly, Howard was still up even though it was pressing hard for nine o'clock. But he said he was feeling all right and just wasn't sleepy. Buttercup was there. He did that sometimes since he considered himself a member of the family. I never minded over much so long as he kept his mouth shut, something, of course, he never did. I was gratified, however, to see he wasn't as drunk as usual. I figured he'd come in to yarn with Howard about the old days. They did that. At first, when I was about twelve years old, it had been interesting. But any story, after you heard it for one hundred times, generally gets a little stale on the ear.

I got myself a drink and sat down. Buttercup was telling some story and I waited for him to finish, half-listening. Norris was at his desk working and Ben was at mine, looking over the breeding records for the Hereford herd. He nodded at me and I raised my glass back.

''Buttercup is telling us about the great range war back in '69. I don't guess you've heard about that one before. Too bad you missed the first half hour of it.''

I said, ''Well, Ben, maybe you got it by heart and you can tell it to me someday.''

Buttercup was deaf to our sarcasm. He was ending his story. He said, ''An' I kilt all three 'fore they ever figured out whar' I was pottin' 'em from. An' that's why I say a windmill platform is the best place fer bushwacking in this kin' of country they iz.''

He give a triumphant jerk of his head and then gobbled down what whiskey there was in his glass and sat back, presumably expecting a round of hand clapping.

But his last words kept buzzing around in my head. There was a windmill across the road from the auction barn. It was some two hundred yards distant. That was too far for a carbine but would be nothing for Buttercup's Sharps buffalo gun. Me and Ben and Norris had all shot it a number of times and were pretty handy with the monster. It might be handy as hell to have a man up there to pick off whatever stragglers got away from the main party. But I put the idea out of my mind for the time being.

When he was certain Buttercup had finished, Norris swung around in his chair and said, ''Well?''

I waited a second for Ben to disengage himself from the herd book, and then I told them as briefly and simply as I could what was planned. There was a silence after I finished. I took a drink of whiskey and waited. It was Howard that said, ''It's a good plan, Justa.''

I said, ''It's the best we could come up with to keep them out of town and get us some cover for the fight, if there is to be a fight.''

But Howard was frowning. He said, ''I just don't see why you got to go along with Lew to meet that bunch. Hell, if they was friendly once they ain't going to do him no harm. An' even if they wasn't they ain't got no call to shoot him. They're gittin' what they want. Least they think they are.''

I didn't have a real good answer for that. I said, "I just feel like two men are safer than one. They could shoot Lew before he could plug Sam Sixkiller, but they couldn't get us both. And he'll know that and he'll tell his men to keep their guns in leather."

Ben said, "If two is good, three is better."

I shook my head. "No, it's not. I'll be going as Lew's deputy. They can believe he'd have a deputy but they ain't going to believe he has two. Besides, you and I look too much alike."

Ben said, "This ain't no time to make jokes."

Norris said, "Justa, why can't you use dynamite like you did that time that renegade tried to drive those tick-infested cattle through our range?"

I said, "Norris, we dynamited a herd of cattle. A big herd. Stampeded them. That ain't the same as trying to blow up a small party of men. At most you'd kill one or two. Might blow a couple more off their horses. But the rest would scatter and you'd have tipped your hand and still have the same problem without the element of surprise. Naw, it won't work. But don't think I didn't give it some thought."

Ben said, "I think the auction barn is a good idea. Maybe the only one outside of forting up the town. Which would sort of cut down on the growth of the place."

Buttercup said, "What day we gonna take 'em?"

I looked around at him. It was true I had used Buttercup's ability with his big rifle to good advantage on more than one occasion, but this didn't seem like the ideal spot. In the first place, how the hell would you get him up the ladder to the windmill platform, stove up as he was? So I just looked at him and said, "We, old man?"

"Ya damn tootin', junior," he said. "Ya ain't keepin' me

outen this one. I been layin' fer them renegades fer a helluva long time.''

''What renegades?''

''Thet bunch that's been runnin' off our cattle, you young whippersnapper! Who tha hell you reckoned I was talkin' 'bout?''

I tried to keep the smile off my face. I said, ''Oh, that bunch of renegades. Yeah, they are getting to be a worry.''

''Worry, hell! I don't call no hunnert head of cattle a worry. Half this country is winterin' offen our beef an' we jest sit here.''

Howard said, kindly, ''Shut up, Butterfield. Justa is figuring this out.''

Buttercup subsided muttering, but he got in one final ''Ain't leavin' *me* outen it. An' that's a fack.''

Ben said, ''Reckon they'll bite?''

I shrugged. Wasn't much more I could do. The same question had been plaguing me ever since I'd come up with the idea. I said, ''All I can do is hope. If I was Sixkiller I'd think it sounded like a pretty good idea. We're going to promote the take at the barn to about eighteen thousand dollars. Maybe even twenty. Depends on how dumb they look.''

Norris said, ''I can't see how they'd have any idea how much cash an auction barn takes in. Though I would be mighty careful not to let it slip that a good bit of that is in checks.''

I said, ''I don't reckon they even know what a bank check is. But I won't let it slip.''

Ben said, ''How many will we be?''

''Nine,'' I said, glancing at Norris.

He gave me a firm look. He said, ''I'm not Buttercup. So don't try and come that game on me. I'll be there.''

Ben said, ''Well, we ought to do pretty good from cover. We ought to get half of them on the first volley.''

Norris surprised me. He looked over at Ben and said,

"How do you know five men won't be aiming at one man and the other four some other renegade? You planning on getting them to wear numbers and then having our side draw lots for them?"

Ben had been caught out and a slight flush come over his face. He said, "Oh, now Norris is a gunfight expert. Fine. I'm mighty glad to know he's on our side."

"Here!" Howard said. "You boys don't get to squabbling. Been enough of that 'round here fer the time being."

I said, "We'll have our men split up into several parties. We'll have them fire at the bunch closest to them. Biggest worry for me is that we can't let none of them get away. Two or three make it clear of the ambush they could hang around in this country for weeks, playing merry hell with outlaying ranchers and farmers, before we could run them down. I'm still trying to figure out a way to trap them all."

Howard said, sort of grumbling, "I still don't like the idea of you going out there with Lew and meeting that bunch out on the bald-ass prairie."

I said, "Pa, I got to. I have got to get a look at Sam Sixkiller. And I've got to get a look at his men. I need to know, in advance, what we're up against. I'm not trying to be a hero and I'm not trying to protect Lew." I said the last with a slight glance at Ben. I said, "I just want to look them over. I got to see what kind of man Sixkiller is."

Ben said, "You ever find out if there was anything between Lew and him?"

I lied. I said, "Nothing I didn't know before. We all know Lew fell in with bad company back in his boyhood days." I finished my whiskey. I said, "I better be going. I'm already in dutch for being late for supper." I started toward the door and then remembered about the ranch in Boling. I turned back into the room and told Norris about it.

He said, not getting it, "What! What ranch in Boling? When did this happen?"

Now Ben was smiling because Norris had put his foot in

it. He said, "You ain't getting it, Captain. It's what Justa is telling Nora so she'll let him go out and play and not worry her. You getting dense, Norris?"

Norris give Ben a look. He said, "I would have got it, baby brother, if he'd have told it the way he meant it. The way it come out sounded like he was really negotiating on a ranch. Want me to explain that to you?"

I walked out before they got cranked up good.

The nights were getting warmer and warmer. It wouldn't be long before early summer was full upon us. I strolled along puffing on a cigarillo and thinking on the events just around the corner of the week. There was no question it was going to be dangerous, and I wondered, with a little guilt, if I had the right to keep on mixing myself into such situations. I wasn't a wild and free cowboy no more; I was a married man with responsibilities and a baby on the way. The only way I could justify it was that somebody was going to have to help clean up the country and I was no different than Millen or any of the other ranchers or townspeople. I was just better suited for the job than most, and I owed my unborn child the chance to grow up in a peaceful place without having to worry about renegades and marauders interfering with the even flow of life. I hated lying to Nora, but I didn't see any other way, especially given the situation and how dangerous it was. I'd tried to tell her a little, but that hadn't been enough. She'd just kept on, wanting to know everything. Naturally she couldn't know that, for her own sake, so I'd had no other choice but to shut down any information.

I walked on. After a while I got to smiling about Lew Vara and his muddy thinking about Sixkiller being his half uncle. But I reckoned if a young boy got something fixed in his head, no matter how wrong, it wasn't all that easy to remove. But now Lew was angry about the matter, and I was going to have to caution him severely about not letting it show when we met Sam Sixkiller. He was going to have to do some play acting and no mistake. If he let anything slip he was liable to get us both shot.

I felt a little guilty about not stopping by and having a talk with Harley about the cow situation. But I was afraid the news would be bad. Either we were losing more calves than usual or they were dropping faster than the crews could keep up with, or we were losing mama cows on account of difficult births. Harley was a first-class hand at pulling the long face and shaking his head dolefully, and I just didn't want any bad news right then. I had enough on my plate, and even if things were going slick as goose grease, Harley would make it sound like they were just barely keeping up and doom and gloom were just around the corner. I'd asked him one time if his daddy had been an undertaker, but he hadn't got it and I sure didn't bother to explain.

Nora was asleep when I came quietly into our room. I undressed as silently as I could and slipped into bed. If she woke up she'd want to talk, and she was absolutely the last person I wanted to hold conversation with right then. She stirred a little as I got under the covers, but her breathing stayed regular and her eyes never fluttered. I kissed her gently on the cheek and then lay back on the pillow.

I was just finishing breakfast the next morning when Ben rode up to the kitchen door. He came rushing in without a knock. He said, "Justa, you better come quick. The Hereford herd has got into the salt grass and we got cows down."

"Damn!" I said. "Go saddle me a horse, quick, while I put on my boots."

Salt grass grew along that part of our land that fronted on Matagorda Bay. That was a one- or two-mile-wide marshy strip where the salt water from the sea seeped in. The grass was called salt grass because it was salty. All cattle love salt and a certain amount is good for them. From time to time we'd let cattle drift into that grass but only under close herding conditions. When they'd eaten as much as we deemed was healthy, we'd drive them out. But you couldn't just let a cow into that stuff on its own because it would just keep on grazing until it bloated up and foundered.

And, naturally, it had to be the Hereford herd, the pure-breds, which weren't as strong as the crossbreeds. Anytime you keep on breeding for a pure strain you will weaken the animals because, no matter how hard you try or how careful you are with your records, a certain amount of inbreeding is going to happen.

I couldn't understand how the Hereford herd had gotten into the salt grass. Last time I'd seen them they'd been in the northwest pasture, a good six miles from the marshy land. Ben brought my horse out of the little barn and I swung into the saddle. I said to him what I'd been thinking about where the Herefords had been. He shook his head and said, "No, we been drifting them east toward the warmer weather. It's about time for them to start throwing calves."

I said, grimly, "I don't know who was on night herd, but he's fired."

Ben said, "You might want to think about that, Justa. It was James Kline."

Kline was one of the men I'd hired extra as a gun hand. I said, "I'll be damned!"

We were riding at a hard gallop toward the scene. Ben yelled over the wind, "Justa, he's a new man. It ain't like he knows all about that salt grass like our regular hands do. He don't even know the range that well. He and Boyd only been on the payroll a little over two weeks."

"Was he warned?"

"Of course."

I said, "Dammit, dammit, dammit. That goddam Sixkiller is running up one hell of a bill."

It wasn't the first time that such had happened and so we did have a treatment of sorts. I didn't reckon it was in any veterinarian's book, but what we did was sluice them out. We had a bunch of great big bulbs made out of India rubber, with rubber tubes about four feet long coming out of the

ends. What we did was take that bulb and suck up a great
big load of soapy water out of a washtub and then stick that
tube down the cow's throat and irrigate the stomach.
Sometimes they throwed up everything they'd eaten for the
last week, and sometimes we just diluted the harmful
effects. The important thing was to get the stuff in them
before the salt could reach their second stomach. If a load of
that got in there it was like they'd taken poison.

I yelled at Ben, "Is anything being done?"

He yelled back, "Yes, they been at it from close on to six
o'clock. Harley has got about half the hands out there."

We topped a slight rise and I could see the little herd
ahead of me on the prairie. The biggest part of it had been
driven back west, and they were milling around and grazing.
But near the salt grass line I could see an awful lot of cattle
laying on their sides on the ground. Parked in their midst
was a buckboard, and as we neared, I could see several
washtubs in the bed. Every once in a while a cowhand
would run over to the buckboard, jam the tube of his
apparatus in the soapy water, fill it up, and then run back to
a cow.

We come thundering up and slid to a stop in the soft,
marshy earth. Harley saw me and hurried over. "About
thirty down, Boss. We done got about five up."

"How are they looking?"

Harley shook his head as he always done. "Don' look
good, Mistuh Justa."

"Well, get back to work."

About then James Kline came up. He said, softly, "Mistuh
Williams, this is my fault."

I said, "Was you sleeping?"

He shook his head. "No, sir. I jest wadn't as conscious of
whar' the herd was as I shoulda been. Ain't makin' no
excuses. It was my fault an' no mistake. First I noticed was
when I could tell my horse was walkin' in wet ground. I
pushed the cattle back as fast as I could but the damage had

been done. Some of 'em was already gettin' down. I shoved
the herd on west as fer as I could an' then figgered to ride
for help.''

I said, maybe a little too harshly, "Well, this ain't no time
to discuss it. Get back to work.''

Ben and I fell in with the rest of them sluicing out the
cows. It was dirty work and hard work and heartbreaking
work to see a valuable steer or cow give out right under your
hands. We had three prize bulls in with the herd and it was
nip and tuck on one of them. We must have sluiced him out
a half dozen times before he let out a bawl and got to his
feet. He looked pretty angry about the whole matter, being
forced to cough up all that nice salt grass. But he finally
trotted off docilely and rejoined the main herd.

We worked on the cattle for going on five hours. When it
was finally over there were five dead ones laying on the
prairie. I stripped off my gloves and yelled at Harley,
"Well, at least we'll eat good off this. Butcher them out.''

Me and the rest of the cowhands were a mess. I had cow
vomit all over my front, and my boots weighed about twenty
pounds from all the mud they'd picked up in the churned-up
marshland. I turned for my horse, figuring I ought to be
thankful that we'd only lost five. Still, at a minimum,
counting the calves that three of them were carrying, the
loss was better than two thousand dollars.

As I got to my horse James Kline came up to me again.
He was as filthy as I was. He said, "Mistuh Williams, I
know you took a pretty good lickin' here and I want to do
what I can. I reckon you know I ain't got the kind of money
these fancy cattle cost, but I'll stay on here and work it out
until my debt is paid. An' that includes that two hunnert you
was gonna give me fer my gun.''

I looked at him curiously. It was an offer I wouldn't have
expected from a drifter. I said, "Kline, these things happen.
This is the ranching business. I wish it hadn't happened and
I know you do too, but ain't a damn thing can be done about

it. You don't owe me anything. You said you wasn't asleep. This is a big range. You don't know all of it." I swung into my saddle. I said, "We'll say no more about it."

He said, stubbornly, "Least I can do is offer my gun fer regular wages. Never mind about the two hunnert."

I looked down at him. I figured to speak to Harley about keeping him on steady once the calving was over. I said, "The one ain't got nothing to do with the other. You're a good man, Kline. Let's say no more about it."

Then I turned my horse and spurred for home, aching to get out of my filthy clothes. I pulled up in the backyard, seen to my horse, and then started for the kitchen door. Before I could reach it Nora opened it and stepped out on the stoop. She put her hand to her mouth. She said, "My heavens alive, Justa Williams! Look at yourself! Don't you come a step closer to this house. You get yourself cleaned up! You are a disgusting sight."

I said, "I was just coming in to get some clean clothes. Then I was going to wash myself off in the shower bath."

She said, "Wash yourself off with your clothes on. I'll get you some fresh things."

I went into the shower bath wearing even my boots. The only thing I took off was my hat. Then, for a good five minutes, I sluiced myself down. Then I soaped up and washed my clothes off, ending up with a good rinse. I figured they were clean enough for the wash. I took everything off, pitched my boots outside to dry in the sun, and slung my socks and jeans and shirt over the wall of the little booth. After that I took a regular shower bath and then stood there drying until Nora opened the stall door and handed me in some clean clothes and a towel.

She said, "How did you get such a mess?"

I told her in some detail. She said, "Uugh!" and then there was the sound of her running away. I figured she was going to do a little emptying out herself. Well, she shouldn't have asked me if she hadn't wanted to know.

I got dressed and went into the house. Mrs. Parker was in the kitchen fixing lunch while Juanita got in her way. She said, ''Why whatever come over Nora? She come through her white as a sheet and went and laid down on the bed.''

''Oh,'' I said, ''I reckon learning about the cattle business was a little more than she could stand.''

═══ Chapter Eight

RIGHT AFTER LUNCH I saddled a horse and rode out to see Charlie Johnson and Brad Millen to let them know what their orders were. I was leaving it to Ben to inform Boyd and Kline when we'd be leaving the ranch for the auction barn.

Johnson's place was an hour's ride off so I just took my time and let the horse test out his gaits as he took it into his head. He was a young colt and much given to shying. Once some loose grass blew across his path and we went off to the races. I let him run hard just long enough for him to see there was no gain in such behavior and then pulled him down into a gallop and finally into a slow canter.

I got lucky and found Johnson without much trouble. He and two of his hands were working a branding fire on the northern corner of his range. He got up from branding a calf when he saw me coming and walked slowly my way. He didn't appear overly glad to see me and I couldn't say I blamed him. I'd played him a dirty trick by giving him no selection as to whether he wanted a part of the fight or not. He met me about fifteen yards from the fire. He didn't ask me to step down. He said, "Well?"

I outlined what we were going to do as simply as I could. I said, "You can come on your own or ride over to our headquarters and go in with my brothers. Either way you need to be at that auction barn no later than noon. I can't count on them not playing us for the fool and coming way early.''

He nodded. He said, shortly, ''I'll be there. Anything else?''

I said, ''No. Not that I can think of right off. Bring a rifle besides your sidegun.''

''I'll be getting back to my work.'' He made to turn back toward the fire.

I said, ''Charlie, I wish you'd take this better. You and I been neighbors a long time. I ain't being harsh about this because I want to be.''

He said, ''You could have fooled me.'' Then he did turn around and walk off.

I made the ride to Brad Millen's in a poor humor. I hated to be put in the position of bullying my neighbors with the Williams' money. But I hadn't seen anybody volunteering. Nevertheless, it put me in poor spirits.

I ran across one of Millen's hands hazing some stock southward. He said that Millen was at his ranch house, probably in the barn working on a wagon that had lost a wheel rim. I got there pretty quick and rode on the place. The barn doors were wide open, and I could see Millen inside working at a little forge doing some blacksmithing. I got down and tied my horse and went into the cool dimness. ''Hello, Brad,'' I said when I was about halfway to him.

He turned around, a hammer in his right hand and a sheet of thin, glowing iron held by tongs in the other. The blaze from his charcoal fire made his face even redder than it usually was. He said, ''Oh. Hello, Williams.''

I could see that he was about as glad to see me as Charlie Johnson had been. I said, ''Can I help?'' I gestured at the forge.

He shook his head. ''No. I'm just brazing a piece of iron over a split in a rim.'' Then he give me a look. He said, ''We got to make do around here.''

It was obvious he was saying, ''We ain't rich like the

Williams family, who probably get a new rim rather than fix the old one.''

I let it pass. I'd been running into such thinking ever since I could remember. He said, ''What do you want?''

I said, ''I come to tell you about the plan me and the sheriff have worked out and how we'll need you and where you ought to be.''

For answer he laid the strip of iron over the corner of an anvil and set in to hammering it, stopping to look at its shape every few blows. Finally, when he got it the way he liked it he shoved the red-hot iron down in a bucket of water to temper it. The iron made a loud hissing noise and steam rose up around Millen. Only then did he turn back to me. He said, ''Well?''

I told him essentially what I had Charlie Johnson. When I was through he gave me a good hard look and said, ''You don't ast much, do you Williams? All you want is fer a man to leave his work, leave his way of putting food on the table, and go off an' give hisself a good chance to get kilt. Leave his wife a widow an' his chill'un without a daddy.''

I said, evenly, ''I'm not asking you to do anything I'm not going to do myself.''

He said, ''You forget. You didn't ast, Williams. You ordered. Do it or you'd call in my note.''

I said, ''I'm not proud of that, Brad. Maybe I spooked. You want me to let you back out?''

''Why don't you go to hell.''

I said, ''You can back out. But I want you to remember that if that bunch of renegades ain't stopped there won't be no bank to call in your note. In fact there won't be no bank at all to do business with. And likely there won't be no mercantile or other stores to get your supplies at. They take to the torch there might not be any town at all. Might be a real big cemetery. But I won't call your note in, Millen, if you don't show up. You do like you feel right about.''

He just stood there staring at me. After a second or two

I turned on my heel and started out of the barn. I was nearly to the sunshine when he called after me, "Hey, Williams."

I stopped and looked back. "What?"

He said, "I allus wondered. Me an' other folks. Where'd you get that front name of yores? That Justa?"

I said, "Ever hear of that old hymn? 'Just a closer walk with thee. Grant it Jesus, hear my plea.' From that. Just a, Justa."

"*You* was named after a hymn?"

"That's what my daddy told me. My mother set great store by religion."

He said, "Well, I'll be damned."

I walked on out of the barn and got on my horse and rode off. I wasn't at all sure that Brad Millen was going to show up. And if he talked with Charlie Johnson I was liable to be short two gun hands.

As I rode I reflected on the fact that my mother had been a great hand at naming things. She'd named the ranch the Half-Moon and she'd also, accidently, named the town of Blessing. That had been thirty-five years previous, when Howard had brought her down from Tennessee as his bride. Blessing, which wasn't even a town then, had been a railhead, the place where the tracks stopped on their trip south. But ten years before that there hadn't even been a railhead there. The MKT line, the Katy, went as far as Wharton and stopped there. Only the determined efforts of Howard and the few other cattlemen in the area had persuaded the railroad officials to extend the track so that the ranchers didn't have to drive their cattle so far to ship them to market. In the years that followed Blessing gradually changed from a few shacks occupied by railroad hands to a real town. Howard, because he had been the leader in getting the railroad to recognize they were overlooking some mighty profitable business, had been asked by the officials to give the place a name so they could sell tickets to it. Dad had remembered what Mother had said when she'd finally got off that sooty, rackety freight train, which was all that was running on the line then. She'd said, when she first put foot to ground, "What a blessing to be off that damn train."

I reckoned he'd picked Blessing over Damn on the grounds that it would probably have more staying power.

In the days that followed time seemed to go at two different rates. When I got to dreading what was coming it would flash by, going like hell; when I'd get to wanting the mess over and done with, no matter what the outcome, it would act like it had been crossbred to a turtle. I had to assume that Axel had been sent on his way. I'd had no word from Lew and I knew he'd let me know if anything had changed. All we could do was hope that Axel would carry out his part of the bargain and deliver the message. After that it was in the hands of a renegade, mistrustful, cunning, murdering, thieving desperado. Which didn't exactly make me feel all that good.

Nora, thankfully, hadn't said any more, and I spent my time going about the ranch acting like I was supervising the calf operation. I didn't have anything else to do except try and not act anxious around Nora, and try not to worry about the outcome of a very shaky plan.

On Thursday night my brothers and Howard again expressed their worry about me going with Lew to meet Sixkiller. We were in the office, like always, having a quiet drink and discussing business and the day's events. I frowned. I said, "Well, I don't know what you'd have me do. Lew's going, making a hundred dollars a month. And Kline and Boyd are going to risk their lives for two hundred a piece. Not counting Johnson and Millen, whom I threatened. Seems to me we are the ones got the most to lose. I don't see how I can not go."

Ben said, "Let me go in your place."

I give him a laugh. I said, "I grant you, Howard would rather lose you than me. I know more about ranching. But think of the hearts it would break among the young ladies in about a thirty-mile circle of here.''

He colored slightly and said, ''You got to make a joke out of everything?''

I said, ''You know, I just now figured out why you taken an interest in horseflesh at such an early age. That was the only way you could keep up with your courting. How many horses have you killed getting from one girl to the other?''

''Aw, go to hell,'' he said. Howard and Norris laughed. Ben did not like to be kidded about his love life. He said, ''I was just trying to help. You ain't as good with a gun as I am.''

I said, seriously, ''Nobody can be good enough when the odds are seventeen to two. But I'm good enough to convince Sam Sixkiller that there will be three of us get shot if any of his bunch pulls a gun.''

Howard said, ''Well, I just wish it hadn't come to this.''

''Well, it has. Lew doesn't think that Sixkiller will trust a message from Axel enough to come to the auction barn. And I agree with him. We got all our eggs in an auction basket and it's risky but I don't know what else to do.''

Riding home that night I mightily wanted to make love to my wife, but I was fearful about it on account of her condition. Also there was the matter of Nora's mother in the house, and she was never comfortable with that. But I was mighty glad her mother was there. She'd been a comfort and company for Nora, and I could visibly see her returning to her old self. Besides, her mother was a valuable, if unknowing, ally in my lies.

I left out early Friday morning before dawn. Nora had wanted to get up and fix me some breakfast, but I had told her I'd eat in town before Norris and I took the train. The night before I had specifically obliged him to either leave early enough where it would look like he was trying to make the train or to not let Nora see him either going or coming.

He'd chosen the latter. Norris never had been a man who was much for greeting the sun on its first appearance.

It was a chilly morning when I set out, but it warmed up considerably as the day bloomed. My horse stepped along lively and we made it into Blessing in just over an hour. It was a quarter of seven when I pulled up to the hitching rack in front of Lew's office. He was waiting for me, looking fidgety. I didn't dismount. I said, "Let's take our horses on down to the depot and leave them and then walk back up here to Crook's and have some breakfast."

He said, "You mean you can eat?"

I said, "Don't give me that, Lew. You ain't any more scared than I am. Get on your horse and let's go."

He mounted and we rode on down to the depot which was about three hundred yards away. As we rode I remembered what Nora had said the evening before. She said that her mother didn't want to leave her daddy alone on Sunday and could I please see that she got taken into Blessing sometime Saturday afternoon or evening. As she'd said it I had reflected that the whole issue of Sam Sixkiller would have most likely been resolved by then.

We got down to the depot and I told the clerk I wanted our horses loaded in a stock car and that I'd pay for a whole car, meaning I didn't want any other stock put in with our animals. I said that me and the sheriff would just ride in the car with our horses. Lew said that by rights the county ought to pay for the transportation since we were on county business, but I said that the ranch would get it.

Walking back up to Crook's he handed me a deputy sheriff's badge. He said, "Consider yourself swore in. I don't feel like going through the whole ceremony."

I put the badge in my pocket. Just the knowledge of what it signaled put a few butterflies in my stomach. Truth be told I was more worried about this meeting on the prairie than I was about the possible battle at the auction barn. I knew what was going to happen at the auction barn; I couldn't guess what Sixkiller might get up to on the prairie when he had what he'd reckon was all the law in the county right there in his grip.

We both had ham and eggs and coffee and toast. There was plenty of time, but it seemed like we were both rushing through our meal as if to get the ordeal over with sooner.

But we still rushed right through our breakfast and then sat there, sipping coffee. Lew said, "I wisht I'd have had biscuits. How come you ordered toast? You always order biscuits. Toast sits heavy on my stomach."

I said, "I only order biscuits when I have just biscuits and gravy or biscuits and syrup. I always eat toast with eggs."

"No you don't. I've eat breakfast with you a hunnert times and you never eat toast."

"Hell, Lew, don't tell me what I eat. I been eatin' breakfast with myself all my life. And I'm telling you I was eating toast with eggs before half the folks around here even knew what toast was."

"Well, when did you start puttin' sugar in yore coffee? You never done that before."

I said, "Lew, are you awake? I always put sugar in my coffee if there's sugar. You've seen me drink it straight because we've been on the trail so many times and they wasn't no sugar. I use cream, too, if it's to be had. You see me drink it black over in your office because you ain't got no cream or sugar. I just never said nothing about it."

He looked sour. "I'll lay some in."

"Not on my account," I said. "If you'll notice I never take more than half a cup and almost never finish that. Only thing that helps your coffee is whiskey. Of course it ruins the whiskey, but the coffee is nearly drinkable."

Lew said, "Then, hell, if you don't like it don't be wasting my coffee. I like it. I wouldn't make it that way if I didn't like it."

"Now you're going to tell me you like coffee that's half grounds and so strong you could use it for axle grease?

You're going to tell me you make coffee like that out of preference? Bullshit, you just don't know how to make coffee."

He said, "I've been knowing how to make coffee since I was six year old an' I can make it any way I want to. At the jail I make it to suit me, an' them as don't like it can jest go to hell!"

We sat there glaring at each other for a few seconds and then I had to smile. I said, "I reckon we're a little more nervous than either one of us expected."

"Yeah," he said. He looked away and shook his head. "We ought to just ride up and plug that bastard and then take our chances with the rest of the bunch. With Sixkiller down they might just cut and run. Ain't any of them over-smart."

"Want to take that chance?"

He got up. "Reckon not. We ought to go. It's about twenty till eight."

We walked on down to the depot. The northbound train arrived at about the same time as we did. The engine came in pulling its assorted lot of passenger cars and freight. It come screeching to a halt a little beyond the depot and then sat there like a winded horse, panting out steam and making hissing noises. Lew and I walked along the platform toward the back of the fifteen or so cars that made up the train. We seen a railroad hand coming with our horses, the stirrups tied together over the seat of the saddle so they wouldn't swing around and spook the horses. Another employee was putting a ramp in place at the open door of the stock car, and another one was bringing hay. I doubted very much our animals were going to have much time to eat hay, but it'd be there for the next batch that took up residence.

When our horses were loaded Lew and I climbed aboard and sat down on the floor with our backs against the side of the car. I got out a cigarillo and lit it. While I was getting it drawing Lew said, "You got any whiskey?"

I said, "I'm settin' here in a pair of jeans, a shirt, and a light jacket. You see any part of a bottle of whiskey sticking out?"

He nodded his head toward our horses. "Could have one in your saddlebags."

"Well, I don't," I said. "Never thought of it. You?"

"Naw," he said. "I don't drink nothing stronger than beer before nine of the morning."

I said, "We'll get a drink in Wadsworth."

"Saloons won't be open."

"Might."

"Might not."

The train didn't tarry long in Blessing. Pretty soon we could hear the couplings of the cars ahead being jerked together as the engine began to grind slowly out of the station. Then the jolting caught up with us, and we swayed against the side of the wall as the slack got taken up in our own car's coupling. We'd left the big sliding doors open, and outside, we could watch the sameness of the landscape sliding by. For people who cared for mountains and trees and rivers and such, Matagorda County wasn't much. But if you wanted grazing land and were in the cattle business it was a mighty fine place to be and was, to a rancher, about the finest scenery around. It rained enough to make the grass grow, but not over much. It never snowed. It might freeze every once in a while, but it was so seldom that folks marked time by the last freeze. It would get a little hot in July and August and September, but if you stayed in the shade as much as you could there was always enough of a breeze to keep you cooled off.

I sat there looking out the doors of the car and thinking those thoughts. I reckoned I was thinking in such a fashion because I was maybe going into danger. It seemed like a man never appreciated what he had until he faced the chance of losing it.

Lew and I didn't say much on the half-hour ride. We

pulled into Wadsworth with a great deal of bell ringing and whistle tooting and screeching of iron wheels on iron rails. We'd no more than come to a stop before a couple of railroad roustabouts came up with a ramp for our car. Lew and I untied our horses and led them down the ramp and onto the platform. From there we walked them off onto solid ground and then mounted up. My horse did like every other one I'd ever give a train ride to; he started off like he wasn't sure where he was supposed to put his feet. Horses get caught up in the swaying motion of the train and learn to brace themselves against it; when they get back on ground they haven't quite figured out yet that the ground is not going to sway, and it leaves them confused for a bit.

But we rode into town and took up residence in a saloon and cafe. Wadsworth was not quite as big as Blessing. Blessing had nearly a thousand souls in or near the city limits. Wadsworth wasn't half that big.

We both ordered a beer. Lew said, "We better take it easy. We got a long wait."

We'd had to come early because there wasn't another northbound train out until four of the afternoon, and that would have been too late.

I said, "What time you figure we ought to ride out across the prairie?"

Lew said, "Oh, I reckon after we have some lunch. Say we eat about eleven, eleven-thirty and then take off. It's ten, twelve miles to the Colorado?"

I nodded. "About that. Course the road is crooked as an Austin lawyer."

He said, "We get away a little before noon, take our time, save our horses. We ought to run across Sam by one or two in the afternoon. What time does that train leave out of here for the run back to Blessing?"

"I think it's five. Or a little after. Here in a minute I'll jingle on back to the depot and book us a car. I should have done it right off when we come in but the biggest part of them clerks is too busy to wait on you when they got a train in the station.''

Lew said, ''Well, if it's five o'clock we don't want to visit too long with Sam.''

I said, ''I don't want to visit with him at all. And I sure as hell don't want to prolong the stay. We say what we come to say, look them over, and get the hell away. You understand I ain't unfriendly, I just like to pick the times I feel like being friendly.''

We were both nervous and it was showing in the way we were talking. Lew and I had always been fair hands at kidding each other, but this was different. We were talking to keep our minds off what was ahead of us. There might have been men who wouldn't flinch about going up against seventeen armed renegades out in the wide-open midst of nothing, but I wasn't one of them. And there might have been men who'd say they weren't afraid of getting shot. I wasn't one of those either. Nora always thought I sought out danger. That was just plain foolishness. I hid from danger, didn't like it. And anytime I got a chance to put the odds more in my favor, I grabbed at that chance and clung to it, no matter if it might seem unfair and ungentlemanly or even dishonest. I didn't give a damn what it was. If a man was forced to fight then he ought to fight to win no matter what methods he had to use. Hell, if Sixkiller's bunch would have agreed to come through the door of the cafe we were sitting in one by one, I'd have been pleased to shoot them down in the same order and never give it another thought.

But on that prairie they'd have the edge, we wouldn't. And both Lew and I knew it.

We finished our beers, and then I went out, mounted my horse, and rode back to the depot. Our ranch had a standing account with the Katy so it was an easy matter to arrange for a stock car back to Blessing. The train did, indeed, leave at five-fifteen, which would put us back into Blessing a little before six. That meant I'd be late for supper for sure. But I counted on Mrs. Parker to square it for me because I was going to claim prolonged business and she seemed to understand that.

I was also counting on getting back to Blessing. Still breathing.

We had some lunch, eating the Blue Plate Special at six bits the plate. It was good, but neither one of us had much of his mind on food. When we finished we ordered up a couple of shots of whiskey, said, "Luck," and knocked them back as befits the toast. Then Lew got out his watch and looked at it. "Quarter till noon," he said.

"I reckon we better get."

We paid our bill and then went out and mounted up. I was riding my roan gelding. He was the oldest horse I kept up to my place, being a hard four. He was also the steadiest and had quick speed though he wasn't as much of a stayer as my other gelding and the colt. But if we had to get away from Sixkiller and his bunch in a hurry, the roan gelding was the horse I wanted between my legs.

Lew and I rode out of Wadsworth and struck the north road that led to the Colorado River and then on to Bay City and points north, Houston being the end of the road. I let us get good out of town before I asked Lew how he wanted to play it. He said, "I guess just on the fly. Take it as it comes. You better pin that badge on your shirt before you forget it all together. You don't look much like a deputy as it is. And without that badge you couldn't fool Axel."

I said, "Oh, yeah? What do I look like then?"

He spit over the side of his horse. He said, "Rich."

I laughed. I said, "Oh, bullshit. Me and you is wearing the same clothes because we buy them at the same place. My horse ain't no better than yours and neither is my saddle. Where do you get off with that?"

He shook his head. "I don't know. You just do. Maybe it's because I know you are. But put on the damn badge."

I dropped the reins around the saddle horn and got the

badge out of my pocket and pinned it to my shirt. It was a hard job and I pricked my finger several times. It hung heavy on my shirt. I said, "What the hell is this thing made out of, lead?"

"Tin," he said. "Cheap tin. Won't stop a bullet if you're thinking that."

We just let our horses shamble along, raising little puffs of dust with their hooves. It had come on to be passing warm, warm enough for an early summer day. I took my jacket off and turned around and shoved it in my saddlebag. I said, "You reckon Axel is going to be with them?"

"I dunno."

"If he is you reckon he's told Sixkiller anything might cause us trouble? Like us threatening to hang him."

"I dunno." Then he looked over at me. "Us?"

"You going to claim you didn't threaten to hang him? You going to claim you didn't have nothing to do with the whole idea?"

"Hell, yes. Wasn't me paid to have that gallows scaffolding built. How long you plan to leave that ugly thing up, anyway?"

I said, "Never can tell when we might need it."

Then we didn't talk for a while. I tried not to think about Nora or her condition or what would become of her and maybe the kid if anything happened to me. I reckoned I was more nervous on her account than anything else. It was damn sure the first time I'd ever gone into danger with a pregnant wife.

We just kept slouching along. The closer to Wadsworth we met Sixkiller and his bunch the better off it was for us. Of course I wasn't just nervous about the personal danger; I was considerably nervous about whether or not Sixkiller would take the bait. I said, "Lew, one thing we can't do is let them take us prisoner. If they do that the town is wide open. It would be just as bad as being shot."

Lew said, "Not quite. But I ain't ever heard of Sixkiller making a habit of capturing people."

I said, "I just wanted to point out to you that if they try and surround us you better get your gun in your hand because that's where mine is going to be."

"I hear you," he said. He glanced sideways at me. He said, "Justa, you got to understand that it's been years since I seen Sam. You know about as much about what he's liable to do as me. Hell, I wasn't with that bunch that long. And that was different country, that was Oklahoma Territory. Wasn't no local law, wasn't no sheriffs or town marshals. They was just federal marshals and they was damn few and far between. All I know to do is watch each other's backs and put our proposition up to Sam and hope he agrees."

"We got to convince him that the town will fight. We got to make him settle for the auction barn."

Lew said, "You don't want to try and *convince* him of anything. You go to doin' that he'll just narrow them eyes of his and figure you are trying to push him. He'll go the other way."

I said, "Hell, I'm just the deputy. It's you that will be doing most of the talking."

He gave me a faint smile. "You be sure an' remember that."

We had ridden for a little over an hour without sight of anything except rolling, grassy plains dotted here and there with a clump of mesquite trees or a lone stunted post oak. It was dull riding; even the horses acted bored. My roan was too old to be shying at anything, but we made a curve in the road so that he got a good look at his shadow and he jumped sideways. I think he did it more out of something to do than anything else.

Lew said, "Maybe they ain't coming."

I took off my hat and run my sleeved arm across my forehead. I said, "Colorado can't be but a couple of miles on further. We been at it better than an hour and a half. And even going this slow we are way beyond halfway."

It was the roan took notice of them first. With nothing visible on the horizon he suddenly raised his head and pricked his ears forward. After a few seconds Lew's horse did likewise. I said, "Reckon it's them?"

Lew said, "It's somebody."

Up ahead we suddenly heard the faint sound of a horse neighing. After a minute another horse let go and then another. My roan answered back and wanted to quicken his stride. I pulled him back to the shambling walk.

"Whoever it is there's more than one."

Lew said, "Ain't like Sam to have horses that would give him away."

I said, "Maybe he just stole 'em and ain't had time to train them to the outlaw ways."

We rode on, and, directly we topped a little rise in the prairie, we caught sight of a band of men on horseback coming up the road at a slow canter. It was difficult to see them clearly because little shimmering heat waves kind of distorted the view.

Lew said, "Well, that would be them."

"Want to speed up?"

"I don't. Let's save these horses all we can."

Inside of ten minutes they were close enough to pick out individual figures. I studied the bunch, watching them as they neared. I said, "It's hard to do, way they are bunched together, but I count sixteen. And I've done it several times."

Lew said, "Hang it, I get a different count every time the way they keep jostling around each other."

Finally we pulled up when they were about a quarter of a mile away and then just sat our horses, waiting for them to come on. I eased my revolver up and down in my holster. I had its mate in my saddlebag and a .30–.30 carbine in a saddle boot.

The nearer they got the better I could count, and I finally convinced myself there were sixteen. That meant one was missing. I figured it had to be Axel, but I had no way of knowing what had happened to him and I damn sure wasn't going to ask.

They got about fifty yards off, and a big man in front raised his hand and they dropped down to a walk.

Lew said, quietly, "That's Sam."

They were close enough to study. Sixkiller was a big, broad man who didn't appear to be too tall. He was wearing a yellow canvas duster that reached down both sides of his horse to his boot tops. The duster was open, and I could see he was wearing a big revolver on his right side and a sheathed Bowie knife on his left. He had a carbine in a saddle boot and an extra revolver slung off his saddle horn in a holster. As they got closer I could see he was bearded and that he was wearing a flannel shirt. He had on an old black slouch hat and his beard was sprinkled with gray.

They pulled up about five yards from us. For a second nobody said anything. Then Sixkiller grinned a big smile so that I could see his bad teeth and the gaps where he didn't have any teeth. He said, in a loud voice, "Why, looky yonder, boys, thar's my nephee I been tellin' y'all about. He be the high shur'ff of that thar' town."

It scared me hearing Sixkiller refer to Lew as his "nephee." I was afraid Lew might get angry and make some remark. But Lew just said, as cool as you please, "Hello, Sam. Long time no see."

Sixkiller said, "Has been a spell, ain't it, Lew?" He kept on with that grin like he wanted everybody to see the condition inside his mouth.

While Lew and him exchanged small talk for a minute I studied Sixkiller. I knew he was a half-breed; Lew had told me so. But he was a different kind of breed. His mother had been white. In most cases a half-breed was the product of an Indian mother and a white father. But Lew had said that

Sixkiller's mother had been an Irish whore. From that I didn't know if ol' Sam had been a love child or bought and paid for in advance.

Lew said, "I see you got my message."

"Oh, yeah," Sixkiller said. Then he grinned even bigger. "But we wuz a-comin' anyways. Say, I heard you throwed my little messenger boy in jail. How come you to do a thang like that?"

Lew spit tobacco juice over the side of his horse. He said, "'Cause he come in slingin' his mouth around and talkin' a little big for his size. Besides, how I supposed to know he was one of yours? Anybody could say it. I put him in a cell an' let him think about it a bit."

Sixkiller grinned. "Wa'l," he said, "that ain't quite the way the boy tol' it. But it don't make no mind."

Lew looked over the bunch. He said, "Whar's he at? Don't seem like I see him."

Sixkiller didn't bother to even look back. He said, "Likely he's a-layin' up somewhar's drunk. You know them young'uns. Cain't hold they liquor." Then he shifted his gaze toward me. He had his forearms resting on the pommel of his saddle. He flicked a finger out. He said, "Who be this?"

Lew said, "That's my deputy. Name of Ray."

I couldn't see why Lew had felt the need to change my name, but I didn't say anything. My eyes were busy running over the rest of Sixkiller's gang. They were a pretty ragtag crew, dressed in all manner of rough jeans and khaki. Some of them were wearing blanket coats, but most had tied their cold weather gear behind their saddles. But if they weren't all that well turned out, there was no mistaking the oiled look of the holsters that held their big revolvers. And it was easy to see, by the few that held their carbines across their saddles, that these were tradesmen who took mighty good care of the tools of their trade. And they were as well mounted as they were armed. I judged the most of them to

be in their early twenties with a few, like Axel, in their late
teens.

Sixkiller said, "Wa'l, dog my cats. I reckon thet means
thet all the law is out'chere with us. Man could jest walk in
an' he'p hisself thar' in Blessing. I mean, I don' reckon a
leetle ol' town like that's got mor'n one deputy."

Lew said, "Town mostly takes care of itself. It's a
vigilante town. We get a lot of steady trouble up from the
Mexican border so most of the menfolks keep their guns on
about half cock."

Sixkiller giggled. It was an odd sound coming out of so
big a face. He said, "Heh, heh, heh. How 'bout the lady
folks? Them stay on half cock too? Or they like the whole
thang?"

Underneath me my horse shuffled impatiently, but I paid
him no mind. Sixkiller's words sent a cold chill through me.
If I'd ever seen a man that was capable of anything, I was
looking at him.

Lew said, "Look here, Sam, I've come out here to make
a deal with you."

Sixkiller cocked his head sideways. "Yeah, nephee?
What kind of deal you figger you kin make with ol' Sam?
Ain't going to tell me I ain't welcome in yore leetle ol' town
be you?"

Lew said, "Tomorrow's Saturday. That's auction day in
Blessing. The auction barn is about two miles north of town.
There's considerable money gets taken in there of an
auction day. You can wait until the crowd clears out and
then go in there and help yourself whilst they are getting the
takings ready for the bank."

Sixkiller said, "An' what time would that be?"

I said, "Auction is over by three of the afternoon, maybe
a little later. Then the crowd scatters and I go out there to
escort the money in to the bank about four."

"How much money?"

I shook my head. I said, "I don't know."

Lew said, "I took it upon myself to find out. Generally runs between eighteen and twenty thousand. Might be a little more this time of the year what with all the stock around."

Sixkiller stared at him for a long half a minute and then looked down and started shaking his head. Finally he said, "Wa'l, I swan! What a nice present you brung yore ol' uncle." He turned in his saddle and looked back at his bunch. He said, "Say, boys, ain't thet a nice present my young nephee brung me? Jest a lettle passel of money. All wrapped up an' tied with a ribbon as neat as you please."

But then he turned back to Lew. He said, "But it's a puzzlement to me. Yes, sir, a puzzlement. Now why would my nephee want to do thet fer his ol' uncle?" Again he turned to his bunch. "Ain't it a puzzlement, boys? Huh? Ain't it?"

This time there was a low murmur of voices, but their faces stayed as flat as they'd been since they rode up.

Sixkiller narrowed his eyes at Lew, and I could see what Lew had meant about him being suspicious of everything. He said, "So, nephee, whyn't you jest up an' answer that one fer yore ol' uncle."

Lew said, "Sam, I got a good, easy job in Blessing an' I don't want no trouble. Y'all come into town an' that gives me two choices; either I got to lead the fight, if I want to keep my job, or I got to git. An' I don't want to git. I'm offerin' you a nice payday without no trouble. My deputy will be escortin' the money back into town. Won't be but two other folks an' neither one of them is a gun hand. And my deputy damn sure ain't going to give you no trouble."

Sixkiller favored me with his grin. He said, "That right, depity?"

"Yeah," I said.

"You mean you'd jest let ol' Sam an' his boys take them nice folks' money an' not put up no squawk?"

I let my eyes run over the faces of the bunch. A more

mean-looking, sharp-featured, hard-faced bunch it had never been my displeasure to see. I said, "That's about the size of it."

Sixkiller slapped his thigh. He said, "Wa'l, if that don't beat all." He turned in his saddle. "Don't that beat all, boys. Huh? Don't it?"

They murmured, but they never took their eyes off of me and Lew.

But then Sixkiller turned back to me and Lew. The false grin was gone off his face and his eyes had hardened. He said, "What makes you boys thank Ah ought to settle fer some chickenshit leetle auction barn when I kin have the wh'ul damn town? Prosperous town like that there Blessing. Axel tol' me they was a right nice leetle bank thar'. An' lot of stores an' whatnot. Whata ya thank of that?"

Lew said, "I don't think it's a very good idea. I done tol' you that the town will fight. The money from the auction barn is safe and sure."

"But it jest ain't enough, nephee. Why, they's sixteen of us here. Leetle ol' piddlin' eighteen thousand greenbacks won't go whar' near payin' fer all the trouble 'n' commotion we spent gettin' down here all this ways. See, I takes a third. That jest wouldn't leave much fer the boys."

Lew said, steadily, "It'll be bloody, Sam."

There was a threat in Sixkiller's voice. He said, "Why, they won't e'en know we's a-comin'. The wh'ul town'll be asleep." Then he leaned forward. "'Lessen somebody wuz to tell 'em. You wouldn't tell on yore old uncle, would ye, nephee?"

Lew said, making up lies as fast as he could think of them, "I told you we had considerable trouble from the border. Town's got a night patrol. Ain't got nothing to do with my office. Part of that vigilante outfit. They take turn about and patrol all night. Any sign of trouble they ring the bell in the Catholic church an' the whole town turns out."

"Hmm," Sixkiller said. "First I've heard 'bout such. Y'all wouldn't be funnin' me, would ya?"

I said, "Your man was right, Mr. Sixkiller. This Axel boy. It is a prosperous town. And they intend to keep it so. Lot of money around the place. Lot of big cattle ranches with a lot of hired hands. Place has got quite a reputation. I'm surprised you ain't heard of it. There's a sign in the middle of town that says, 'Stranger, you are welcome to ride straight on through.'"

Sixkiller said, "Hmmm" again. Then he said, "Funny that boy Ah sent, Axel, never said nothin' 'bout that."

I said, "I didn't know he could read."

Sixkiller looked at me for a long second and then he suddenly grinned. He hit the pommel of his saddle and said, "Why that's a fack! Poor ol' Axel cain't read, kin he? Now whyn't I thank of that?"

I didn't answer, just looked at him.

Sixkiller said, "Say that crowd at the auction leaves out 'bout three of the afternoon?"

"Yeah," Lew said.

I could see a dark cloud forming up to the west. With the wind blowing in the direction it was, there was a good chance that thunder and lightning might bring our meeting to an early close.

Sixkiller said, "Might be we ought to get there early so as to work the crowd fer they pocket money."

Lew shrugged. "If you want trouble . . ."

Sixkiller grinned that awful smile of his again. He said, "Say, I don't recollect you ever answerin' my question 'bout would you tell on yore ol' uncle. Seems to me you went to ramblin' on 'bout some vigilante outfit."

Lew said, "Ain't nobody in town knows about you. I intend to keep it that way if I can."

"What 'bout yore depity?"

Lew glanced my way. I don't reckon either one of us was

liking the way things were going. Lew said, "He does what I tell him. We're in together."

Sixkiller said, "Wa'l, ain't that sweet." He stared at us fixedly for a moment. Then he said, "Nephee, whyn't you tell me why I oughtn'ta git rid of some law right here an' now?"

Lew didn't flinch. He said, "Because they ain't no point to it. We ain't gonna get in your way. Y'all take you a payday out of the auction barn and ride on and no harm done."

Sixkiller said, "Oh, we intends to take us that payday outten the auction barn, ar'right. But the fack iz, nephee, I cain't see us stoppin' thar'. 'Specially iffen we ain't got no what ye might call official law to deal with."

I could feel myself tensing up. Lew said, "Ain't a smart play, Sam."

Sixkiller said, "Wa'l, it's a sight smarter'n you two boys comin' out here ta meet us." Then he straightened in the saddle and made a motion with his right hand. Instantly the bunch behind him began fanning out, separating into two wings that started toward us on each side. It was clear they intended to surround us where we stood.

=Chapter Nine

Lew AND I started backing our horses the second we took notice of their intentions. I put my hand at my side, holding the reins in my left. Lew said, "You better think this over, Sam."

Sixkiller started his horse forward at about the same pace we were backing ours. The riders on each side of us had not quite come up to the line of our retreat.

Sixkiller laughed. He said, "You boys don't reckon you kin outrun a bullet, do you?"

I said, evenly, "For every hole you make, Sixkiller, we'll make two. And guess where they going to be heading."

Lew said, "You better stop these here boys of yours, Sam. You're crowdin' us an' we don't like it."

Sixkiller took his time, coming toward us in a slouching walk. My horse was getting tired of walking backwards and was starting to fight the rein. Then Sixkiller raised his hand again and said, "Whoa up."

His riders stopped. The ones that had lifted rifles into their hands put them back across their saddles. Sixkiller laughed. He said, "Why, nephee, would ye have shot yore ol' uncle? That thar' depity of yor'n iz mighty mean. Kin he back it up?"

Lew said, "You don't want to find out."

When we saw that Sixkiller's men had pulled up, we let our horses back for a few more yards and then pulled them to a stop. Lew said, "All right, Sam, what's it to be? An easy payday? Or trouble? It's yore pick. I done explained my position in Blessing. Don't give me no hard time."

Sixkiller grinned. He said, "Why, I reckon we's a-gonna take yore advice, nephee. Won't none of them folks in yore leetle town e'en know we been about." Then he looked at me and his grin got bigger. He said, "Reckon Ah'll see you at tha auction barn, depity."

I shook my head. I said, "No you won't."

"Ye ain't gonna be thar'?"

"No," I said. "You look like the kind that might hold a grudge. You can have it all to yourself." Then I took a chance. I said, "You want to see me, I'll be back in town sitting up in some second-story window with a .30–.30 carbine and a lot of cartridges."

Sixkiller slapped his thigh and said, "Boy, howdy, nephee, you got yoreself one alligator bear fer a depity. He's somptin', ain't he?"

Lew started backing his horse. I followed suit. Lew said, "We'll be goin' now. You do it whichever way you want to, Sam. I went out of my way to set the matter up for you, but you do it whatever way you think is right."

Sixkiller had gone back to resting his arms on his saddle horn. He said, "You boys don't rush off."

I said, "You want some easy pickings there's always Wadsworth. Just up the road four or five miles. No law there."

Sixkiller laughed. We now had a good thirty yards between us and them. He said, "Oh, I don' reckon we'll be payin' that leetle piddlin' town no mind. I reckon we got more money then that thar' place. Ain't no use raisin' a fuss if they ain't no profit in it."

Lew said, "Let's go."

As we whirled our horses and spurred away I heard Sixkiller call after us. He said, "We'll be seein' you boys. Tomorrow."

We let our horses stretch their legs for a quarter of a mile and then pulled them down slowly through a gallop and finally down to a canter. After about a half a mile we slowed to a walk. I said, "I'd have liked to shoot that bastard on the spot. I was about halfway hoping they'd try something."

Lew give me a look. He said, "I don't know what you been drinkin', but you better switch brands. Talk like that."

"Yeah," I said. "Lord, that has to be the trashiest son of a bitch I've ever seen in my life."

Lew looked back, studying the horizon. He said, "Well, they ain't coming. Reckon what Sixkiller is thinkin'?"

I said, "How would I know? He's yore half uncle."

He give me a hard look. "That would be just like you to pass such a remark. As if it hadn't grieved me enough years."

The truth be told we were both so glad to have the ordeal over that we were more than a little lighthearted, and that even though there was some serious work ahead. But it ain't no church social to go up against sixteen heavily armed renegades led by a misfit that would be considered dangerous in any company. I said, "Well, what do you think? You reckon he took the bait?"

Lew was silent for a moment. Then he said, "You know what I hated? I hated spurring our horses into a run when we left. I bet that give the old bastard a laugh. I wish we could have just loped away."

I gave a short laugh. I said, "Well, you go right ahead and feel bad about it all you want. I'll do the exact same thing next time. I ain't a big hand on showing off when the odds is dead against me. You get a good look at the faces of that bunch? Hell, some of 'em ought to be in Bellville where they put the crazy people. Even running our horses, the middle of my back was itching waiting for that rifle bullet. Wouldn't have taken much thought for one of them inbred son of a bitches to up with his long gun and take a pop at us."

Lew said, "Still . . ."

I said, "Forget that. It's over. We got the next step. Do you think they bit?"

Lew said, "I don't know. Sixkiller is a snaky old bastard. He's liable to do anything. But, yeah, I think he'll go for the auction barn. I also think he's got it in his mind to not leave off there but to go on into town. How'd that vigilante stuff sound to you?"

"Sounded pretty good," I said. "When'd you dream that up?"

He said, "Aw, it come over me riding out. Lot of them little towns up in the Oklahoma Territory had such. Since they wasn't no law it was the only way they had to protect themselves against men like Sixkiller's. I knew he'd understand. I wouldn't be at all surprised if it wasn't such organizations that sent him south."

I said, "Well, if he'll visit that auction barn we might can cut his plans off right then and there."

We'd picked up the pace again, almost letting our horses canter. Lew said, his voice jouncing a little with the motion of his horse, "I just hope we got enough guns to handle that bunch. They been shot at before. Some of our bunch ain't. An' just because we'll have cover don't make it no pigeon shoot."

I said, "And the thing is, we got to get them all."

Lew said, "What kind of smart-aleck remark was that about you'd be back in town waiting in a second-story window with a carbine? And lots of ammunition. Was you trying to provoke Sam?"

I said, "I got kind of tired listening to the bastard and watching him toying with us like a cat with a mouse. Wonder what happened to Axel?"

Lew shook his head. "That would be hard to say. Wouldn't be surprised if Sam stretched him out over an anthill just for pleasure. You don't ever want to figure what that renegade is liable to do. No, likely Axel delivered the message out of fear of your half-Indian, half-wildcat you said was trailing him. Then I reckon he took off.''

I said, ''Well, I'm glad this business is over, that meeting. I don't mind saying I didn't like the situation or the odds.''

Lew said, ''Aw, I wasn't worried. Hell, ol' Sam wouldn't of hurt his 'nephee.' Half-breed bastard!''

The black cloud I'd seen forming in the west had spread and was closer. I looked back over my shoulder at it. I could see flashes of lightning and hear faint thunder. I said, ''We better get a move on or we are going to get a good drowning. They's enough rain in that thundercloud to raise two crops of cotton.''

He took a look. He said, ''I hope to hell it catches Sam and his bunch with nothing for shelter except a bare-limbed mesquite tree.''

We put our horses into a gallop. They responded willingly, having had a good deal of slow work and standing around. The storm caught us a mile out of Wadsworth in spite of our haste. We rode our horses straight to the railroad depot, riding through the driving rain. The railroad had a little shed there where they could keep stock and freight out of the weather, and we rode straight into the open-sided little building.

''Shit!'' Lew said.

I climbed down off my horse and then untied my slicker.

Lew said, ''Little late for that, ain't it?''

I said, ''I don't want to get no wetter.''

He said, ''Hell, you couldn't get no wetter.''

I looked at my watch and was surprised to see it wasn't quite four o'clock. I'd have bet my last shirt it was two hours later. It seemed like we'd been out there on that prairie, either riding or talking to Sixkiller, for hours. But maybe it was the way the thundercloud had made it so dark that had misled me. I said, ''One hour to train time. You want to stay here wet without a drink or you want to walk over to the cafe and get wet on the inside?''

He said, "Like I say, we couldn't get no wetter on the outside. Let's go."

We went on over to the little saloon and cafe and went inside shaking off the rain on their already wet floor. Everybody in the place looked like the thunderstorm had caught them out. We sat down at a table and ordered a bowl of chili apiece. Outside the storm was passing over and the thunder was growing distant as the clouds moved on east.

The chili came and we set out to eat, though neither one of us was much hungry. I said, "Lew, we got to get every one of them."

He said, "If they show up. And if our gun hands show up."

I took a drink of beer. I'd wanted a whiskey, but I figured to eat first. I said, "There's a windmill across the road from the auction barn."

Lew said, "I know that."

I said, "I'm thinking about putting a man up there."

He looked up. "Who?"

I chewed a minute and then washed the chili down with beer. I said, "Buttercup."

Lew had his spoon halfway to his mouth. He lowered it. "Buttercup? That ol' man? How the hell will you ever get him up there on that platform?"

"Haul him up," I said.

He said, "Shit, you can't put an old man in a desperate fight like that."

"I don't know nobody can shoot that big rifle of his better'n he can. Besides, he's gonna raise hell if he's left out. And it will give us one more gun."

Lew gave me a sour look. He said, "Next you'll be wanting to bring yore daddy along. Hell, Buttercup ain't drawed a sober breath in ten years. He'll roll off that little platform and fall on his head. No, sir. No, sir. I can't have it."

I didn't say anything, just went on eating chili and

drinking beer. Presently Lew said, "It ain't a good idea, Justa. That old man could get killed. They'll spot him up there for sure."

I finished my chili and then got out a cigarillo and lit it.

Lew said, "Well, he can shoot that damn thing. And I know he's been a help in the past. He might could pick off a straggler in case we don't cut them all down first few volleys."

I said, "Let's get a shot or two of whiskey in us before it's time to take the train. We got to be careful we don't take a chill what with the wetting we got from that rainstorm."

Lew said, "You'd have brought him anyway, wouldn't you? No matter what I said."

I signaled to the waitress and ordered the whiskey. By my watch we'd nearly killed enough time to wander back on over to the Wadsworth depot.

We got back into Blessing a little before six. When they had the ramp in place we led our horses off the train and mounted up. Lew said, "Com'on down to my office. I got a piece of a bottle left."

I said, "I better get on home."

"You don't want to ride seven miles without a drink. You're already in trouble with Nora. Fifteen minutes one way or the other ain't going to make no difference."

"All right," I said. "But just one."

Truth be told we were both cooling out from our adventure that afternoon. Man doesn't raise his nerves up that high and then just come straight back to normal. Takes a little whiskey and a little talk.

We rode up Main Street and turned in to the hitching rack in front of Lew's office. He said, "Well, I'll just be damned!"

There, huddled up on the boardwalk by the office door, was Axel. He slowly rose as we dismounted. I said, "Axel, what the hell are you doing here?"

He rubbed the sleeve of his grubby old coat across his nose and said, "Din't have no place else to go."

Lew said, "Why the hell didn't you stay with Sixkiller?"

Axel give him a cunning look. He said, "I git the feelin' ol' Sam is in fer a mighty warm welcome from you gennelmen."

Lew unlocked the door to his office and went inside shaking his head. He said, "Hell, this ain't a sheriff's office. It's a damn orphanage. You still got that gun, Axel?"

"Yes, sir." Without another word he went under his coat and handed over the big Navy Colt. Lew put it in a drawer.

Lew said, "Go on back and lock yourself in a cell."

Axel rubbed his nose again. "Reckon I could have a drank of whuskey?"

Lew grumbled, but he got out his piece of bottle and a tumbler and poured the kid a full measure. He said, "Now go on."

"Reckon I could git somethin' to eat. Ain't eat fer a day and a half."

Lew said, "I'll get you something after a while."

"Iffen I had me some money I could git it myself."

"Here," I said. I took two silver dollars out of my pocket and handed them to Axel. I said, "Now go along and don't get into trouble."

When he was gone Lew poured us out drinks, still shaking his head. He said, "That kid. Boy, he beats all. I wonder how he got away from Sam."

I sat down in the chair across from Lew's desk, and we made the toast to "Luck" and then knocked them back. Lew poured out again. I said, "I ought to be heading for home."

Lew kept pouring. He said, "I done told you—you're already in dutch. Might as well make a good job out of it. And, besides, here you been out playin' hero an' you ain't gonna get a damn bit of credit for it."

"I better not," I said. "I think Nora would have rather

I'd been out running around with another woman. I swear, Lew, since she got on the brink of being a mother seems like she can come up with the damnedest ideas. And her nerves are just shot to hell.''

"Well, drink up. Tomorrow we are gonna find out jest how the cards stack up. I don't reckon you are letting that bunch's appearance fool you? I mean them raggedly lookin' clothes.''

"No," I said, "I taken notice of their firearms and the way they was kept. Pretty hard-looking bunch of old boys.''

Lew said, "You got to be hard to survive up in that Oklahoma Territory. You got every bandit in the country hidin' there. Hell, it's worse than the Mexican border. If that's possible.''

I said, "Well, I reckon we'll see you here at the jail. We'll try to get here around eleven o'clock or so.''

"Don't run it too late.''

I had one more drink and then I headed it for home. The grandfather clock in the parlor was tolling eight when I walked in the door. My supper was on the kitchen table covered with a cloth. I half expected liver again, but it was a steak and some succotash and mashed potatoes. It was cold as an eskimo. Neither Nora nor her mother were anywhere in sight.

I didn't know much about cooking, but I knew I wasn't going to eat that meal in the condition it was in. And I damn sure wasn't going to call Nora. I figured she'd be colder than the steak. Our stove had what they called a dutch oven. I stirred up what coals remained with a poker and then stuck my plate in the oven and closed the lid. There was coffee in the pot, but it was cold. I figured to just make do with well water.

After I figured the meal had had a little time to heat, I got the plate out of the oven, using a dishrag to keep from burning my hand. I put it on the table and then sat down to eat. It was pretty tough going, everything but the succotash being pretty well dried out. I figured Nora was in the parlor with her mother. Either that or they were both in bed. I kind of hoped for the latter. If there had to be trouble I was just as willing to have it the next morning. I figured it would kind of prepare me for what was to come in the afternoon.

I finally managed to make a meal, though it took three glasses of water to wash it down. When I was through I walked across the hall to my office, poured myself out a drink, and then stepped into the parlor. Nora was sitting on the divan, crocheting furiously. She didn't so much as favor me with a glance when I came into the room. I sat down in my big overstuffed chair and said, "Well, hello. I didn't hear a sound out of you. Figured you was in bed."

Without looking up she said, in a voice about as cold as my supper had been, "Is that where you've been? In bed?"

I looked at her blankly. I said, "What?"

"You heard me." Her fingers were flying with the knitting needles or whatever they were. "I'm not quite as dumb as you think I am. Oh, I know I don't look as pretty as I used to. I know how you must feel. I know I'm swollen and ugly. But, Justa, while my mother was here!"

I didn't know what she was talking about and told her so. I said, "What is all this?"

She finally looked up. She said in an overly sad voice, "Oh, Justa, don't lie. That just makes it worse. At least have the courage to admit your wrongdoings. That way I'll have some respect for you."

I said, "What in hell are you talking about? You are going to have to take me on lead on this one because I'm in a storm."

She let her hands drop in her lap. She said, "Mother and I went up to the main house to see about someone taking her in in the morning. I *was* doing better and I know how she's been worrying about Daddy. So I thought she could go in early and fix him some meals."

I said, "What the hell's that got to do with this? With me?"

Nora said, "Norris was already home. It was five o'clock. *He* left the office at four o'clock. You didn't get home until *eight*."

Well, I was in a tight place and no mistake. I said, lamely, "Hell, Nora, I had a few drinks with Lew Vara. So what? You never objected to me seeing the inside of a saloon."

She commenced shaking her head. "For four hours?"

"How about the ride home?"

"All right. For three hours?" She shook her head again. She said, "Oh, Justa, this is going to wreck us. I can stand anything but your lying to me."

Well, my heart was in my throat. It looked like she'd caught me out. But I couldn't figure how she'd got anything out of Norris. He knew I'd half kill him if he gave me up. I said, desperately, "Well, what did Norris say?"

Her eyes were starting to show signs of tears. She twisted her hands in her lap. "Oh, he backed you up about the land proposition, all right. But he got mighty awkward when it came to telling me what else you'd been up to."

I said, "I told you, I was having a few drinks with Lew Vara."

"Oh, yes you were! That's all you've been doing lately is having drinks with Lew Vara. Every day it's the same thing—you go into town and then you're late getting home. And with my mother here. Oh, it makes me so ashamed!"

I was near frantic. I said, "What does your mother have to do with it?"

Nora had taken out a lace handkerchief and was holding it first to one eye and then the other. She said, "That she has to think she has a daughter whose husband goes into town to, to, to floozies!"

And then she burst out crying.

I just sat there openmouthed for a few seconds. I thought Norris had given me away about what was really transpiring, and instead, I was being accused of philandering. I wanted to laugh I was so relieved. But Nora was taking it hard and I knew I'd better do something. I jumped up and ran over and sat down by her on the settee and tried to put my arm around her. She kept shrugging it off. She said, between sobs, "Don't you, you dare touch me."

I said, "Honey, I ain't been with any floozies or any other kind of woman for that matter."

She wouldn't look up at me, just kept crying in her handkerchief. I said, "Did your mother put this idea in your head?"

"We haven't talked about it," she said, her voice quavering. "I've been too ashamed."

I said, "Your thinking has got all catawampus. I swear I've been tending to business. I swear I haven't been seeing other women."

"Wait until I'm all ugly and fat and then you, des-des-desert me. Ooooh, what a horrible man you are, Justa Williams!"

I said, "Now, wait—"

But she said, "Never in our life have you been late to supper so often. And gone to town so much. Now I know why! And don't you dare tell me it's a coincidence."

"Now listen, let me—"

"No, you wait until I've lost my looks and then you're not interested anymore. You don't have to write me a letter. I can see the handwriting on the wall. You haven't even really kissed me since, since I can remember."

I said, "Now just a damn minute! When you had that there seizure you took down with, Dr. Jackson told me it would be best if I didn't get too close to you. And you know what I mean. He said that for a while you was going to associate me with all that pain in that false labor."

"Oh, sure! A likely story."

I looked wildly around the room, looking for a Bible. I said, "Dammit, I'll prove it to you!" I finally saw the Good

Book on a shelf of a chest that was against the wall. I jumped up and ran over and got it and then came back and stood in front of Nora. Holding the book in my left hand I raised my right and said, "Now look here, Nora. Look up here. Look at me, dammit!"

She slowly raised her head until she could see me, but she kept dabbing at her eyes, which were red and still trickling tears. She said, her lower lip trembling, "Well?"

I said, "Now I admit I ain't much of a one for going to church, but you know I ain't about to damn my immortal soul by swearing to a lie on this here Bible."

She said, "What are you going to swear?"

I said, "I swear on this Bible that I never so much as looked at another woman after you and I got serious. And I double swear I never even so much as looked, touched, or even much thought about any other woman since we been married. I ain't been around no floozies or no women of any kind. I ain't cheated on you in any shape, form, or fashion."

About then, out of the corner of my left eye, I seen Nora's mother come out of her room. She had on a robe and had her hair up in some kind of net. She said, "What is all this commotion? Nora, what are you crying about? Justa, what are you doing with that Bible?"

I said, "Your daughter thinks I have been philandering on her. She don't believe I've been late because I've been doing my work."

Her mother said, in a kind of disgusted voice, "Oh, pshaw! Nora, you are not the first woman who's ever had a baby. I wish you would collect yourself and get over this foolishness you keep on inventing." Then she turned around and went back in her room and closed the door.

For a second neither one of us moved. Then Nora started crying again, really sobbing this time. Well, that perplexed me. I said, "Now what's the matter?"

She said, "Oh, I feel so sorry." She looked up at me and raised her hand to mine. She said, "Oh, honey, I'm so sorry.

I don't know what came over me to doubt you like that. Can you please forgive me? Mother is right. I'm acting so silly.''

I took her hand in both of mine and squeezed it. Then I sat down beside her and put my arm around her shoulders and pulled her to me. I said, "There, there, sweetheart, it's all right. Ain't no harm been done."

Hell, she ran through so many moods I couldn't keep up with them. She changed faster than Texas weather. But I was so damn glad that she'd accused me of something that I could truthfully swear on and hadn't caught me out about the other business with Sixkiller that I was near weak with relief. When she'd first lit into me I'd thought I was a gone goose. It would have never entered my mind that she might think I was philandering. And with floozies. It made me want to laugh, but I had better sense than that. So I just held her against my shoulder and patted her and kept saying, "There, there" until she kind of quit sobbing and just gave a kind of little snuffle every now and then.

She finally pulled back and looked up in my face. Her eyes were swollen and red. She said, "Oh, how hateful I've been. I even made you eat a cold supper."

I said, "Aw, that don't matter. I warmed it up in the oven."

I thought she was going to burst out with a fresh set of tears on that one, the idea that I'd had to heat my own supper up. But she held it in and said, "Mother is right. Maybe I don't deserve you. You work so hard and then have to eat a cold supper. She told me I was doing wrong when I didn't wait to cook yours when you got in. She said she was going to bed and washing her hands of the whole mess. Why, if it hadn't been for her your supper wouldn't even have been covered up and the flies would have got at it."

We carried on like that for a considerable time. When I finally got her settled down it was after ten and too late to go over to the main house. But it didn't matter. I had given Ben instructions to keep Kline and Boyd back from going to the range next morning and to look for Johnson and Millen. I'd told them to expect me sometime after breakfast.

We finally went to bed and I held her close. I could tell she wanted me to make love to her, but my mind was so on the possibilities and probabilities of the next day that I just couldn't get my mind on it. To keep her from thinking I didn't find her as attractive as ever I spent considerable time soothing her and stroking her and telling her she was still the prettiest girl in six counties. Before long her breathing got quiet and even and I could tell she was asleep. As gently as I could I disengaged myself from her arms and turned over on my side and thought about what the next day might bring. It was going to be a risky time, and there was a damn good chance that a lot of men would hit the ground facedown. I could only hope that all of them would be on Sixkiller's side. Just before I dozed off I remembered that I hadn't told Buttercup he was to go. Near as I could figure he'd be the only one glad to take a hand in the business.

Nora got up and fixed my breakfast the next morning even though I protested I could make do with coffee. Her mother came into the kitchen while I was eating and said, straight away, "Well, I hope all this stuff and nonsense is over with. Nora, you ought to be ashamed of yourself."

I hastened to her defense. I said, "Mom, she just got a little carried away. I've already give her a good talking to."

And, indeed, Nora was as contrite as if I had given her a lecture. She'd taken extra pains to fix her hair and powder and rouge her cheeks and was wearing one of her prettiest frocks. I was mighty glad she didn't know what I was up to or where I was bound for. I said, "Mom, I know you want to get back and see to Lonnie, but I wonder if I could get you to wait until this afternoon to go into town?"

She looked uncertain. She said, "Why, I suppose I could. Whatever for?"

I said, "Well, today is auction Saturday and I've got to go into the auction barn. I probably won't be back much before five o'clock and I don't want to leave Nora alone that long.''

She give me a look. She said, "Now, Justa, don't you start getting silly. Nora is not going to break. She's not some little china doll.''

And Nora said, "It's all right, honey. I'll be fine. Go ahead and tend to your business.''

Well, I couldn't very well tell her I didn't want her mother in town until the "business" was tended to, so I said, "Mom, I know that. But it's Dr. Jackson's orders. She ain't supposed to be alone for a little more time.''

Mrs. Parker said, "Oh, what do doctors know? Women were having babies long before there were any doctors. But, all right. Lonnie's not helpless. I did want to get there early enough to fix him a good lunch and a good supper, but as long as I get there early enough to make supper I guess it will be all right. Besides, it being Saturday he'll probably keep the store open late.''

I said, "It'll make me feel better. I'll tell them over at the main house to come get you in the early afternoon.''

I said adios to Mom and kissed Nora just like I did every day, just like I was going out to work cattle. She didn't say anything about me wearing a gun, knowing, by then, that I always wore a gun to town.

I went outside and caught the two-year-old gelding. He wasn't as steady as the four year old I'd rode the day before, but he was a hell of a lot steadier than the two-year-old colt and hell for quick speed. He also had pretty good staying power.

I rode over to the main house, dropped the reins, and went inside. Ben and Norris and Howard were sitting around the dining room table drinking coffee. I sat down and one of the Mexican women brought me in a cup.

Howard said, "So this be the day.''

I nodded, blowing on my coffee to cool it off.

He said, "You reckon it dangerous?''

I shrugged. I said, "We'll have cover; they won't. It ought to be a lot more dangerous for them than us." Then I looked at Ben. I said, "Unless somebody decides to get foolhardy."

Ben said, with a little heat, "Don't be referring to me."

I said, "I never. Must be in your mind."

Norris said, "What time will we be leaving?"

"About ten-thirty. Ben, did you speak to Kline and Boyd?"

"Yeah. They're waiting in the bunkhouse. Harley like to have throwed a fit about losing two men. And, of course, I couldn't tell him why."

"Where's Ray?"

"He was in here a while ago. He wandered off somewhere. Say, what about your mother-in-law? She and Nora came over last night about getting her into town. I nearly had to put on my dancing shoes about that one. Do you want her in town?"

"No." I turned to Howard. I said, "Dad, when she gets tired of waiting she's liable to come up here. Anytime after four o'clock you can send her in with one of the vaqueros off the horse herd. By the way, where's Buttercup?"

Norris laughed. "You're asking for Buttercup?"

"Yeah," I said, "I'm going to use him in this fight."

Howard said, "Oh, no, Justa. I wish you wouldn't do that."

I explained what I had in mind and how valuable Buttercup could be in picking off stragglers. I said, "And he won't be in no danger. They won't look for him up on that platform, little as he is. And we'll be so hot on their tails they won't have time to look for anything but the way back to Oklahoma."

Norris said, "Well, you must have already told him."

"Why?"

"Because I went back in the kitchen a while ago and the door was open to his room. I could see him sitting on his bunk cleaning that old rifle of his and checking his cartridges.''

Ben said, "What about Johnson and Millen?"

I just shrugged. I said, "Either they show up or they don't."

"You really going to call in their notes if they don't?"

I shook my head. "No. In fact I wish I had never said it. But what's done is done."

Norris said, "What a curious place Texas is. I'd hate to have to explain it to some of my northern friends. Especially how we could be faced with such a situation."

Ben said, "How so? Texas is Texas."

"No," Norris said, "it is not. It is a combination of many different types of country, and I do not mean the terrain. That is obvious. I mean the temper of the different parts. Here we are in this huge section in the southeast, the coastal plains. It is largely unsettled and largely uncivilized. It is so uncivilized that bands such as this Sixkiller gang can roam with impunity. Yet areas around Houston and Dallas and Fort Worth and San Antonio and even East Texas are settled and have organized law and order where such a thing as these depredations of Sixkiller wouldn't be possible and ordinary citizens wouldn't have to come to their own defense."

Ben said, "Yeah, but you're talking about big cities and their surrounds. We ain't got no big cities."

Norris said, "Houston is not much over a hundred miles from here, but it's twenty years ahead in civilized behavior."

I said, "What about West Texas? There ain't no more law there than there is in the New Mexico and Arizona territories. And what there is is about as crooked as the bandits."

Norris said, "That's my very point. Texas has been a state for over forty years and it doesn't seem like we've made much more progress than those two territories. I can understand about West Texas. There isn't anything out there except cactus and rocks, nothing to attract civilized settlers. But this is a lush land. We ought to be doing better with it, better than us sitting here preparing ourselves to go and defend it against a bunch of wandering bandits.''

Ben said, ''Next he'll be wanting to have a opery company in here.''

I said, ''No, next we'll be having nesters and farmers who will cut this state land up and we'll see the last of the free grazing on that government land. The day of the fence is just around the corner.'' Norris was beginning to sound too much like Nora, with his talk of ''civilized'' living, to suit me. It was a source of irritation that we had to fight our own battles, but I was more ready to do that than I was to see the range chopped up with fences. We had some fences, but they were drift fences, not enclosures, just fences to keep the cattle from drifting too far in a direction we didn't want them to go.

Howard said, ''This country will be a long time in becoming settled mainly because it is not farming country.''

We all looked around at him. If Matagorda County wasn't farming country I'd never seen any. There were thousands of acres of flat land with hardly a tree or a rock to intefere with the plow. I said, ''How so?''

He said, ''This land is leeched out by the salt that has seeped through the ground from the sea. It will grow grass, yes, and mighty damn good grass. But it won't grow crops. I remember when your mother set out to make a little vegetable garden. We had to haul river soil in here from the Brazos River to sweeten up the dirt. An' then we had to add a bunch of cow manure to fertilize it where it would grow much of anything. You can do that with some little vegetable garden, but you damn shore can't with a 160 acres they give squatters.''

Just then Ray came in. I was glad enough to leave the subject. He said, ''Johnson an' Millen jest rode up.''

I said, ''Invite them in for coffee. We still got a while.''

He left and I got up. I said, "Norris, either you or Howard have a little talk with them. I'm going to make myself scarce. Make it clear I was feeling a little desperate when I first brought up their notes. Hell, offer to extend them or cut down on their payments. Do whatever you have to to get them feeling better about matters."

Norris said, "So you want me to clean up after you?"

Before I could say anything, Howard said, tartly, "Of course it's not as if Justa ain't ever cleaned up behind you."

Norris pulled a face. "All right, all right," he said. "The point is taken. I'll do my best."

I went out through the kitchen and then swung around toward the front of the house. I could hear Johnson and Millen going in through the front door. I walked on, heading for the bunkhouse. I didn't have anything to say to Boyd and Kline, but I wanted to make sure they were ready. I stuck my head in the bunkhouse door. They were playing some card game on one of their bunks. I said, "You boys seen to your weapons and horses?"

They looked up. Kline said, "Yes, sir."

I had a roll of bills in my pocket. I said, "We'll be starting pretty quick. You boys want your money in advance?"

Kline said, "I don't, Mistuh Williams. But if somethin' was to happen to me I'd be obliged if you'd send it to my old mother. I writ her address out an' left it in my other clothes."

I said, "Nothing going to happen to you, Kline."

"Jest in case," he said.

"All right." I looked at Boyd. "What about you?"

He shrugged. "Give it to the boys for a good drunk on me. I ain't got no folks. Least none I know of."

I pushed away from the door. I said, "Hold yourself ready."

Then I walked back to the house and entered through the kitchen. Just off to the left, and obviously tacked on to the main body of the house, was Buttercup's room. When I stepped to his door I could see he was still wiping and polishing his old buffalo gun. He looked up. He said, "We be ready to go, young'un?"

I said, "Wherever in the world did you get the idea that I'd take an old drunken fogey like you on serious business such as this?"

He snorted. He said, "Shoot! Who be you joshin', chil'? You couldn't *not* carry me 'long. I is still the bes' shot of the bunch of you. An' you knows it."

I give him a look. I said, "You don't mind patting yourself on the back, do you? Make sure you don't break your arm."

He said, placidly, "Man ain't braggin' iffen he kin do it."

I said, "You got your buckboard hitched up?" It was too long a ride into Blessing for his old stove-up legs to sit a horse.

"Been waitin' fer word." He got up and I swear I could hear his old joints creak. "I'll tend to that matter right now."

I looked at my watch. It was going on for ten o'clock. I said, "I'd get high behind was I you. We'll be leavin' in fifteen or twenty minutes."

"Then git outen my way."

I walked through the kitchen and back into the dining room. Johnson and Millen both looked up in a friendly way and nodded. I reckoned that either Norris or Howard had done their work. I sat down. I said, "Well, we either got time for another cup of coffee or two shots of whiskey." There was a bottle setting in the middle of the table. I reached for it. I said, "I know which I'm going to have. But every man to his preference."

Ray Hays said, "Boss, be all right if I have my whiskey in my coffee? Thet way I can have both."

I just give him a look. Ray did and said things like that

just to plague me, which he was doing better than anyone else.

I poured myself out a shot and then raised my glass around the table. I said, "Luck" and then knocked the drink back as befits the toast. We might well need it.

═══Chapter Ten

WE RODE SLOW and mostly silent. There didn't seem to be much left to talk about. I had described to the others in as full a detail as I could without actually being in the auction barn what my plans were. They were pretty simple. We'd let Sixkiller and his bunch enter the auction barn and then we'd shoot as many of them as we could. Lew had not said what we could do if they just rode up and came in without pulling a gun. He had not said, and I had not asked about, our course of action in that eventuality. My position was that if they didn't pull out a gun there they'd do it somewhere else, somewhere we weren't so prepared for them. I planned to see a gun whether one was drawn or not. Sixkiller had clearly stated his intentions plain enough for me during our meeting out on the Wadsworth Road. I didn't need any more to go on than that.

Near town I had us split up into smaller groups. I told Millen and Johnson to go along with Buttercup's buckboard and head out to the auction barn. I told Ray and Boyd and Kline to go to Crook's but to not drink anything but beer. Ben and Norris and I would go to Lew's office. I told Ray, "Keep an eye out the window. When you see us heading out, come on right then. But don't catch us on the road. Come in like we weren't together."

I didn't put it past Sixkiller to have snuck a spy into town, and I didn't want it to look like we were gathering up some sort of posse. It might scare the bandits off, and worse than the fight, I dreaded them getting spooked and holding off. That would just put the option in Sixkiller's hands as to when to raid, and leave us in fear and readiness for weeks, perhaps. No, if it had to be done I wanted it got to and over with.

Buttercup and Johnson and Millen bore off to the right, headed for the auction arena. I had Hays and the two hired hands just hold up the prairie while Ben and Norris and I rode on ahead. I told them they could come on when they seen us in town.

We went straight to Lew's office and tied up out front. When we went through the door we found Lew behind his desk and Axel huddled up in a chair along the wall. I jerked my thumb at the boy. I said, "What are you going to do with him?"

Lew shrugged. "He says he wants to go along. Says he wants to see Sam get his."

That kind of took me aback. I said, "How does he know what is going to happen?"

Lew said, "He knows. Claims he knowed all the time."

I said, "Well, this is a pretty mess. Reckon he told Sixkiller?"

Axel spoke up. He said, "I never tol' that sum'bitch nuthin'."

Norris said, "Who is this?"

I said, "This is the famous robin, Axel, you've heard me talk so much about. Sounds like he's had big ears."

"No, sir," Axel said. "I never heered nuthin'. I jest knowed y'all two fine gennelmens wadn't gonna let that murderin' half-breed come into yore town an' make free like he's allus doin'. An' I been up an' down that thar' road a fair number o' times. Thet auction barn looked like the place ta me."

Lew looked at me and shrugged. "Thinks just like you do, Justa."

I said, dryly, "Glad to hear that, Lew. Now put him in a cell and let's go."

Axel said, "Awwwww. Please, Mistuh Justa. Please!"

Lew said, "I don't see any reason not to let the boy go. He's got a powerful hate on for Sixkiller. Lease he acts like it."

I said, "That's what I'm thinking. He *acts* like it."

Lew said, "What I was thinking was that neither you nor I would recognize the rest of that bunch. The only one we can tell on sight is Sixkiller himself. What if he was to send half the bunch to hit the auction barn while he led the rest into town? If we seen a half a dozen men riding up we wouldn't know if they was Sixkiller's men or not. Might be honest farmers or traders coming in to auction day. Been a lot of new folks moving in around here. But Axel would know."

"Shore would," he said.

I considered it. It was true he'd know the other members of the gang. And there seemed little enough harm he could do. I said, "He's not carrying a gun."

Lew gave me a look. "Of course not."

I said, "And what are you going to do if he lets out a warning yell just as they ride up?"

Lew reached into his boot and came out with a short skinning knife he always carried there. He held it up. He said, "It'll be the last yell he lets out." He said, to Axel, "Understand?"

The boy said, "Yes, siiiir."

Norris said, "Why does he slur that sir out like that? Something wrong with his mouth?"

Ben said, "He looks like he's been put together out of spare parts."

Lew said, "Now y'all don't rag the boy. He's been considerable help in his way."

I said, "We better get going."

Axel said, "Kin I have some whuskey?"

Lew looked at me. I shrugged. I said, "Hell, we've all had a little dose. Why not him? At least it won't take long."

Lew poured the boy out a tumblerful and handed it over. Axel gulped it down, then held his empty glass out like a hopeful child. But Lew said, firmly, "No. You kin have one later. Right now we got business." Then he rammed the cork home in the jug and put it back in a side drawer. After that he opened the center drawer of his desk and took out a big, .44-caliber Colt revolver and stuck it in his waistband. It reminded me to take my second gun out of my saddle-bags. Once the fighting started there wouldn't be time to reload.

Lew said, "I'm ready."

"We'd best go."

Axel's horse was out front so it was pretty plain, even though he'd made a show out of asking me, that Lew'd intended to let him go along all the time. We mounted up and then rode two by two with Axel a lone one between the two pairs. As we passed Crook's I saw Hays looking out the window. As soon as he spotted us he stood up and made a motion to Boyd and Kline to get up. But I taken notice he took time to finish his mug of beer, gulping it down, before he made a move toward the door. Which didn't surprise me. Hays had a positive fear of leaving any kind of alcoholic drink unfinished. He said it meant sure bad luck.

We rode on, taking it slow and easy. Just as we were passing the last shacks that marked the outer boundary of the town I looked back and could see Hays and the other two trailing us by a couple of hundred yards.

Nothing much got said on the ride to the auction barn. But about a hundred yards away I said to Lew, "I reckon you'll speak to the crowd?"

"Your auction barn."

"You're the sheriff. I'll speak to the manager and the auctioneer, but you got to tell the crowd what to expect, and what to do."

"Fair enough."

As we got close I could see Johnson and Millen and Buttercup. I said, "First thing, we got to get Buttercup up on that windmill."

Lew said, "I got to do some deputizing first. This thing is damn near illegal. I got to give it some stamp of authority."

At the front of the auction barn we all gathered around Buttercup's buckboard, sitting our horses, facing Lew, who said, "Justa is already deputized. The rest of you consider yourselves the same. I ain't got enough badges to go around so we'll let that part go. What do you want to do next, Justa?"

I pointed across the road. I said to Buttercup, "I want to get you up on that platform so's you can command a pretty good field of fire. I reckon it to be about twenty some odd feet off the ground. I figure to draw you up there with lariat ropes."

Buttercup looked at the windmill. He said, "Shit! I'll either climb that little ol' ladder or lay down and die for a hoss thief."

I shrugged. One thing could always be said for Buttercup; he'd give you an argument no matter if he agreed with you or not. I said, "Let's go on over. Though brittle as your old bones are if you was to fall off that thing you'd scatter over about three counties."

He was wheeling his buckboard around. He said, testily, "You jest tend to your bidness, whippersnapper, and leave this here kind of work to me."

We sat around at the base of the windmill and watched him make his way laboriously up the rickety old wooden ladder. He had a coil of rope over his shoulder to pull up his gun and his sack of cartridges once he was in place.

It seemed to take forever, but he finally popped out through the opening and crawled out on the platform. The platform was a circular affair made out of sturdy planks about four and a half feet in diameter. Its purpose was to give a man working on the windmill blades or the gearbox a place to stand and have room to set his tools or his grease pot or spare parts down on something.

Buttercup lay down flat on the platform and then threw his rope down. We tied on his buffalo gun and his sack of cartridges. As he pulled them up I yelled up at him, "Now listen, old man, take a good look at us and make sure you don't shoot the wrong folks."

He said, "You just tend to yore bidness, smart aleck."

I said, "And wait until they are coming out. Don't fire when they first ride up."

He fair yelled at me. He said, "Git on away from here! Want to give my position away!"

We rode on over to the auction barn. Before I dismounted I looked back at the windmill to see what a rider would see. Unless you were looking for him Buttercup was nearly invisible. I knew he'd gone up there with a bottle in his jacket pocket so I figured he'd be comfortable while he waited for the fight to start.

If there was to be a fight.

We walked through the main entrance. On each side of us the benches went up four or five rows, rising above our heads until they fetched up to the round walls of the barn. There were windows at regular heights along the lower part, but there were also a few well-spaced windows up top where the stair-stepped benches ended.

We made our way down the little entryway. It was about five feet across and ended twenty-five or twenty-six feet later at the little four-foot wall that surrounded the auction ring. I knew there were two other openings in the barn; one to the right, where they brought the stock into the ring, and another, to the left, where they ran it out. There were pens on both sides, some for horses and mules, some for cattle.

We went on up to the little wall and stopped. A pen of six crossbred heifers was being auctioned. One of the hands that worked for the barn was cracking a bullwhip to keep them moving around. Up on his little perch, halfway up the bleachers, Tommy Aldine, the auctioneer, was going through his spiel. He said, "Got thirty, thirty, thirty, who'll make it the half? The half, the half, now looking for the half. Got thirty, thirty, thirty, who'll make it the half? Thank you, sir. Got the half, got the half, half, half, half, who'll make it thirty-one? Thirty-one, thirty-one, thirty-one, lookin' for the half. I'm going to sell these prime steers at thirty-one. Don't lose 'em, boys. These are range-bred cattle that are good rustlers. All twos and young twos. I got thirty-one, thirty-one, thirty-one, thirty-one. All done? All through? Sold, to Ol' Man Mullins! Now this next lot is—"

But Lew cut him off. He vaulted the little fence and was in the middle of the arena even before the pen of steers was cleared out. He held up both hands and turned slowly so everyone could see him.

There was a faint murmur as the crowd of forty or fifty ranchers and farmers scattered around the bleachers took notice of this interruption. Somebody yelled out, "You here to arrest the livestock, shur'ff?"

A few chuckled, but most were interested in what was going on. By now they had discovered the bunch of us standing in the entryway. Most looked toward us and then made some comment to their neighbors that we couldn't hear. The auction barn's office was a little room under the bleachers just off the alleyway where the stock went out. The door opened and the manager, Edgar Marsh, came running out. His ear must have heard an interruption in the normal flow of business, and he was coming to see what it was all about. I yelled at him. I said, "Edgar! Edgar!"

He stopped and looked and recognized me. I said, "It's all right. The sheriff has got an announcement. Stay there and listen to it. Then get back to your office."

He nodded though he looked plenty mystified.

Lew said, "Quiet! Quiet! *Quiet, dammit!*"

When at last he had their attention he said, "I've got some information you need to know so pay strict attention. There's a damn good chance we are going to have a band of robbers visit us here today. I—"

But he was cut off by a sudden murmur among the crowd. He yelled, "*Dammit, shut up! I mean git quiet and stay quiet!*"

When they were silent again he said, "Pay strict attention. Your very lives may depend on it!"

Well, that sobered them down right quick. Lew wheeled slowly around in a circle before he began speaking again. Even the arena hands with their whips and the gate boys at each end of the sales circle were standing quiet and attentive. Lew said, "Like I say, there is a damn good chance that a bunch of renegades is planning on robbing this place today. We think they'll be coming sometime between three and four o'clock but we cain't be dead certain."

That caused a little stir, but Lew ignored it. He said, "Now, we've made a plan for this and nobody ought to git hurt. At least not on our side." He pointed toward our little group. He said, "Yonder is my duly authorized depities. They is the only ones that will be allowed to do any shooting. Any of you carrying weapons you are to keep them in leather unless you are directly attacked. Is that plain?"

Somebody called out, "Who are these here bandits, Lew? Whar'd they come from?"

Lew waved his hands. "That part don't matter right now. What's got to be handled now is the way you are to behave and what I want you to do." He paused and looked slowly around the crowd. He said, "Now them as wants to can leave. I won't stop you."

Somebody yelled out, "Hell, shur'ff, I come twelve mile to this here auction, drivin' fifteen head of yearlin's. I need the cash money. I cain't drive 'em back an' then wait two weeks 'n' drive 'em in again."

Lew said, "Nobody is askin' you to leave. In fact if everybody was to leave an' them renegades was to come early we wouldn't be able to suck them in because it would look like a trap. But if you stay you got to do exactly what you be told. An' you got to do it without no hesitatin'. That clear?"

Somebody else yelled out, "What we supposed to do?"

Lew said, "We're hoping you don't have to do nothin'. We're hopin' they'll come when the place is jest naturally cleared out. But if they come early I'm going to jump out here in the ring and I'm going to go to waving my hands like this." He demonstrated by holding his arms out with his palms downward and pumping them toward the ground. He said, "You see me do that, you are to get under these bleachers and go to ground. Go right on down to the floor and lay flat and don't look up. You don't need to see. We'll tell you later what happened. Could be this is all fer nothin'. I hope so. But if it ain't, wal', it's best that we be prepared."

A voice said, "How you know about this, shur'ff?"

Lew said, "This county pays me one hunnert dollars a month to know about such. How I do it ain't fer publication."

"How many will they be?"

Lew said, "Not more than we can handle. Now, if they be some of you that wants to leave, now would be the time. Otherwise we are going to go on with the auction."

I saw three or four men get up silently and steal toward the exits. But I said, "Lew, don't forget about Tommy."

Lew said, "Hell, Justa, he works for you. Likely it would be best for you to tell him."

I went over the wall and crossed the ring to where Tommy was positioned. He was about four rows up. I said, "Tommy, I got a hard thing to ask of you."

"Yessir, Mistuh Williams."

I said, "I need you to just keep on auctioneering until the first shot is fired." Tommy was seated behind a little lectern or podium, a kind of walled-in table where he kept his notes and his bid and asked quotes and whatever other paperwork he needed for his job. I said, "They are going to be leery. And if they hear you right suddenly break off in the middle of your auctioneering they are going to get suspicious. You got a voice that carries, reckon that's why you are an auctioneer. You willing to do this for me?"

Tommy was a little bald-headed man in his late thirties. He had been our auctioneer almost from the first day we'd opened the place some eight years before. He said, "Just keep on a-talkin' until the first shot?"

"Yes."

"What if they ain't no stock in the ring?"

"Make some up. They'll be able to hear you outside. But after that first shot you get down behind your little podium there and then you stay quiet."

He said, "What if that first shot gets me?"

I said, "Then we will see that you get a damn fine burial."

It got a laugh from the house. Tommy shrugged. He said, "I reckon I can do that, Mistah Williams. Don't know if I can do it without my voice cracking."

"Do your best," I said. I nodded at Lew and went over and leapt back across the wall.

Lew said, "That's just about it. Except to warn you not to get excited and fire a gun. You scatter this bunch before we can get them rounded up, and neither yore stock nor yore families will be safe for months. Now get on with the auction."

They started up again, but it didn't quite have the zest it had before. I could see a number of men in the upper seats looking out through the windows. I called up to them, I said, "Here, you men looking out those windows! Turn around. Pay attention to what is going on in the ring."

Lew said, "Let's get up top. Com'on, Axel."

"What do you want him for?"

"Spot any of the bunch we don't recognize."

We climbed up the benches, weaving our way through little groups of men who seemed more interested in us than they did the pen of heifers that were being auctioned below. We finally got to the top bench and kind of sat sideways looking out through a little half window. It was dirty and streaked, but we still commanded a good view some two or three miles up the Wadsworth Road. There wasn't a rider in sight. I got out my watch. It was a quarter until one. I said, "I hope to hell they do like we told them."

Axel, who was standing in the little aisle between rows and leaning in between us said, "Ol' Sam ain't ever gonna do what you reckon. Or hope fer."

Down to our left Lew noticed a couple of men climbing up to look out the next window. He said, to them, "Dammit, I tol' you to stay away from them winders. Now go back down there and buy a cow or somethin'."

We watched them scramble back down to their seats. Lew shook his head. He said, "If this crowd panics . . . ," letting it fall off into an unexpressed fear.

"Yeah," I said. "It will be wholesale killing. And the more danger to us because we'll be between Sixkiller and the crowd. All we need is for a few of these cow-pasture farmers to get to thinking they're Jesse James."

Lew was still staring out the window. He said, "I could have them pass their guns down."

I shook my head. "Likely you wouldn't get them all. And, besides, it ain't quite fair to disarm a man with danger imminent. We just got to hope they do like they've been told."

Lew said, "How far you want to let them get in? Sixkiller's bunch?"

"Just in," I said. "This place ain't all that big. Likely they'll leave a couple of men outside holding the horses and to bring warning if trouble comes in that direction. I'm counting on Buttercup to take care of them."

Lew said, "I figure them to come in more than one door."

I agreed. I said, "I just hope they come in two ways. They come in all three, it is going to cut us kind of thin."

Axel said, "Cain't I have a gun?"

Without looking around Lew said, "No. And don't ask again."

I said, "I figure we put the most of our men, say, five, on the main entryway, there in the front where the customers come in. We'll get on each side and hide behind the benches and fire down that aisle toward the door."

"Not get behind the wall inside the ring?"

"No, because then we'd have to raise up to fire."

"What about them other two openings, where the stock comes in and goes out?"

I said, "The other four will be kind of a flying squad. As soon as we see them commit themselves, they'll go for that entry."

"And if they come in both of them?"

I said, grimly, "Then we are going to wish we had more men. And our bunch at the front door is going to be getting shot at from two directions. I got to figure that's where Sixkiller will bring in the biggest part of his men. To get to them back doors you got to climb through stock pens and you know some of them cow brutes are going to raise a ruckus. Might even be a few bulls out there."

Lew said, "Well, so far so good. I jest wish I knew fer sure they was coming."

I said, "I got to go down and talk to Ben. I figure to put him in charge of the party covering the back. That is if it's all right with you."

Lew made a little "Huh!" deep down in his throat. He said, "I was kind of hoping to have Ben alongside of me."

"Me too," I said. I pushed away from the window and stood up. I said, "I also left my rifle in my saddle boot. I reckon I better bring it in."

Lew snorted. He said, "I reckon the work in here is gonna be a little close for rifles. Shotguns, maybe."

I started down the benches. Tommy was going on about a lone saddle horse that had been run in the ring. He said, "Now this here is a three-year-old cow horse give to settle a debt to Ben Allison by a cowboy who don't work for Ben no more. The horse is gentle and had been working for a good nine months. Now what am I bid for this good animal? Who'll start the bidding at sixty dollars? Sixty here in the front row. Now who'll give sixty-five? Sixty-five, sixty-five, thank you sir, who'll give seventy . . ."

Our group was still in the entryway down by the wall. I sought out my brother and pointed across the ring toward the two openings. I said, "Ben, I'm going to give you the worst of it. We won't know until the last second what they're going to do. Your job will be to take three men and defend the back."

He said, "Can I have Hays?"

I shook my head. I said, "It makes sense that the most of them will come in the front. Lew and I will take Kline and Norris and Ray. That leaves you with Boyd and Johnson and Millen. I figure all three of them to be good, steady hands."

"Any sign of them yet?"

I shook my head. "No. Now you do understand we don't want none getting away?"

He nodded. "I understand you. Do I wait for y'all to fire?"

"If you can," I said. "But if they get too close you'll have to shoot whether our side is ready or not."

Over his shoulder I could see the others watching and listening. They didn't look nervous, but they did look like they were anxious to have it over. I said to them, "We will be firing from cover. The advantage is on our side so long as you don't get carried away and expose yourselves. And don't snap shoot. Pick a target and hit it. You'll be hid along each side of the little alleyway just behind the end of the

benches. Stay as low as you can. The ones on the right shoot
at the bandits on your side. The ones on the left do the same.
That way you won't all be firing at the same man.''

Johnson said, ''I brought a double-barreled shotgun
loaded with double-aught buckshot.''

I said, ''Then use it. By all means. Ben, I'm going outside
to get my rifle and check on Buttercup. Go tell Edgar I said
to stay in his office. Tell him to get under his desk if he
can.''

I walked outside and looked around. There were a
number of wagons parked around and thirty or forty horses.
I went over to mine and pulled my carbine out of its boot.
I jacked a shell in the chamber and then looked across the
way to the windmill. The day was sunny and mild, and the
blades of the windmill were turning slowly. I could see a
little something on the platform, but I couldn't tell it was a
man. I hoped to hell Buttercup hadn't gone to sleep. But if
he had I reckoned the gunfire would wake him up soon
enough.

Just as I started back into the barn three men came out.
Two hurried to their horses, but the third stopped me and
said, ''Mistuh Williams, I done bought two cows. But I'm
scairt to go over to Mistuh Marsh's office 'n' settle up,
feared the guns will commence goin' off 'bout the time he's
writin' me out a bill o' sale. What in hell am I suppose to
do?''

I said, ''Ferlin, don't worry about it. All the business will
get handled when this other is settled.''

He said, ''Yeah, but I needs to be gettin' on home. I tol'
my ol' woman I'd be back before milkin'. An' I'm a good
two hours from home.''

I said, ''Then go along. We ain't worried about you
paying what you owe.''

He turned to go and then stopped. He said, ''You
un'erstan' I ain't takin' off on 'count of them bandits? It's
the milkin'.''

"I understand."

"My old woman has got the rhumatiz in her hands 'n' she cain't milk."

I patted him on the back. I said, "I understand. Now go along."

I watched him go over to a wagon, unhitch his team, climb into the wagon seat, and then wheel his team out of the yard. I called after him, I said, "Don't head north."

He gave me a frightened look over his shoulder and veered sharply east, heading cross-country rather than taking the Wadsworth Road.

When I went back in I saw there was a small crowd of men bunched up in the alleyway that led to the office. I said, to Ben, "What the hell's that all about?"

He shrugged. "I don't know. They just started coming down a few minutes ago. I can guess, though. I'd guess it's them as got money coming and they want to get it and take off."

"Damn fools," I said. "Sixkiller could show up at any minute." I made my way around the outside of the little wall and stepped into the aisle. In the ring Tommy was auctioning about six Longhorn steers. To the first man crowding to get at Edgar's door, I said, "What are you men doing? Get back up in the stands."

A big, blustery small rancher that I knew as a man named Brown turned around to me. He said, "Listen, I sold me twelve head at fifty dollar the head. I got six hundred dollars comin' less commission. I want my money so's I kin git out of here."

I said, "You can leave, but we ain't got time for you all to complete your transactions. And it wouldn't be fair to accommodate just one. Now get back up on those benches or get out."

Brown shoved up to me. He said, "I want my money."

Behind him others were crowding forward yelling the

same thing. I saw that there was no reasoning with them. I stepped back to the gate that let the cattle out of the ring into the alleyway that led to the outside pens. A young man named Luther was manning it. I said, "Luther, swing open that gate and let them Longhorns through here."

He said, "But, Mistuh Williams, they ain't through being auctioned."

I said, "I don't care." Then I called to the hired hand swinging the bullwhip in the middle of the ring. I said, "Joe, drive them cattle out of the ring. Open that gate, Luther."

It got the crowd in the alleyway's attention. A Longhorn steer's no bargain when a man is mounted and out in the middle of a pasture. He's a dead loser to be hemmed up with in a tight place. Before Luther could unlatch the gate the whole bunch of them had either gone bustling out the back entry or gone by me and climbed back up into the stands. I said to Luther, "Never mind, son."

Then I climbed the wall and got a ways out in the arena. I said as loudly as I could. "Do not worry about your transactions. I will guarantee your money."

Somebody yelled. "What if you get kilt?"

"Then my family will honor it. If we all get killed our estate will honor it. For those of you who don't want to wait around until this is over you can leave and I'll see your money is delivered to you."

Well, that seemed to calm them down considerably. I stepped back over the wall just as one Longhorn began giving me a pretty threatening eye. Ben said, "You reckon this bunch of fools has got any idea the trouble and expense you been out to save their sorry asses?"

I said, "That ain't the point, Ben. We're also looking out for ourselves."

Just then I felt a tug at my sleeve. I looked around. It was Axel. He was pointing up at Lew. Lew was signaling me vigorously to come back up to the window. I said, to Ben,

"This could be it. Y'all stand by to get on the other side. Don't nobody forget to check their weapons."

Then I turned and went up the benches as fast as I could. Axel was right on my tail. I got up beside Lew and leaned down on the bench and looked out the window. I said, "They coming?"

"One is," Lew said. "Axel says he's one of the bunch."

Behind me Axel said, "Name of Casper. Mean sumbitch. Took ten dollar offen me oncet."

I looked. A solitary horseman was riding our way. He was still a quarter of a mile distant, but he had the look and was dressed like the men in Sixkiller's bunch.

Lew said, "Likely he's a scout. What'll we do if he comes in?"

I stood up and yelled down to Ben. I said, "We might have a scout coming in here for a look-see. Y'all take seats and act like customers." Then I raised my voice. I said, "Rest of you be easy. Don't pay him no mind."

I went back to the window. Lew said, "I can't make out the main party. Ought to be able to see them."

There was a slight rise in the prairie about two miles away. I said, "That hump could be hiding them."

But even as we looked we saw a large party of men, without a doubt Sixkiller and his bunch, rise up out of the prairie and come our way. They were taking it at a slow walk, obviously giving their scout time to do his work. I felt some butterflies take wing in my stomach.

The scout kept coming on, but we saw Sixkiller raise his hand and stop his gang. They were about a mile off. A hundred yards away the scout had also stopped. He sat his horse, seeming to be studying the layout. Behind me I could hear Tommy going on with his auction. Now he had a matched team of mules in the ring. I would almost have bet that the advance man could hear him even as far off as he was.

Finally, the scout put spurs to his horses and came closer.

At a walk he veered off to the right and started around the barn. He wouldn't go far because he'd run into the pens that stretched back and to his right. They were full of stock waiting to be bid on. Lew and I didn't bother to go down to another window to keep him in sight. Sure enough, after another moment, he came riding back heading around to the other side of the barn.

Lew said, lowly, "He's liable to run the horses off."

I said, "I figure them to do that, but not him."

We kept him in sight until he rounded the left side of the barn. He was blocked off that way, too. When he came back in sight we saw him stop directly in front of the main entrance. We saw him look back toward Sixkiller. The marauder lifted his arm and waved it. Lew said, "I bet he's coming in."

Sure enough the rider swung off his horse. I stood up and made motions with my arms for everyone to take it easy. Our bunch crawled up into the benches and tried to act like customers. Lew pushed Axel down so that he was laying at our feet and couldn't be seen.

We watched the alleyway. The benches were high enough we wouldn't see him as he first came in, but as they sloped down, if he walked far enough, we'd get a view of him. A minute passed and I thought I heard a door creak. Tommy was going on with his business, though I saw him glance toward the entrance, and then I thought I heard a little waver in his voice. Then I saw the top of an old slouch hat. It didn't come far enough for me to see what was under it but stopped and seemed to be taking a slow look around. I saw some of the crowd look that way and I gave them a silent curse. The damn fools didn't know what kind of danger they were playing with.

Then the hat was gone. In a moment or two more we saw the scout emerge from the barn, mount his horse, and ride at a gallop back toward Sixkiller. He came up to them, and then a little time passed while the scout spoke with Sixkiller. Lew said, ''Wonder what he's telling him.''

I said, ''We'll know soon enough.''

It wasn't a half minute later that Sixkiller raised his hand and his whole gang started forward, heading straight for the auction barn.

═══*Chapter Eleven*

"WELL," LEW SAID, "this looks to be it."

"They're coming," I said.

Lew said, "We better get down there."

I was still crouched by the window, careful to stay far enough back so that I couldn't be seen. As I watched I took the second revolver that, like Lew, I'd stuck in my waistband, and opened the cylinder and checked the load. I had six cartridges in it, same as I did the one in my holster. In the saddle or jostling around I never carried a bullet under the firing pin, but on this occasion I wanted all the fire power I could get. I'd left my rifle laying at the bottom of the risers, next to the entrance alley.

Lew said, again, "Justa, we better get down there. They ain't that far off."

I said, "You go signal to the crowd to take cover. I want to see if he splits his forces and how he does it, if he does."

Lew and Axel clambered away. I watched out the window. Even though they were coming slow Sixkiller and his bunch were no more than a quarter of a mile away. By now they had fanned out until they were riding line abreast sixteen-men long. As I watched they all started looking up at the sky.

A voice at my elbow said, "Looks like it's sprinkling."

I looked around. Ben had made his way up to join me at the window. I said, "You better be for getting ready."

He said, "Just wanted to get a look at 'em. Reckon how it will rain? Hard?"

Little drops were splattering against the dusty window. It was that time of the year when we got a regular dose of afternoon thunderstorms. The skies were already beginning to darken, and back toward the southeast, we could see little flashes of lightning and hear the faint rumble of thunder. It did not stop the riders. They paid no more attention to it other than that one glance skyward.

I heard the faint noise of men scrambling around and turned to look. Lew was in the middle of the arena making downward motions with his hands, and the crowd was slowly making their way underneath the bleachers. I was pleased to see they were doing it orderly and without undue haste. Axel was standing right behind Lew imitating him.

When I turned back to the window I saw that Sixkiller was also making hand motions. At his direction five men from the right end of the line broke off from the rest and started toward the back of the barn. Ben saw it and said, "I better git. Looks like my side is going to open for business."

I said, "Station two men at each entryway. When you see what they're up to combine your forces if they are just coming in one way."

"I can figure that out." Then he went down the bleachers, taking two benches at a time.

I watched until Sixkiller and his remaining men were only about a hundred yards away. The five he'd sent to the back were already out of my vision. I got up hurriedly and started toward the floor of the building. Across the way Tommy was still auctioning imaginary cattle in an empty ring, although now he wasn't sitting erect but barely had his head above his podium. I got to the foot and hurried to the end of the benches. Lew was already there on my side, positioned about three benches up, peering around the end, looking down the alleyway. Axel was just a little below and

almost beside him. Across, Hays and Norris and Kline were
on the first, second, and third benches, with Hays at the
bottom. I found that by ducking my head down and looking
under the seat part of the bench I could see through a crack
caused by the way the bleachers were constructed and get a
good view of the front doors. They were double doors
opening to about the width of the aisle. It gave me the
chance to see when Sixkiller came in without exposing
myself. I looked back across the ring. Ben was peering
around one entryway while Johnson was looking out the
other. Boyd and Millen were set to go either way. I signaled
Ben and pointed at my revolver indicating I'd fire the first
shot. He nodded. Then I made the same motion to Hays and
the other two across the aisle. I pulled the revolver out of my
waistband. I could tell Lew had done the same because I
could see his other gun in its holster. Just then Axel turned
around to me and whispered, "Ol' Sam won't come through
first. He'll make some other'uns take the chancet."

I put a finger to my lips and the boy turned back. Behind
me Tommy was still going a mile a minute. ". . . now I
got thirty, who'll make it thirty-two, thirty-one then in
the second row, lookin' for thirty-two, thirty-two, thirty-
two . . ."

Outside it seemed I could hear the sound of horses and
then the creak of saddle leather as men dismounted. I looked
back. Ben and his men were out of sight. The ring hands had
taken cover. The marauders wouldn't be able to see anything of the inside until they got right to the end of the aisle,
where it entered the business part. By then it would be too
late for them. I peered through the crack, watching the
doorknob of one of the doors. It slowly began to turn.
Seeing it begin to happen made me sort of draw in my
breath.

The door opened slowly, being pushed inward without
any undue haste. A man stood there. It was easy to see it
was one of Sixkiller's men. He had a revolver in either

hand. There was no longer any question that they were there on mischief. For a minute the man just stood there looking around.

". . . now thirty-one, now thirty-one an' a half, who'll make it thirty-two? Com'on, gen'lemen, this is a fine batch of year-old heifers. Do I hear thirty-two, there's thirty-two an' now . . ."

Finally the man took two steps forward. He still wasn't in far enough to see that the bleachers on the far side were empty, but even if he had, he might have just thought the crowd was elsewhere.

He took another step. It was starting to make me nervous. If he came too many more paces I was going to have to do something.

But then he suddenly turned around and pulled the other door open. I could see the whole gang of them. They were all holding at least one gun and they started forward rapidly. They were coming at least three or four abreast. I figured to let them all get in before I fired. I wanted Sixkiller with my first shot, but he was so buried in the crowd I didn't see him at first. Then I spotted him about six men back, recognizing him more by his bulk than by his face. I could see what appeared to be the last man coming through the door. In another second I was going to fire. At that range I figured we should take down half of them on the first volley and create such confusion that the rest would just mill around while we shot them down.

Then, and it happened so fast I wasn't quite sure what I saw or what I imagined, Axel was suddenly in the aisle, revolver in hand, facing Sixkiller and his band. I had just raised my eyes from the crack, getting ready to lean around the end of the bench and fire when it seemed I saw Axel jerk Lew's gun out of his holster and spring into the open. I was going to yell, "Axel!" but I was too late. He was already leveling the big revolver Lew carried. He yelled, "Sam, you sumbitch!" Then he fired, and even back in the crowd, I saw Sixkiller grab at his arm. But then the marauders opened up such a fusillade that poor little Axel was knocked, by the force of all the bullets striking him, clean back to the fence gate leading into the ring.

But I had no time. Lew and I leaned around the end of the benches and began firing as fast as we could thumb off shots. Across the aisle Hays and his bunch were doing the same. The bandits, those as were still standing, were returning fire as they backed toward the exit. I fired all six shots in my revolver, dropped it, jerked out the one in my holster, and kept on firing. Out of the corner of my eye I saw one of ours pitch out of the bleachers across from me, but the smoke was becoming so dense I couldn't see very plain. It was just all bedlam and noise and confusion. Behind me I was dimly aware of more gunshots, and I figured Ben had engaged the ones on his side of the barn. Now the smoke was so thick I couldn't see at all, but I kept firing nevertheless. When my revolver clicked on an empty chamber I jammed it down in my holster and jerked up my rifle. But before I could get off a shot Lew had jumped out in the aisle. He yelled, "Hold your fire, hold your fire! They're out!"

I jumped to the floor and was starting to run toward the doors when Lew grabbed me by the arm. He said, "Don't be in such a damn hurry! They liable to be waiting for the first damn fool to come rushing out."

I said, loudly, because my ears were still ringing with the explosions of the gunshots, "They're getting away! We didn't get them all!"

I pushed by Lew and went to the front doors. They were standing open. Even as I looked through I heard a *boom* and knew it was the sound of Buttercup's buffalo gun. I looked out the doors. I saw five men already across the road and heading east cross-country at a hard run. I could tell one of them was Sixkiller. Then there came another *boom* and one of the five fell. His horse veered off and ran north. The other four kept riding. They were about a quarter of a mile from me when I heard another shot from Buttercup and saw a horse go down. But the rider was up immediately. From the looks of the man I thought it was Sixkiller, and then I was certain because the other three riders pulled up and one spurred back to the lone figure and helped him up behind him. So Sixkiller would be riding double unless they could find another horse.

Then I taken notice they'd made an effort at running our horses off. Some had scattered pretty good, but I taken notice that Ben's had stopped about fifty yards off and was standing there ground-reining himself. Then I noticed one of Sixkiller's bunch laying in the road. He didn't look like he was going to get out of the way if a wagon came along. It appeared to be some more of Buttercup's work.

But we had four desperados loose in our country and one of them was Sixkiller. That was trouble a-plenty. I ran back through the door to get a catch party organized. Lew was just coming out. He said, "We killed six in here. Ben's coming over."

I said, "But we got four loose. We got to get after them."

Lew said, "We lost Kline. And Axel."

Of course I knew about Axel, but I was sorry to hear about Kline. I picked my way back through the bodies. Kline was laying on his back, his arms outflung. He'd been hit right above the nose and his face was a mess. I looked down and shook my head. But then, glancing around at how the lower bleachers were chewed up and at the holes in the little wall, I figured it was amazing that more hadn't been hit. Hays was suddenly standing by me. He said, quietly, "Norris has been hit."

I whirled. Norris was sitting on the lowest bench. His face was white and there was a splotch of blood on his shoulder up near his neck. Somebody had ripped his shirt open to expose the wound. With relief I saw the little furrow the bullet had made as it plowed through the flesh. I said, "You're all right. It's just a deep scratch."

He shook his head and opened and closed his mouth. He said, "It's not that. Not the wound. It was the sound the bullet made. It came right by my ear."

I glanced at my feet. There, like a bundle of old clothes somebody had discarded, was the body of Axel. I wished mightily he hadn't done what he had done, spooked them before I was ready, but I couldn't much blame him. He'd at least proved one thing; he really and truly did hate Sam Sixkiller.

Ben came up, vaulting the wall. He said, with satisfaction, "We got all five of the bastards. Caught 'em climbing a fence. I made damn sure every one of them was dirt."

"Get anybody hurt?"

"Not a scratch." Then he looked down and saw Kline. He said, "That's Jim Kline."

"Yeah," I said. "We had four get away. They're loose around the countryside, including Sixkiller. Axel fired too early and spooked them before we could draw them in far enough. We had to wait for the ones in front to fall before we could get at the ones in back."

Ben frowned. He said, "Axel? What the hell was he doing with a gun?"

"It's a long story," I said. "I'll tell you later. Meanwhile, they scattered our horses. Yours is the closest. Get him and then get mine and Lew's and Hays's animals. We got to get after them. And hurry."

It seemed awful quiet in the barn after the din of the battle. My hearing was returning, and I could hear and see the farmers and ranchers coming out from under the benches. They commenced yelling questions; I ignored them. I went to Norris, and said, "Norris, Ben and I have got to organize a chase party. You take charge here if you're able."

He was coming out of his shock. Some of the color was returning to his face. He said, "I'm all right. Get going."

Lew was staring down at Axel. When he was aware of my presence he said, "Pore little feller. He ain't big as a minute, is he?"

I took him by the arm. I said, "Com'on, Lew. Norris will get things organized here. We got four renegades loose in the country. And we no longer got the element of surprise. They already got a long lead on us. Load up your guns and let's go."

He nodded. "All right. Who'll it be?"

I told him and he nodded again. "That's best. Keep it small."

I gathered up Ray Hays, who was studying the dead men that littered the entryway, and we started outside. But going through I couldn't help but glance down at the bodies. There were five of them. Some had been shot to pieces, catching five and six slugs. These were the ones unlucky enough to be in the front.

Hays said, "What come over that kid? If he'd have waited thirty seconds more we'd have kilt every son of a bitch of them."

I shook my head. I said, "Not really. The ones in the back would still have had time to get away. The ones in front just wouldn't fall fast enough. Besides, that kid had a lot of hate built up and he did wing Sixkiller."

Lew said, "I thought I saw that, too. But I was so busy I couldn't be for shore. Reckon he got Sixkiller pretty good?"

I said, "Beats the hell out of me. He was so shuffled up in the crowd. But I saw him grab his arm. For the kid's sake I hope it broke the bone. By the way, Buttercup downed a horse. Sixkiller is riding double with someone."

Lew whistled. He said, "Poor horse. Carryin' that big bastard and somebody else."

At the door I remembered and yelled back at my brother.

I said, "Norris, send into town for Peabody, the undertaker. Tell him to bring more than one wagon."

Norris was up and looked busy. He nodded at me. He said, "I've already had that thought, Justa. Do we go on with the auction? Lot of cattle still in the pens outside."

"Whatever you think," I said.

We went outside just as Ben arrived riding his horse and leading ours. I swung aboard my mount and shoved my unused rifle back in its boot. Then I reached around in my saddlebag and came out with a handful of cartridges. While the others were doing the same I reloaded both of my revolvers. When we were ready I led us across the road and toward the windmill. Buttercup was up and looking toward the southeast. He saw us and yelled down, "Is that the balance of them?"

"Yeah."

He said, gleefully, "I got me two 'n' a hoss. An' they never cottoned to whar' I wuz."

"Are they out of sight?"

He looked down at us. "Hell, yes. If you plannin' on givin' chase you better be fer gettin' after it."

"Which way?"

He pointed his arm. "Right yonder. Got about two mile on you."

I said, "Stay up there until somebody comes to help you get down."

He said, "Shit! I got myself up here, don't reckon I need no he'p gittin' down."

I didn't have time to argue with him. I said, "Let's go," and spurred my horse into a slow gallop. Ben and I glanced at each other. Nothing had to be said. The direction Sixkiller had taken was aimed straight at the headquarters of the Half-Moon ranch. They'd be looking for an extra horse or even fresh horses, and there wasn't a ranch or a holding between them and the Half-Moon. Our only hope was to try to overtake them and turn them back toward the west or the southwest. I thought of Nora there by herself or, at best, there with her mother. It nearly scared me to death. And there would be no help from our ranch hands or Harley. They'd be scattered all over the far south range working the calf crop.

We rode hard, but not so hard as to wear our ponies out. Near as I could tell they were going to have a hard day of it. I reckoned it to be about eight or nine miles cross-country to the Half-Moon headquarters. We had to figure that Sixkiller and his men were just riding across the pastureland looking for any ranch or farm where they could find fresh horses. We had the advantage of not only knowing the land, but also not being encumbered by having one of our number riding double.

Ben ranged up alongside of me. He said, "We got to push harder!" He had to yell to make himself heard over the sound of the hoofbeats and the rush of the wind.

I shook my head. "Not yet."

"We got to outrun them to the ranch. We can get fresh horses there ourselves."

Fortunately for us the grass had gotten up to such an extent that the path of Sixkiller and his men was as plain as a wagon trail across the prairie. And, because of the rain, the ground was soft. We could almost pick out the horse that was carrying double by the depth of his hoofprints.

I yelled at Ben, I said, "What about their stride?"

He leaned toward my ear, standing hard on his left stirrup. He said, "They are alternating. Look hard and you can see they were loping their horses along here. But back a ways they had 'em in a walk."

But all I knew was that they had to be a considerable distance ahead of us. The prairie was mostly flat, but here and there were long, low depressions and then a rise or so. The only trees were scattered mesquite and, here and there, a clump of post oaks. There was no place for them to hide. Then we topped a rise and I thought I saw some dim dots in the distance. They couldn't be cattle because we'd cleared that part of the range to bunch the cattle to the south and make the calf work easier.

Hays, who I swear could see like a hawk, sang out, "I think that be them."

In answer Ben put spurs to his horse and set him up at a high gallop. The rest of us had no choice but to follow even though I thought it would surely founder the animals before we could come up to our quarry.

But the extra speed was paying off. The next time we topped a little rise I could see that Sixkiller and his men were appreciably closer. But I could also feel my horse starting to strain. I figured we'd come some five miles from the auction barn. As close as Sixkiller was, maybe a mile, I thought we could rest the horses by walking them for a spell and then make a final dash and close with them. I was slightly in front on the left, wide of the others. I held up my hand and said, loudly, "Slow down!"

We gradually pulled our horses down until they were in a walk. I could hear all four of them blowing and snorting. Between my legs I could feel my horse swell as he pulled air into his lungs. Ben said, "Justa, this ain't good. Better to kill the horses than have them sonsabitches get at Howard or Nora."

I said, "We got room and we got time. Look yonder at them. They are walking their horses too. And that one carrying double is lagging."

Ben said, "Then it's time to get high behind and overtake them."

Lew said, "If we could just get them in rifle shot."

"That's a ways coming."

We kept on like that. After a little we noticed that whoever was riding double would slip off the back of the horse he was on and be taken up by another rider. They were switching around the extra load to keep one horse from being more tired than the others.

Then we rode down into a long, wide meadow and they went out of sight. In the six-inch-high grass I could see bluebonnet flowers and Indian paintbrushes beginning to emerge. That and the budding of the mesquite trees was a sure sign that spring had really and truly arrived.

As we came up out of the meadow Ben said, urgently, "We got to git!"

My horse's breathing had almost come back to normal. I said, "We'll lope them." I brushed my horse's belly with the rowels of my spurs, and he instantly responded by hitting a trot, then a canter, and then breaking into a rocking lope. He and the other horses were pretty well lathered up, but I figured they had plenty left in them. I had taken time to look at my watch and been surprised that it was nearly four o'clock. So much had happened, but it had gone so fast that I'd thought it to be no more than two. In two hours it would be dark, and then we would have hell running down our targets.

As we hit the flat prairie again I looked ahead, expecting Sixkiller to be even closer. The prairie was bare except for a little knot of trees here and there. "What the hell!" I said.

Hays yelled, "They've gone to ground."

But that didn't seem possible. The grass wasn't high enough to conceal men, let alone horses, and there were no clumps of trees in sight that would do for a hiding place.

Lew said, "We better be careful. If they've seen us they could be laying an ambush."

We kept on. Ahead, perhaps a quarter of a mile, was a small clump of oak trees, just little stunted specimens no more than eight or ten feet high and no more than six inches in diameter. I was examining them as we tore across the prairie, trying to decide if they would hold horses and men in concealment, when, all of a sudden, I saw puffs of smoke bloom up and then heard the whizz of bullets passing close. I yelled, "Hold up!" But even as I did, Hays's horse went down and Ray went tumbling headfirst across the prairie.

We all skidded our animals to a stop. I jerked my Winchester out of the boot, jumped down, and then pulled my horse's head almost around to his neck so that he either had to come down on his side or have his neck broke. He staggered sideways a few steps and then kind of sagged and fell to the prairie. I saw Ben and Lew's horses doing likewise. I sheltered up behind my horse and began firing into the clump of trees as fast as I could work the lever of my carbine. By then Ben and Lew had got their rifles into the action. Hays was snaking along the ground back to his dead horse. He got there, got his rifle, and joined the shooting. It had to be getting pretty warm for the folks that were in the trees. There just wasn't that much cover. We'd fired maybe twenty shots. Only a few were coming our way. All of a sudden we heard a cry.

Ben said, "We got one."

Lew said, "That or they're playing possum."

Then their firing stopped. I was on the left, and as I watched and waited, I suddenly saw three horses come riding up out of a little low place behind the oaks. They'd hid their horses down there. Now I could plainly see that there were only three of them. I jumped to my feet and sighted at the retreating party. It was too long a shot to do much more than pray for luck, but I yelled, "Fire at their horses!"

We let loose a volley. Nothing happened. We fired again, and the horse on the right suddenly started staggering sideways and then went to his front knees. We saw the rider jump off, run to another rider, and jump on behind him.

Ben already had his horse up and was mounting. He said, "Let's go!"

Lew said, "My horse is hit."

"Bad?"

He was standing by his animal's side, looking at where a wound was pumping blood. He said, "It just cut flesh, but he's bleedin' pretty bad. He won't make it far."

I said, ''We got to head for the ranch.''

Ben said, ''But they'll get away. They might even get to the ranch ahead of us.''

I shook my head and pointed. Sixkiller had aimed his party due south. They'd pass our headquarters a half a mile to the west. I said, ''They ain't in very good shape themselves, horse wise.''

Hays was getting up behind Ben. He said, ''Boss, they are liable to run into them crews working that south pasture and turn back north or northeast.''

''Let's get to the ranch,'' I said. ''Take it easy. I want to check that knot of trees.''

While the others went ahead I rode to the little grove of trees. One of Sixkiller's men was laying on the ground behind a thin tree. He had a hole right in the middle of his forehead and one in the toe of his boot. His rifle and revolver were gone. Likely, if I knew my quarry, so was any cash he'd had on him.

I turned my horse and caught up with the others. Lew's horse was still pumping blood. He couldn't go on much longer without the wound being closed in some way so that the bleeding would stop.

In less than half an hour we had the main house in sight. We could still make out Sixkiller and his two men, but as they were going south and we were heading to the east, the distance between us increased with every step.

Lew said, ''What'll happen if they run upon one of your branding crews?''

''I don't know,'' I said. ''But it worries me greatly.''

Privately, though, I was more worried that they'd see all our men working and turn back as Hays had suggested. That would put Nora and Howard in danger.

When we finally got to the horse barn Lew's animal was visibly weak. I dragged my saddle off my tired animal as the others did likewise. The gate to the little horse trap opened right into the big, dim barn. I gave my horse a slap on the rump and sent him into the corral to hunt up some hay and water. Then I said, "Ben, you and Hays get me and Lew fresh mounts just as quick as you can catch them."

Ben had taken a step before what I'd said hit him. He said, "What about us?"

I said, "I'm going to ask you to do a hard thing, but it has to be done. And all the squawking in the world is not going to help. Lew and I will go on with the chase. But I can't leave Dad or Nora unprotected. As soon as we're gone, Ben, I want you to go and watch my house. I don't want Nora to see you. Hays, you stay here."

Ben said, "But—"

I shook my head. I said, gently, "Can't be no buts, Ben. I know you want to be in at the end, but it can't be. Those renegades could turn back. I can't chance it. Now go on and get our horses. And then do what you can for Lew's animal."

Ben grimaced, but he said, "I got some tar salve that will stop that bleeding. He'll be all right in a few days."

While Ben and Hays were getting us fresh horses Lew and I went outside the front of the barn to a barrel of drinking water that had been set there for the hands. We passed the dipper back and forth until we'd both drank our fill. I'd been powerfully thirsty. Gun fighting and chasing folks is mighty thirsty work. While we drank I surveyed Lew. He was wet and muddy all down the front from flopping down on the wet prairie. I figured I looked the same although, by the smell, it appeared that I'd found some cow manure to roll around in. I also reeked of gunpowder. It was a smell that took a time to get rid of; not even immediate soap and water would help. And with all the shots fired, and in such close quarters, I figured I had it better than skin deep.

Ben brought me my horse, a four-year-old roan that had plenty of staying power. He said, "You might be on the trail a good while. He's the best I got."

I knew he was out of Ben's personal string. While I saddled the horse I told Ben about Kline and about his request in case anything happened to him. Ben said, "Why you telling me? You not planing on coming back?"

I said, "Just wanted you to know. Be real careful not to let Nora see you. You know she's not supposed to know what I've been doing."

"She won't," he said. "But I'll just bet you you ain't fooling her. By the way, you reckon Norris will be back out tonight?"

I pulled the girth tight and said, "Don't see why not."

"Well, if memory serves me right, he ain't never been shot before. He looked mighty pale to me."

Hays said, "Boss, you sure I cain't go? Hell, the crew will be returnin' in less'n two hour. An' those son of a bitches shot the best horse I had."

I swung into the saddle. "No," I said. "Do what I told you." Then to Ben I said, "What about the crews? Reckon they might jump one of them for their horses?"

Ben shook his head. "I don't see it. We're near to the end of the calving and Harley has got the men bunched together. We've got some horses running loose on that south range, but they are green stock and wild. They ain't going to run any of them down as tired as their animals be."

Lew was mounted. He said, "Justa, we got to git."

"Yeah."

Lew and I rode away, quartering toward the southwest, hoping to cut Sixkiller's trail. The ground was still soft, and we saw plenty of cow sign and here and there scattered horse prints, but nothing like two horses carrying three men. Lew said, "I think we ought to try further west."

"Why? This was the direction he was headed when we saw him last."

We were walking our horses so as to better study the ground. There was no use hurrying until we had a scent. Lew said, "Because Sam will turn back north sooner or later. He's going to loop to the west and then circle back north.''

"Why?''

"Because north is home ground. Indian Territory is north. Oklahoma. He come down here with seventeen men and he's going back with two. He wants to get about five hundred miles north of here and lick his wounds. We got to find him before that or we are liable to have us another reunion like this next year.''

We turned farther west and increased speed. I was getting worried about night coming on. If we didn't locate his trail before dark we'd have no idea where he'd gone or what kind of mischief he was up to. It was a plaguing thought.

I let my mind rove back to the auction barn and the chaos and smoke and gunfire of the battle. I'd hated to have to leave in such a hurry, but I didn't see where I'd had much choice. I could only hope that Norris had been up to handling matters and clearing up the mess. I said, to Lew, "You know, I only saw one of them renegades I shot. After that the gunsmoke was too thick.''

Lew said, "I didn't even see one. I just fired into the smoke. Axel distracted me so by jerking my pistol out of the holster that I was behind in getting off that first shot.''

I said, "Well, it was a dumb thing for him to do but—''

Lew said, "Hold up! I got something over here.'' He stopped his horse and looked at the ground to his right. I was to the left of him so I had to circle his horse to see what he meant. Then, there on the prairie, were two sets of horse hoofprints, one set a little deeper than the other.

I said, "I believe this is it.''

In the growing twilight the tracks led off to the west by southwest. Lew said, "They are definitely coming around to head back.''

That was luck for Johnson. If they'd have held more to the south they'd have struck his ranch in another mile. And then he'd have been glad he'd been involved earlier. I looked around, getting my bearings. I said, "How far south of town you figure we are?"

Lew said, "On their line of march I'd reckon them to be going at least a mile south. Town should be three or four miles yonder."

I said, "We better move it along. Looks like they plan to make a big sweep around Blessing."

Lew said, "They could be lost. Hell, they don't know this country. I bet Sixkiller has never been anywhere near this range."

We put our horses into a canter. I looked at my watch. It was six o'clock lacking five minutes. We had really been dogging it along. I said, "Damn, I'm hungry. We ain't eat."

Lew said, "I'd rather have a drink. I didn't provision up fer a long pursuit, figured the whole business would be over at the barn."

We kept on pushing our horses. Legally speaking we had to catch up with them in Matagorda County for Lew's badge to be in effect. But I figured we could always say we didn't see no marker boundaries.

Then, just before dark we came upon the remains of a small camp fire. We both got down. Lew cautiously put his palm against the coals. He said, "They're still warm though they be damp."

"Coffee grounds," I said. "They stopped for coffee."

But Lew was looking at some dark stains on the ground near the ashes. He said, "This appears to be blood. I think they stopped to heat a knife to cut a slug out of somebody. Sixkiller likely. Then they took the opportunity to have coffee whilst they was at it."

I got up and circled the fire, noting that they'd ridden off in the same direction they'd arrived. There was an empty bottle of whiskey in the grass. I picked it up and showed it to Lew.

I said, "They could at least have saved us a little."

"We better get moving." Lew said.

We mounted and set off in pursuit, but now dark was coming fast and it was getting harder and harder to see the tracks. When it got plumb dark we had to resort to riding a couple of hundred yards in the direction we thought was right and then getting down and casting about for sign, sometimes having to get down on our hands and knees.

Lew said, "If the damn moon would just get up. Suppose to be full. We are losing all kinds of time."

We made slow pace, but we kept pushing on. We noticed that Sixkiller was turning more south. We couldn't figure if that was his intention or he'd lost his way in the dark night with no stars out. The sky was still overcast, but Lew and I knew our directions from having been over the country so many times.

Then, sometime later, the clouds began breaking up and the moon came shining through, lighting up the way and casting weird shadows on the prairie. We put our horses into a faster gait. I could now see, plainly, that the two horses were struggling. It was clear that, even walking, they had shortened their strides. Well, even the best horse will break under enough strain, and Sixkiller had put his animals to a hard day's usage.

Lew looked over his shoulder. He said, "Damn that moon. It has got us set up like we was standing in a door frame with the light behind us."

The words were no more than out of his mouth when there came the crack of at least two rifles and bullets whizzed over our heads. The only reason they hadn't taken their deadly effect was that, at the instant the shots were fired, we'd started down into a little wide ditch. It had been pure luck because the parties shooting at us were not that far away. We jerked our rifles out of their boots, then flung ourselves off our horses, ran up the facing side of the ditch, and threw ourselves to the ground. We peered over the top. Ahead I could see a little stand of trees some two hundred yards distant. If they were in there they'd fired too soon. But closer, and off to our left was the falling-down remains of a small barn. I whispered to Lew, "We must be on the Adcock place. I remember he used to store hay in that barn until he moved his outfit further south. If that's so we're way on south of town."

The remains of the barn were just two walls and part of the ceiling. I reckoned the wood to be rotten enough that a rifle bullet would pass through. I fired a shot and was instantly answered by a quick crackle of fire. One of the bullets hummed through the grass near my shoulder. I ducked back and looked toward our horses. They were deep enough in the ditch that they weren't exposed to fire.

Lew said, "They're trying to give their horses a blow. They've been there for some time. We come up on them too quick."

I said, "I'm glad they fired before we got closer. Might have been the end of the chase."

Lew said, "They don't know we're just two. Far as they know we might be spread out in a line. They fired to make us go to ground and stop."

I levered a shell into the chamber of my carbine. I said, "Let's make it a little warm for them."

Lew put out his hand. "Let's listen for a minute or two. Likely they are on the floor or behind some pretty good timbers with their horses the hell out of the way."

So we laid there, staring at the old barn etched against the sky. The clouds were thinning with every passing minute, and a little gulf wind had sprung up to send them scudding across the sky. We waited five or ten minutes. There wasn't a sound from the barn or the sign of any movement. Lew glanced over at me. He said, "Want to wait until morning?"

I said, "Naw. Let's stir them up a little."

We fired two shots apiece, just aiming randomly at the wall of the barn facing us. After the echo of our shots had faded away we listened intently. There was no sound except the noise of night insects. I said, "What do you think?"

"Either they are playing possum, they left, or they are saving their ammunition. Or we killed all three."

"Could they pull out without us seeing them?"

"Say there was some low land the other side of the barn. They could keep the barn between us and them and lead their horses quite a spell before we caught sight of them."

I said, "I don't reckon we ought to get rash and take a rush at them."

Lew said, "My job don't pay that well fer such antics."

We waited. After a while we tried a couple of more shots. Nothing come of that except more echoes. We waited some more. Finally I said, "Hell, we got to do something. We just can't sit here."

"What do you reckon?"

I said, "I can't see but one thing to do. And I don't much like it."

Lew said, "What, snake up there on our bellies?"

"All I can think of."

Lew shook his head. "Pretty risky. That grass ain't very high."

I said, "Lew, they are going to get plumb away from us if we don't do something."

He heaved a sigh. "I reckon you are right. But you ain't as thick as I am. Yore butt don't stick up as high."

I eased out over the top of the ditch. The moon seemed to get brighter with every foot forward I went. I figured the old barn to be about 150 yards. I said, "You swing out to the right and I'll do the same to the left."

It was slow, nasty going. The ground wasn't as wet as it had been, but it was wet enough. And there were still patches of nearly fresh cow manure to be encountered. But after what seemed like an hour and a half I finally come up to the corner of the barn. The back wall was down so I was able to peek right around the still-standing wall that had been facing us and see inside the gloom. As soon as my eyes adjusted I could see the place was dead empty. I stood up and yelled at Lew. I said, "They're gone. You get the horses and I'll look for their trail."

I picked my way through the debris and walked through where the south wall would have been. I could see from the manure where they'd tied their horses. I walked on out into the prairie, looking for sign. It wasn't hard to find. I found clear evidence that three men had led two horses due south, keeping the barn between them and us. I kept walking and following the sign until Lew came up with my horse. I mounted and then we walked along, keeping the tracks between us and looking down. They had led their horses some quarter of a mile, led them until the prairie had dipped down to where it would have put them out of our sight. We could see where they'd mounted. Once astride their horses they'd radically changed course, heading almost due west. Either they'd meant to try and throw us off track by heading south or they'd had to wait for enough stars to figure their direction.

Lew said, "Bet you anything they go west until they strike the railroad tracks and then turn north."

We moved out rapidly, pushing our horses into a canter. It made the sign hard to track, but both of us had a pretty good idea where they were heading and it was important that we head them off before they could reach their objective. As we rode I got out my watch and was able, by the light of the moon, to tell it was near ten o'clock. It had been one hell of a long day and it was a hell of a long ways from being over.

Lew said, "I can't figure out how their horses are holding up. They should have foundered by now."

I said, "I've seen men make a horse last by cutting him with a knife and then rubbing salt into the wound. I guess you do that when you figure the horse is dead anyway."

"Yeah," Lew said. But he wasn't listening. He was too intent on the sign and making time up on the three desperados. Their trail led just as straight west as if they'd been following a compass. We kept urging our horses to a faster gait. Even they were beginning to tire. I figured we'd ridden some twelve miles since we'd left the Half-Moon headquarters, maybe more. And, before that, I'd ridden at least another seventeen or eighteen. It made for a lot of saddle time.

And then the trail stopped. We'd reached the gravel of the railroad bed and the tracks. Now the trail turned due north. Lew said, grimly, "Ain't hard to figure out what they got in mind."

"No," I said, "they know these tracks lead to a town. I don't know if they know it's Blessing but they know it's a town."

Lew said, "And a town means horses."

"And fresh provisions. And maybe a chance to do murder or get money."

Lew said, "They'll go for the horses first. How far to Blessing you reckon?"

I looked around. "Maybe three miles."

Lew put rowels to his horse's belly. He said, "We better hurry. We got to catch them up before they can do any mischief. Ain't got to worry with a trail now."

I said, as I came up alongside him, "Don't get into too big a rush, Lew. They know we're behind them. They laid one ambush for us. They can do it again. Let's take it easy and be alert."

We pulled our horses down to a trot. I figured it was at least twice the speed Sixkiller was making.

══Chapter Twelve

THE ROOFS OF Blessing were rising from the dark prairie when we came upon their dead horse. He'd nearly made it, but he'd come up about a half a mile short. I dismounted for a second to make a quick examination. There was still foam around his mouth and his sweat wasn't close to being dried. They'd taken the saddle and bridle. I said, "He ain't been dead more than a quarter of an hour. He's warm enough to melt suet."

Then I noticed the shallow slashes on the animal's shoulder, the side I could see. I looked closer. I said, "They cut him. And they rubbed salt in the wounds to keep him going on the pain."

Lew said, "Let's go. I want my hands on that bastard."

We rode slowly toward Blessing, doubly alert now. Blessing was mainly a one-street town. It started to the north off the Wadsworth Road near the railroad depot and then ran south for a little over a mile until the last house, where the main street turned into the Tivoli Road. There were houses on both sides at both ends. The business establishments were placed in the middle of the town. A few side streets went off at right angles to the main street, and here and there, a haphazard lane wandered back into the prairie land, but what you were looking for was right along that main street: the hotel, the mercantiles and general stores, the grocery stores, the blacksmith, the livery stables, the saloons, and the churches.

We stopped as we came to the first of the houses. Looking up the street, I was astonished to see not one light or one sign of movement. Blessing never had been a late town, but there wasn't even a tethered horse to be seen. A man would have at least expected to see a light on in Crook's. I said, "Lew, I'm afraid we're too late. They've already stole three horses and are gone."

He shook his head. "I don't think so. All the horses are either locked up or in a corral with a loudmouthed dog. And I ain't heard no dog bark."

I said, "But Crook's ain't even open."

He said, "I see you ain't been to town on a Saturday night in a while. The church folks made all the saloons shut down at ten o'clock on Saturday night. Only way some of them women figured they could get their husbands to church next morning." He got out his watch and looked at it. He said, "It's a little after eleven. Town looks about right. Besides, tomorrow's Easter."

I said, "So it is."

Lew dismounted and I followed suit. He said, "I reckon we better proceed on foot."

There was an elm tree handy to the road and we tied our horses there. Lew said, "You take yon side and I'll work it from here. Take it slow."

I said, "I got an idea where they are. I think we ought to move along right smart."

"Where?"

I said, "If you were a stranger in a strange town and needed three horses, where would you go? Into somebody's yard and wake that loudmouthed dog you was talking about? And how would you know you'd find three horses? What if there was only two, or one? And you'd already woke the town up."

Lew nodded slowly. "Only one place you could be sure of three good horses. The livery stable."

"Yeah. And I'd know that a hotel stable would have good

horses because no man that can afford to stay in a hotel sets out traveling on a bad horse.''

Lew said, ''We better check them both. The blacksmith's livery comes up first. And I still think we better check both sides of the road. They might have left one of their number back as a rear guard.''

I crossed the road and began working my way down along the row of houses. I raised a bark here or there, but since I didn't try to get too familiar with the houses the dogs were content to just give a token yelp to let their masters know they were on the job. I went along that way for about forty houses and then faded out toward the street. I could see Lew under a tree motioning to me. I made my way over to his side. He said, ''Jacob's place is next. You take the right side and I'll take the left.''

We separated, and I crossed a wide space between houses and hunkered down in the shadows. Set about thirty yards back from the street was Jacob's blacksmith shop and stable. Above the big double doors of his smithy and stable was a sign that said, ''LIVERY TO RENT.'' I watched until Lew got in position, and then we both went creeping toward the big barn. We were nearly there when a dog started raising a racket. In a moment a light came on in the house that Jacobs lived in right in front of his place of business. I saw Lew get up swiftly and go to the back door of the house. Through the lighted window I saw a figure go to the door from the inside. There came a brief mutter of voices and then Lew was back, motioning me on. The dog suddenly stopped barking and then the light went out.

We crept up to the barn. It was padlocked with a huge Stanley lock. The hinges were near six inches wide. It was all intact. It would have taken a mighty determined man with the right tools and a lot of time to gain entry through such security.

We checked around back, but there was nothing there.

Lew said, "I reckon you are right. They have to be at the hotel livery."

"And it's never locked," I said. "Because sometimes customers want to hit the road way early."

The hotel was a good three hundred yards down the road, more convenient to the train depot than anything else. Lew and I walked down the left side of the street, pistols drawn, alert to any movement. We passed Lew's office, then Crook's, then Lonnie's Mercantile, then various other stores and a couple of saloons, and finally got to the hotel. There was a dim light on in the lobby, but most of the guest rooms were dark. The livery stable was around in the back. There was a big wide space between the hotel and the next building over, so wagons could be driven in and turned around. The hotel stable did not rent horses. It was there purely for the use of the guests.

As soon as we'd crept around the corner of the hotel and turned into the entrance to the stable I could see that one of the doors of the stable was slightly ajar. By itself that didn't mean much. The last guest to put his horse up could have left them open. But we had a stable boy that tended to matters until around eight o'clock, and he would never have left the doors ajar for fear a horse would get out of his stall and run off.

I squatted down. Lew joined me. The stable doors were about twenty yards away. I said, "I'd bet my good hat that they are in there."

Lew said, "Let's get closer. Over to the right."

We crossed the driveway and got up next to the adjoining building, kind of hiding in its shadow. Going as slowly as we could we eased our way toward the front of the horse barn. Lew whispered, "I wish they'd come busting out of there right now. They'd be easy pickings. I don't relish having to pry them out of there in the dark."

I was of the same sentiment. If we had to go into that barn the advantage would all be on their side. Their eyes would have adjusted to the dark, they would have concealment, and we'd be outlined in the door just as we come through.

I said, "You got any ideas?"

Lew said, "Ain't no back way out of there, is there?"

"Nope. This is the only door."

"Ain't a winder we could sneak through?"

I shook my head. "Not another opening in the whole damn place."

Lew looked around at me. "You ain't in no hurry, be you? You're already mighty late fer supper. Little more won't matter."

I said, "I ain't in no hurry to catch a slug, that's for sure."

Lew said, "They got to come out sooner or later."

"They might not be in there. We might be sitting here waiting while they've found horses somewhere else and are getting away. Let's get an ear up against the side of the wall and listen."

We crept forward the balance of the distance and then, practically holding our breath, stuck our heads close to the side wall and listened. Sure enough we could hear muffled movement. It could have been the horses moving around in their stalls, but then I distinctly heard a few whispered words and then the creak of saddle leather. They were saddling the horses.

I motioned Lew to come back a few yards. I was going to say something to him, but he just held something up for me to see. It was a piece of rope, about fifteen or twenty feet long. With hand signals he motioned me to get in the middle of the driveway facing the doors of the stable. I done so, moving to the dead center of the hard-packed dirt and laying flat, a revolver in either hand. As a general rule I don't shoot very good left-handed, but for what I'd figured out Lew had in mind it didn't much matter. I watched while he crept forward and tied one end of the rope to the door hinge of the right-hand door, the one that was slightly open. Then, paying out the rope to its very end, he backed until he was almost on a line with me. He said, in a low whisper, "I'm going to wait until they start to open the door. Then I'm going to jerk it open. We ought to catch them flat-footed."

It was a good idea and substanially reduced our risk. I was about to whisper something back when a church bell all of a sudden let loose and began tolling like there was no tomorrow. I nearly let out an oath, but I controlled it in time. I scooted over a couple of feet closer to Lew. I said, very lowly, "What the hell is that?"

"It's high midnight. That's the bell in the Catholic church. It's tellin' folks they is fixing to have a high midnight mass. I told you it was Easter."

Then Lew got a look of fear on his face. He said, "My gawd, Justa, we can't wait. In five minutes these here streets are fixin' to be filled with ol' women and little chillun. We can't have no lead flyin' around then. That Catholic church is right across the street."

I said, "Then jerk that door open and let's start shooting in there."

Lew came up to one knee and suddenly pulled the door back all the way. The flood of moonlight made the inside a little lighter but not light enough to see anything. As soon as the door came open I started firing, deliberately blasting one, two, three shots into the interior with my left-hand gun. By the third shot they were firing back and I fired right-handed at the flashes. Lew was doing the same. Before I emptied my right-hand gun I heard a cry and the flashes I'd been firing at came no more. I switched to the two on the other side. Another cry came just after I heard something that sounded like a bullet hitting flesh. It's the only sound that sounds like that. It don't sound like a bullet hitting a tree or a rock or a saddle. It sounds like a bullet catching a man in the chest.

Then, suddenly, all firing ceased and a voice yelled out, "Hold yore fire! Hold yore fire! I give, I give!"

Lew yelled, "Come out with your hands up. Don't have no weapon near to hand or you are a dead man."

There was some shuffling around and then the same voice called out, "I cain't raise my left arm. I taken a ball in it."

Lew said, "That you, Sam?"

"Yeah. That you, nephee?"

"I ain't yore goddam nephew! Now git out here!"

Sam Sixkiller come shuffling out of the stable. He had his right arm raised above his head, but his left was in a sling they'd made out of a blue bandana kerchief. He came out, stumbling a little, as if the moonlight was blinding him. Lew said, "Keep coming."

When he was about fifteen yards clear of the stable Lew told him to stop. He said, "Now git facedown on the ground."

Sixkiller said, "I cain't. I tell you I'm hurt."

We were holding ourselves well clear of the barn door in case Sixkiller's cohorts were playing possum. Lew said, "You want me to knock you down with the barrel of my pistol?"

Cussing and swearing, Sixkiller got down on his knees and then eased himself to the ground with his good arm.

I said, "Sixkiller, I'm fixing to go in that barn to see about them other two renegades. If one of them takes a shot at me you are a dead man."

Lew said, "Wait a minute. That's my job."

"We'll both go," I said. "We can still easy shoot Sixkiller if he tries to get up."

They were both dead, as I had felt pretty sure about. One of them had three holes in him. Lew said, "Let's git Sixkiller in jail and then I'll wake up Peabody an' tell him he's got some more business."

People were already coming out to go to church as we marched Sixkiller back down the street to Lew's office. They looked at us curiously, but no one called out or said anything. I guessed they were used to seeing a jail prisoner being paraded down the street. But if they'd have known who he was and what damage he might have done, they'd most likely have been a little more thankful in the church house that it wouldn't be Sixkiller passing the collection plate.

We got to Lew's office and I held a gun on Sixkiller while Lew got the door unlocked and went inside and lit a lantern. I poked Sixkiller ahead with my revolver. He had been silent most of the time since we'd captured him, but once inside the office, he let loose with a torrent of talk. He said, "Nephee, what in hell's comed over ye? What be you fer shootin' my men 'n' shootin' at me? Why we is blood kin! Have you taken leave of yore senses? I—"

Lew had gone to stand behind his desk. He fixed Sixkiller with a cold eye. He said, "Listen, you murderin', thievin', no-good, trashy bastard, don't you ever call me kin again or I'll break every bone in yore body. The only blood between us is bad blood and I intend to see you pay for your crimes. You walked into a trap, you old fool. Now turn out yore pockets and take off yore boots!"

Sixkiller stared at him. He said, "I ain't hearin' right. Som'thin' wrong here. I—"

Lew came around the desk moving faster than I'd ever seen him move. Using Sixkiller's good arm for a lever he slammed the big man's face down on the desk and held him bent over with his left hand. With his right he went through Sixkiller's pockets, throwing out on his desk whatever he found. It didn't amount to much. There was a wad of bills, some loose change, a stub of a pencil, and a page or two of folded, blank writing paper. When he was done he let Sixkiller come erect and then told him, again, to take off his boots. He said, menacingly, "Next time I tell you to do something you don't bother to think. You do it."

Sixkiller had a kind of dazed look on his face. He was a long way from the evil, confident, grinning marauder Lew and I had seen on the prairie above Wadsworth. Now he looked middle-aged. And he looked gaunt and hungry and tired. As he took off his boots he said, "I'm mighty dry. Got any water?"

"In your cell."

"I could eat a bite."

"At breakfast."

I stood there looking at him and a slow anger began to build in me. He had caused me and people dear to me a considerable amount of trouble and expense. I said, to Lew, "How much money is on that desk? How much money did he have on him?"

Lew stirred a finger through it. He said, "Oh, a couple of hundred I reckon."

I went to the end of the desk and sorted through the money until I found a twenty dollar bill. I put it in my pocket. Sixkiller was watching me. He said, "Here! What be you doin' with my cash?"

I stepped up to where I could get my face close to his. I said, "Listen, you son of a bitch, you don't know how light I'm letting you off. For instance I ain't going to charge you for my time or the time of my hired help. I ain't even going to charge you for my brother's time. Or even for the two stock cars I rented to carry me and Lew up to Wadsworth so's we could bait a trap for you. And I'm not even going to charge you for the business you cost us at the auction barn. Or for the four hundred I had to lay out for two gunfighters. I ought to charge you some hide for the scare you caused my wife. I ought to drag you behind a horse for that one. But I'm not going to charge you for that. Or even for the doctor bill. Or even for the wear and tear on my horses or maybe for the calves we lost because we were working shorthanded because you had to come down here to do your robbing and murder."

With every sentence I was leaning closer and closer and he was pulling back so that he was nearly bent backwards over Lew's desk. I had started softly, but as I'd gone on, totaling up the cost, my voice had risen as the bill had gotten higher. At the end I suddenly shot out both hands and grabbed Sixkiller by the collar and jerked him up straight. I said, "*But what I am going to charge you for is my out of pocket expense in building your goddam gallows!*"

Then I slung him across the room toward the window that faced out onto the vacant lot where the gallows scaffolding stood. I followed quickly and grabbed his head in both my hands and shoved his face up against the windowpane. I said, "See it? See it, you miserable shit eater! Take a good look. Cost me twenty dollars. And I am going to *charge you for that!*"

Behind me Lew said, quietly, "Justa. Justa. Justa!"

I looked around, still holding Sixkiller's face against the window. He was making no move to struggle. I guess he figured I was just looking for any excuse to kill him. Which I was. I looked at Lew. "What?"

He said, "I understand how you feel, but I can't let you manhandle a prisoner in my jail. As your friend I can, but not as the sheriff."

I nodded. He was right. I took Sixkiller by the good arm and slung him back over to Lew's desk. I said, "I'd be obliged if you'd get him out of my sight. Now that it's over I'm about to lose hold of myself."

Lew said, to Sixkiller, "Let's go, Sam."

I heard the jangle of his keys and then the door to the cells opening. I was staring at the floor thinking about the past week and what hell that evil old man had put us through. Well, the authorities wouldn't have no trouble finding a volunteer to spring the trapdoor when it come time for him to hang.

When Lew came back he opened his desk drawer and came out with the bottle and two glasses. He poured us both good measures and handed me mine. I said, "Luck," and so did he, and then we knocked them back as befits the toast.

I said, "What the hell time is it? I'm too tired to get my watch out."

Lew said, "Going on for one o'clock. Ten of. Why the hell don't you stay at the hotel tonight, Justa? You've put a lot of miles in the saddle today."

I shook my head. "Nora will just about be having kittens by now. I don't want to make it any worse than it already is."

Lew said, "Well, my horse is down there with yours. I reckon I'd better fetch him. Of course that is your horse."

I said, "Next time you come to the ranch you can swap out."

Lew locked the jail office behind him and we walked south down the middle of the street. The only lights that were on in town were in the church and at the jail. I said, "Wonder how come we got to have both churches and jails."

Lew said, "I don't speculate on such matters."

I said, "Just right then it struck me as kind of odd. Guess I'm so tired my mind has taken off for Mexico."

We got to the horses and I spent a moment tightening the girth. Then I swung aboard. Lew looked up at me. He said, "Reckon I don't know the words to thank you and your family properly."

I said, "Ain't any need for thanks to ever pass between us, Lew. You don't thank a man for doing what he chooses to do."

He nodded. "I appreciate you saying that."

I swung my horse to the right. I said, "Come to supper one night next week."

He said, "Send in word which night."

I took my time getting home. First I went to the main house. The clock in the hall was just striking three as I let myself in. I found a lamp and lit it and then went into Norris's room. I lifted the lamp. He was in bed, asleep. He didn't stir.

I couldn't see his wound because he had the covers pulled up to his ears, but the way he was sleeping it didn't appear he was in any pain. It was also a good thing I wasn't an assassin or burglar.

It was a different story when I went into Ben's room. He was asleep also, but I had no more than raised my lamp than he rolled over and, in one motion, reached for his revolver on the table by the head of his bed. I said, quickly, "It's Justa."

He stayed his hand and half sat up, yawning. He said, "Do any good?"

"We killed two of them. Sixkiller's in jail."

"What time is it?"

"Little after three."

"Looks like you made a night out of it. Wasn't any trouble around here or at your place. I think we ought to give Buttercup and Ray a bonus."

I said, "I agree about Ray, but what does Buttercup need with money? He gets his whiskey and food free and that's about all he needs. But I'll give him one anyway. He get back all right?"

Ben yawned again. Then he said, "He got back but he celebrated all the way. Norris said they had to carry him in and put him in his bunk. Norris said he wanted to sleep with that damn rifle of his."

"Norris go to the doctor?"

Ben laughed shortly. "What for? Hell, he's cut himself shaving worse than that little scratch. He just can't get over how close that slug came to him. He was still up talking about it when I come in about midnight."

"You felt like Nora was safe?"

Ben said, "Her daddy come out about eight. Besides, I heard some shooting to the south, way to the south. I kept going to sleep. I was hid out behind yore little barn. And when Mr. Parker came up my fool horse commenced neighing at his buggy horse."

I said, "I better get. If you don't see me for a few days send for the doctor."

"You figure Nora is going to be that upset?"

"Hell, Ben, it's after three. What am I supposed to tell her? That I been at the auction barn all this time?"

"How about the truth? It wouldn't upset her now that it's over."

I said, "Wait'll you get married, Ben, and then you won't ask that question. If I tell her the truth now I'll be admitting I was lying before. Then the next time something comes up where I have to lie to her she'll throw this up in my face. No sir, the best policy, once you start lying to your wife, is keep it up and make a good job of it."

He lay back and pulled up the covers over his bare chest. He said, "Well git the hell out of here and let me get some sleep. Go on and take your lumps." I was nearly to the door when he said, "By the way, how'd Sixkiller take it?"

I said, "He got kind of upset when I showed him the gallows I'd had built and charged him twenty dollars for the use of them."

Ben said, "Sounds like a bargain price to me."

Out in the hall I turned off the lamp and set it down where I'd found it. Then I went outside and got on my horse and rode slowly home. As I topped a little mound about halfway there I saw that there was a dim light burning in one of the back rooms of my house. Well, that dismayed me. I had hoped for Nora to be in bed asleep and for me to slip in without waking her. I knew that a reckoning was coming, but I was hoping for morning. I was so tired I couldn't even think, and in the morning, her parents would be up and that would spike her guns a little.

But there burned that light. And I didn't figure it was lit to guide me, because Nora knew I could find the house with my eyes closed.

I rode on up to my little barn and took my time caring for the horse, giving him some grain and rubbing him down with a handful of hay. He was about as tired as I was though he'd plainly showed Ben's skill the way he'd performed over a hard night's work.

Finally I went on in the house through the kitchen door. The lamp I'd seen burning was sitting on the kitchen table. By its light I looked down at myself. My whole front was soaked with mud and water and manure. Some of it would have had to go on through to my skin. Just getting undressed wasn't going to clean me up, and I certainly wasn't going out in that cold spring night and take a shower. And I sure as hell knew better than to get in bed in such a condition. I wasn't about to make matters worse by dirtying up the sheets. I figured to just sit up all night.

I turned to the water pump at the kitchen sink and done what I could to my face and neck and hands and arms. But the condition of my pants were such that I knew I daren't sit down in one of the upholstered chairs. It was a wooden chair for me until the sun got up enough for me to take a sprinkling.

I had just finished the business of drying my hands and face on a dish towel when Nora came walking into the kitchen. She was rubbing her eyes with her knuckles. She must have been napping very lightly to have heard me because I'd been being extra quiet. She sat down in one of the kitchen chairs. She said, "You're home, honey."

Well, I figured the "honey" was encouraging. I sat down across from her. I said, "Yeah."

She said, "Can I get you anything? Something to eat?"

I said, "I'd be obliged for a drink of whiskey. I'm too tired to eat."

She got up and went into my office and came back later with a full tumbler of whiskey. I sipped at it while she inspected me. She said, "My, you are a mess. Did your horse throw you or something?"

I cleared my throat. I said, "Oh there was some thunder and lightning earlier and the cattle got restless. We had some runaways. We all had to go hunting them. I roped one and got jerked around in the mud and whatnot."

"I see," she said. "Daddy's here."

"That's good," I said. I was looking at her. She was wearing her sleeping gown with a robe thrown across her shoulders. The robe was open and her nightgown was low-cut so that I could see the swell of her breasts. It gave me that old feeling I nearly always got around her.

She said, "Yes, nobody ever came for Mother. Isn't that funny? I thought you left orders for someone to take Mother in."

"Oh, I did," I said. "I did."

She noticed me looking at her breasts. She said, "So we waited and waited and then Daddy came. He said he heard a lot of shooting out at the auction barn."

"Huh," I said. "Do tell. Somebody must have made a good trade and got to celebrating. Shooting their guns in the air and such."

She was staring innocently into my eyes. She said, "Noooo. Daddy says there was talk around town of a robbery out there. Weren't you at the auction barn?"

I said, truthfully, "Wasn't any robbery while I was there."

She just looked at me steadily for a long moment. Then she said, "How are you going to go to bed like that?"

I looked down at myself. I said, "Well, I just kind of figured on sitting up until I could take a bath."

She got up and left the room. When she came back she was carrying two big fluffy towels. She soaked one under the pump at the sink. She said, "I would heat up some water, but that would take too long. Take off your clothes and I'll clean you up as best I can."

It was kind of awkward because I'd never had such done to me before. But I got my boots and clothes off and stood there while she swabbed me down. The wet towel was pretty cold, but I was kind of heating up inside so I didn't much feel it. About halfway through Nora said, "By the way, how did that ranch deal that's been worrying you and taking up so much of your time come out?''

I looked sideways at her. I couldn't see her eyes, but she appeared to be about half-smiling. It almost caught me short, but I recovered and said, "Oh, it come out fine. Most satisfactory."

She said, "That's good. Maybe now you can put your mind where it ought to be."

I was getting impatient for her to finish. I was ready to go to bed. It appeared to me that her nerves were enough back in shape that she could stand pretty nearly anything I cared to do to her. I said, "Are you ever going to finish? I'm about to freeze to death."

She said, "When are you going to take me to see the new ranch? The one in Boling. I've never seen that country."

"Soon," I said, "Soon."

That was another reason to hang that damn Sixkiller. Now it looked like I was going to have to buy a damn ranch just to keep my wife from finding out what a liar I was.